Down and Dust

Another Odd Thread in the Tapestry of America's Wild Magic
Book 1

A. M. McCray

For every person who has ever felt like an odd one.

Contents

Down and Dust

Chapter 1

A Handyman of a Kind

John's job became much easier when he started telling himself he probably wasn't human anymore. When people asked what he did, he'd say he was a handyman because when he tried to explain what he really did, they'd get the wrong idea about it.

He began the work over a decade ago when a wanderlust overtook him, forcing him to keep traveling. If he ever denied it, a tattoo would beat in his head and grow in intensity like a fever until he had no choice but to continue. Eventually, he'd end up in a place where it allowed him to stop. Then, he'd fix something. Once he got a new assignment, the drumbeat would start again. That was the nature of his work.

At first, the job was frustrating because he didn't really understand it. He figured it out around the same time he got a good horse that liked him. This one was a pretty black mare named Lucky.

Only his left hand held the reins while the right sleeve of his duster hung empty. His felt hat was askew on his head with a plain feather stuck in the band. Like his hat, he sat lopsided on the saddle, but his mare was used to his crooked seat.

John had traveled America back and forth several times since he started this gig, so he thought he'd pass that old farm in the heartlands again. Passing it always made him think that Cyrus, the man who lived there, would be surprised to see him riding.

The closer he got to the farm, the more sure he was that he should stop and make this his destination. It was a strange feeling, just like the same one that compelled him yesterday to shop for the ingredients to cook a roast. The instinct that guided him probably came from the same place that gave him this job.

He adjusted the reins in his left hand, subtly cued with his legs, and Lucky turned toward the farm. John was nervous about what he could find there. Perhaps something had happened to his friend Cyrus in those years. Magic often did strange things to men, especially when handled as clumsily as it was a decade prior.

Since then, there had been the Enchanted War, which lasted two years, and Cyrus emerged from it a war-hero: The Undying Soldier. Based on the stories, John was sure his friend was fine, but if he was supposed to stop here today, then perhaps not. He'd have to check, at least.

Especially because he didn't buy turnips yesterday. Oh, and also it was his fault Cyrus couldn't stay dead.

* * *

JOHN SLOWED Lucky to a walk when he made it to the wooden fences. Coming up to the house stirred up memories of the years he spent here working as a farmhand.

There were fewer animals than there used to be. A small herd of white-faced cattle and a flock of chickens were left. Like always, they were wary of John. It was Cyrus who handled them, leaving John to do what fieldwork he could one-handed.

Half of the garden was weeded and mulched as if regaining control had been an on-going project. In the other half of it, dead-nettle nodded, purple-headed among the bright green carpets of chickweed. Proud field thistles stood with brandished thorns between the rows of young vegetables. New to John: a stone walkway bordered the garden and then a path led off of it, towards the house.

He dismounted Lucky and led her alongside that path. His horse's reins laid in his hand, and he made sure to put no pressure on it save for the small adjustments his fingers made to ask the mare to veer to the left, away from him, when the path split.

The two-story house had an addition built onto it. He stopped leading his horse by putting his hand gently out for her to nudge with her nose. She pressed the white-snip between her nostrils against his palm. "Mahne," he said, softly. When he withdrew his hand, she remained where she was.

He ascended the steps, then paused before the front door to wait for the wanderlust to make its noise, but it stayed quiet. He really was meant to be here then.

He attempted to straighten up his hat, but never quite fixed it to not favor one side over the other. The feather gleamed with a gold shimmer when the morning sun hit it just right. Once he adjusted his duster so it hung better, it hid the shape of his right side more effectively. Satisfied, John brought his hand to the door and knocked three times.

After a few moments, a tan-skinned woman and her gun

answered. "Who are you?" Her dark hair was done up in a thick braid.

John had not expected her; but because he was meant to be here, he knew they were supposed to meet. "I'm John, just John," he said. "I knew Cyrus Cooper."

The way he said Cyrus's name gave the woman some pause. The first syllable was almost but not quite the right sound. She studied his violet eyes and his narrow face with a three-day-old beard. She looked down at the empty right sleeve. Altogether, it allowed her to regard him with fresh patience. Her voice was gentle when she said, "My husband tells me stories about a friend of his named John who has only one arm. Are you that John?"

"I probably am."

"In that case, my name's Abigail. I'm Rus's wife."

"How has he been faring?"

"Rus is doing just fine."

"Cyrus said if I visited someone in this part of the country, it's customary to bring something." The more John spoke, the easier it was to hear the lilt in his voice. He was trying to hide his odd accent. It came out mostly in the roundness of a few of his vowels and the over-pronounced *t*'s. Though he had an interesting cadence to his speech, he was well-spoken.

"He would say that." She finally pointed the gun down and away.

"Allow me to fetch that gift for you, Mrs. Cooper."

"Oh goodness. Just Abigail, please."

"I apologize. Abigail, then." John walked over to Lucky. He opened the saddlebags and pulled out a satchel. It went over his head so it hung in front of him, where he could access it easily.

With everything in place, he climbed up the steps to show his friend's wife what he had.

"Just yesterday, I bought this in the town down the way," he said as he tilted the bag toward Abigail so she could see the large cut of fresh meat, wrapped in butcher's paper. "It's for a roast. And a proper roast is more than meat." He closed the bag, opened it up again, and this time it was filled with brightly scented herbs. "I've gotten herbs as well, and the vegetables. All in a witch's satchel."

"Goodness gracious, magic is rare nowadays. Usually, only rich men have things like this."

"Yes-yes, that's very much true," John said.

"I used to think my husband was making things up when he told stories about you."

He tensed up. "I don't know what all he's been saying about me."

"It's all good things," she said. "And interesting things. Let me put my gun away, then I'll help get you settled."

* * *

Abigail showed John where to put Lucky. As he untacked his horse, he half-expected her to ask him if he needed help like most people did, but she didn't. She just tucked her hands in the deep pockets of her tobacco-colored skirt, watching him with a pleasant smile.

He undid Lucky's saddle and lifted it, effortlessly.

"Rus did tell me you were very strong," she said.

"I suppose I am," John answered. He held the saddle one-handed. Sometimes, he forgot which things were supposed to be heavy for a man of his build.

"It's just amazing to see something like that in person."

"It's hardly so." John put the saddle away.

"You know what's amazing? That horse of yours! Where'd you find a horse that nice?" Abigail asked.

Lucky nickered as John stroked her neck with his fingertips. Everything he did with the mare was gentle and soft. "I was given her as payment for a job."

"Oh, and what do you do for a living?"

"Currently, I'd describe it best as being a handyman."

"A one-armed handyman?" Doubt colored her voice.

"Yes-yes."

"Interesting."

Before Abigail could ask more questions, John said, "I want to see if Cyrus is well."

"He's fine."

"I've a feeling that he may not be fine."

"You know, he told me ten years ago, you performed a miracle on him."

"I might've," John said. "I just want to see how he's been faring. It's part of my work."

"Being a handyman," she said, still skeptical.

"Of a kind."

She was sharp-eyed, taking measure of him. "I know you aren't being completely honest with me."

He focused on the silver tips of his boots. "I try not to be dishonest."

She sighed. "Rus always said you were sensitive about your . . . condition. I'll tell you again that we're just fine. We normally don't take guests unless we're expecting them, but I'll invite you in. I know Rus would love to have you, and he'd be upset if I turned you away. He still talks about you often, like you're a fairy tale or something."

"I'm not sure if I'm remarkable enough to warrant all that. I'm just a plain man except for this old thing." He shrugged his right shoulder.

2 Aprilis 1892

I decided to start a journal because I learned out how to use sinister to write a bit. I hate how messy it looks. My handwriting used to be much better, but now it's a chaos all over the page. I am writing in English because not many read English here in Nyuskom. But especially because Father cannot read English well. Not that he could read this with my penmanship as poor as it is. I used to be right-handed.

The Spring is new at now. It's strange that in English 'Spring' is also the word for 'leap'. But this occurrence happens in all languages. Where the important words we use many times also mean other things. Like 'ver' means 'Spring' but also 'true' or 'truth' here. Sometimes, the same words mean other things in different languages, too. For example, I find it amusing that 'sinister' means 'harmful' in English. Surely what has happened to me is something like that, yet the arm that remains is sinister. I have to ask the English word again from my tutor. I know he's told me but I've forgotten the word.

I've been distracted lately, as it has been a half-month since I woke up with one arm. The other was transformed. My tutoring is to start again on this week. I am nervous how it will go.

My father had for me a cloak made to wear. Elysia was helping me at morn to put it on and fasten the pin. Also to practice how to keep the right side hidden well.

That's another word. To English, they say 'right', meaning 'dexter'. 'Right' also means 'correct' for them. But dexter is no longer correct for me. Father has J Bellamy to return my right arm to normalcy. He is not only my tutor; he also studies magic. He's to come soon to examine me and start to teach me again. I have gotten bored waiting in this room.

Note from J Bellamy

The initial physical exam is scheduled on April 6, 1892 around noon. That should give me enough time to cook and finish my breakfast. The lessons with your son will continue where we left off before his arm got transformed. I can't wait to see it in person. I like these kinds of curses. The ones that change the configuration of a man are rare. Typically, magic doesn't have enough reach to do that anymore. If it was going to happen somewhere in the world, it makes sense that it would happen here.

— J. B. B.

5 Aprilis 1892

Sans this cloak, my father doesn't look at me. His eyes roam around the room. Like he's making sure everything is where it's to be. Maybe he believes himself to be culpable and the sight of it reminds him that he is. Once I'm covered up, he can look at me again.

I cannot ride horses anymore or play with the hounds. The animals all fear me, as if I am a monster because of this thing. Elysia assures me I'm not.

Father says it will be fixed soon. Still, it's been two weeks since it happened, so he had some shirts tailored for me that would fit during me like this. I can't get them on by myself. I don't think it's possible to. They made them with the buttons along my back so the front of the shirt is tailored to look as normal. Normal is inconvenient at now.

I can't get the cloak on properly. I prefer it when Elysia helps me to get it on. When Father did it earlier, his hands kept shaking as he tried to fasten the pin. He asked me if it hurts me to be like this. I told him I miss piano more than it hurts me. I think he'd rather I still played piano than look like this.

My tutoring will begin again tomorrow even though I'm not fixed yet, but my only tutor now will be J Bellamy. He has always been an odd one, but I don't mind his foibles.

Father reminds me of the rules everyday, but they aren't rules I will break anyway.

I'm not to leave this room on my own. I don't want to leave this room until I'm fixed.

I'm not to take off my cloak. I don't want to take off my cloak because it's such a strange thing attached to me on my right shoulder. As well, I still haven't figured out the cloak pin. Elysia has to undo it for me. It's better when she does. Her hands don't shake like Father's.

Chapter 2

From Nowhere

J ohn followed Abigail into the house. He stayed a respectful distance from her, making sure to turn his good side toward her. Her left hand reached up to grasp the pull-string of the overhead light. With a gentle tug, the alchemic reaction within the bulb whirred and then quieted. The glow started up, filling the entryway with its sodium-yellow color. The last time John was inside this home, that light wasn't installed. Alchemic lamps were starting to become common-place, even in the heartlands.

Abigail turned to face him. "Would you like to take off your coat?"

"No, I'll keep it on, thank you."

"Rus did say you'd probably prefer wearing your coat. It's just going to get real warm here, John."

"I can take this off." He doffed his hat to reveal his graying hair in need of a trim. Dark and silver-streaked, it hung in loose curls over his ears. He offered his hat to her.

Abigail took it, with its teardrop crease at the crown, and

hung it near the front door. As she did so, the feather in the hatband shimmered a golden color in the overhead light of the entryway. "Has anyone ever asked you what sort of bird this feather comes from?"

"They have."

"And what do you tell them?"

"It comes from a bird across the sea, you wouldn't have heard of it. It's a rare one."

"Is that where you're from? Across the sea?"

"I'm from nowhere," he replied.

"Goodness, we all come from somewhere, John." She led him into the candle-lit parlor. His heeled boots knocked across the wooden floor following Abigail's quieter steps. The curtains were shut, which was unusual for this time in the morning. He took inventory of the dim room.

The parlor was organized to entertain guests with a baby grand piano in the corner. Most of the furniture in the seating area was new. A coffee table of dark wood was set between matching reading chairs and a loveseat. John put his hand on the high arm of one of the reading chairs before he explored the cushioned upholstery with his fingertips—velvet. From his inspection, everything was expensive and of fine quality.

"Please feel free to sit," Abigail said.

John inspected the chair. He shook his head, unable to imagine himself sitting in the soft plushness between those arms.

"I don't mind standing," he said, adjusting the satchel so that it lay just a little bit differently on his stiff right shoulder.

"I think I understand what you need. Rus *has* told me a great deal about you." She eyed his empty sleeve before going to the piano in the corner of the room. She put her left hand on the bench. "Will this do?"

John looked wistfully at the shape of her fingers against the leather atop the bench. Her golden wedding band stood out brightly against her dusky skin. She had dexterous, well-used hands. He noted she was left-handed. He was as well, not that he had a choice in the matter. Sharing some uncommon traits always made people seem familiar.

"I can figure something else out, John," Abigail said because he hadn't answered her.

"No, this will do. It's, um, the piano wasn't there before."

"Rus got it for me right before he left for the war."

"Yes-yes, sometimes a piano can be good company, I think."

"It can be." She started to drag the bench towards the coffee table inch by inch. The wood complained as it scraped across the floor. "It's a bit heavy because we keep the books . . ."

John picked the bench up as if it weighed nothing by lifting it from underneath the seat. Her eyes rounded at how effortless it was for him.

"Please don't strain yourself. As you can see, it's no problem for me."

Her hazel eyes were burning with questions, but she didn't ask them, thankfully. He didn't feel like answering them. He had a job to do, but he figured she wouldn't cooperate until he had made himself comfortable for her. So, perhaps that was what he had to do in order to figure out why magic wanted him here.

"Where ought I to put this?" he asked.

Abigail pointed to the right side of the loveseat. "Rus sits here usually. You should try and sit close to him if you can."

The seat was tired where she indicated, worn down from

years of a man tucking himself into the corner. The backrest had a few spots of discoloration, but only on Cyrus's side.

John then placed the bench nearby, and positioned himself at the very edge. Once there, he arranged how his duster draped over his limb, only peeking up once to find Abigail had turned away to give him some privacy. "Cyrus must have told you a bit too much about me, I think."

"He has told me a lot. I'm sorry if that makes you uncomfortable."

"Perhaps I'm just not used to it," John said. "Thank you for not trying to get a look at the thing."

"Of course, John."

"Can I meet Cyrus at-tum?"

"At a tomb?"

"Meya kulp—er, I'm sorry. I'm nervous, et this place is nostalgic."

"Oh it's alright John. I just wasn't sure what you meant is all. And to answer your question: Yes, you can meet Rus soon enough."

John took a deep breath to calm himself.

Abigail pretended to be busy, fluffing the cushions of the loveseat. "He did say you were a shy one. I don't mind how you are, really. And he knows you, so you can relax."

John nodded.

"It might take him a while though—getting ready I mean. He'll need my help for that. Also, he can be hard to take right now, and he'll need you to be patient with him. Can you do that?"

"I can. Years ago, he was patient with me. It's only proper that I return the favor."

She went down the hall where there was that room which

was newer than the rest of the house. Some of her words stuck with him. Once upon a time, John always needed help to get ready. He was surprised Cyrus did.

It was Cyrus, after all, who taught him how to light matches one-handed. How to work some chores on the farm. He even figured out how John could use a knife to cut vegetables.

6 Aprilis 1892

My tutor came earlier today. He is learned and he hails from America. He came on a boat last year, when he started working for my father. He smiles too much, but maybe that's how Americans are. He taught his lesson as usual, so it was easier to pretend I was still like normal.

I asked J Bellamy about 'sinister'. He said it is 'left'. 'Left' is also the word for 'that which remains'. My left arm is what is left.

He examined me, as he was a doctor once. I turned my head away when he looked at what my right arm became. He asked if I could move it. I could, so I followed his instructions on how he wanted me to move it. He asked for me to put the cloak back on. I tried, but I couldn't get it to drape right and I still hadn't figured out the pin.

While he watched me to have difficulty dressing myself, he told me that his boy was still in America and he grew up and married a woman with three toes on her left foot. She learned how to dance and he liked how she matched his boy he raised so well. I didn't know he had a son. He didn't seem the type to have children.

My cloak still was a chaos by the time Elysia had come to check on us. She fixed my cloak and fastened my pin for me. My tutor told us that it would be kinder to let me learn on my own.

He said, from what he saw, amputation was the best solution at now and that he could do it. He said he used to be a surgeon once and he could schedule it straight away. It is scheduled before Aurelius would come back from

Albion. Maybe my older brother won't ever have to see it, but I'll have only one arm and that begs an explanation.

Note from J Bellamy

The amputation is scheduled on the morning of April 10, 1892. I also want permission to engage in a vivisection to explore the unique anatomy of your son. If I do not have permission to do so, I will simply not do any of it. There are not many surgeons as skilled as I am. And of those, I don't believe any are familiar with magic. Of course, I will be discreet.

—J. B. B.

Chapter 3

No Turnips

Sitting alone in that parlor, awkwardly perched on the end of a piano bench, made John notice the ache and stiffness in his back and shoulder all the more. He sat up to correct his posture and put his left hand under his coat to support the limb he hid. Because of the way the damned thing was attached to him, he had to lift it up to bring relief to his muscles. It was the only thing that ever felt heavy anymore.

The candles around the perimeter of the room made the shadows float like phantoms. Knickknacks lined the shelves along the walls in maximalist clutter. Two end tables guarded either side of the archway that led down the darkened hall. A pair of matching alchemic lamps, with their cylindrical glass-and-metal bulbs, were centered on each of the walnut end tables. The parlor would be brighter if only they were switched on.

At the end of the hall, the doorknob turned. In response, John adjusted his arthritic shoulder and hunched slightly forward. He patted his left hand against the thigh of his jeans, in case he had gotten some dust on him.

Abigail emerged first. "Careful sweetheart." She guided her husband so his blond head wouldn't knock against the door jamb.

"I ain't an invalid," Cyrus complained. As if on cue, he swayed and had to hold onto his wife to keep his balance.

She supported him until he found his footing again. "You still sure you don't want your chair, Rus? I can just wheel you out."

"Sure as hellfire! I got this!"

She helped get him to the wall to support himself, and then she stepped back to give him space.

Cyrus's arms were tight against his body. His bent wrists tucked his hands into his chest. He had to concentrate to get his legs to cooperate. None of his steps were consistent as he slid his shoulder along the wall, shambling towards the parlor. Abigail's cream-colored blouse was like a beacon behind him as they walked the unlit hallway together.

A controlled breath filled John's lungs, which he exhaled quietly. He had suspected something might be wrong with his friend, but he wasn't prepared to see him like this.

Cyrus stayed at the opening of the archway, leaning against its frame to stay on his unsteady feet. As if keeping up appearances was important, his well-groomed beard didn't have a hair out of place. His eyelids fluttered as he turned his head this way and that, listening. "Abby, someone there?" he asked. The corner of his mouth was turned up slightly in the hint of a smile. He already had an inkling who it might be because a sense of eeriness always accompanied strange things. And this eeriness was familiar to him.

"You're blind Cyrus," John stated as soon as he realized it.

"Sawr-riss! Ha! Ain't nobody else talks like you around

these parts, John! I reckon you don't know what to make of me," he said with a chuckle. "Have you changed as much as me?"

John shook his head.

"He shook his head, Rus," Abigail narrated for her husband.

"So, you're quiet as ever. You're gonna have to get used to speaking up if you're gonna be in my company the way I am right now. I can't hear your head rattle."

"Sorry."

"Ha, don't be sorry, ya silly goose," Cyrus said. "I always tried getting you to talk more. Shame it took going blind to make some progress on that front." He pushed himself against the archway with a grunt. It was a lot of effort for him to stay standing.

"Here, Rus, let me help you get into the parlor. You can sit and talk to John then."

"Alrighty."

Abigail took each of his hands in hers, and walked backwards to the loveseat. With his wife leading, Cyrus moved quicker and with more confidence.

"It's right there now," she said.

Cyrus plopped into the loveseat. "I made it!"

Abigail sat next to her husband on his left side. She put her hand on his slack-clad thigh. He wore a bespoke shirt and vest, with a small handkerchief in the pocket.

The pair of them looked to be a good match, the sort where being married made the wife more beautiful and the husband more handsome. Cyrus's strong chin made Abigail's look more feminine. Her long fingers looked elegant despite the calluses compared to his farmer's hands, made strong and thick from a lifetime of hard work. Her hair was long and dark, while his blond hair was trimmed short and roguishly unkempt. When

Cyrus's body tensed again causing him to grunt, it was then and only then that John realized the married couple were not holding hands because Cyrus could not do so comfortably. His arms still folded his fists against his chest.

However, this time John noticed those arms were well-muscled. He was surprised how strong and fit his old friend looked despite not being able to move well.

"John, come on over here." Cyrus tried to move his right hand to beckon his friend near, but the gesture wasn't fluent. "I wanna take a gander at you. I do have *some* vision. It's just not enough to be real useful yet."

John walked around the coffee table to approach the loveseat. Cyrus tilted his head down and to the side to look from the corner of his eye. It was strange, but John understood when he saw how those flickering brown eyes only calmed their frantic movement when in a sidelong gaze. Cyrus's clenched hands were up against the duster. "John! You're wearing that same ratty old coat!" He shut his lids and sank back into the right corner of the loveseat to rest. "So, you're still cursed then?"

John nodded.

Cyrus chuckled. "I'm gonna guess you nodded."

"He did, Rus," Abigail confirmed.

"Ain't you lonesome, John?" Cyrus asked. "With the way you're all put together like that?"

Normally, John didn't speak about himself, but because his friend was in such a poor state, he humored him. "Not at all. I'm doing fine. As good as something like me is able."

"Well, that best be true."

"What about you, Cyrus? I didn't know you were doing so poorly."

He shook his head and laughed. "Don't worry 'bout me,

John. Believe it or not, I'm doing fine, too. Once I'm up for a bit, things start working again. See, we usually entertain the guests when I'm feeling better. You did drop in unexpectedly."

"I'm sorry."

"Oh don't be! I'm glad you're here. I's so worried we'd never meet again. Look at everything what's happened since I last saw you: I got myself a wife, I fought in a war, and I know I look piti-ful," he said with a smile. "But it's just . . . It takes a while after I wake up. I'm fine, John. Really I am."

John didn't know what to do with that information, but he decided to accept that this was how Cyrus would be right now. "Is it just you and Abigail here?"

"Yeah, but we ain't lonely or nothing. We have all our guests that come by. Speaking of, all of my regular visitors know not to come to my home empty-handed. It's only good manners bringing a gift."

"Yes-yes, I'm aware." John walked over and picked up his satchel where he left it, across the room. "I have brought all of the ingredients required for a good roast." He offered it to Cyrus, but then realized his friend wasn't able to inspect the gift with his tight arms, balled up hands, and unfocused eyes.

"It's fine John. I'll take it. You can sit," Abigail said before things got too awkward.

The satchel traded hands, and John reclaimed his seat on the piano bench. He adjusted his duster again, nervously.

Abigail opened the bag. "Goodness, Rus, if only you could see it right now! It's more than the meat. He's got these vegeta-bles, too: taters and carrots."

She held them out for her husband, one at a time, close to his chest so he didn't need to force his arms forward. He touched the vegetables by putting the backs of his trembling hands against them. His eyes kept moving under his lids, like he was dreaming.

"No turnips?" he asked.

"No turnips," she confirmed.

"He remembered I hate turnips."

She looked at John. "That was really thoughtful of him."

She put the vegetables away, shut the satchel, and then opened it again.

Cyrus grinned. "Oh Abby, I can smell it already. Rosemary, thyme . . . Are these herbs? How's it all smell fresh-picked?"

"It's because it's a witch's satchel," John explained. "Time doesn't pass when it's closed up. You can pack as much as you want into it, but it's always easy to get what you need. The contents change depending on what you're looking for."

"That's amazing!" Cyrus said. "So do I just get the food or the whole kit-and-caboodle?"

"Ah, the whole kitten-a-boodle," John replied.

"Enchanted things're expensive. You're doing well for yourself then with this job of yours. What is it?" As Cyrus spoke, his body kept jostling and fidgeting, never completely able to be still.

"I'm a handyman."

"Really, John?"

He nodded, but caught himself this time. He made sure to speak aloud, "I am. Is it so hard to believe?"

"A bit. Last I checked, you weren't great at being handy. And you still have just one hand, right?"

"I do." He held up his hand. "And it's the left."

Abigail giggled.

Cyrus smiled. "Lordy, I missed you, ya silly goose. Well, do you like doing it? Being a handyman, I mean?"

"Sometimes, I suppose. What about you, Cyrus? Are you doing well for yourself?"

"I reckon I am. See, 'cause I'm a decorated hero, a legend and all, they make sure I'm taken care of. That I'm alright. I get plenty of guests come through, and I get plenty of gifts.

"Look around, I've got these expensive doodads all over the place now. But this witch's satchel you got me is the best one I've gotten in a long while. Mostly 'cause it means on the day that the wind finally blows you on in, we get to feast like kings!"

Letter to Elysia (Translated)

Elysia,

Everyone acts as though this is my last day. They are cooking a feast with all of my favorite foods.

Tomorrow is the surgery. I am not certain how it will go. If something should happen, I want you to know I am very grateful for the kindness you've shown me while it was attached to me. It's been a few weeks, and it's been difficult to be like this.

Once it's gone, let's play on the shore again. Or read books in the library. I miss how we used to put on voices and act, as if in a play, when we read those stories aloud. I still won't be able to play piano the way I used to, but when it's gone, you can play my right hand. I can still play the left. Both of us can fit on the bench then, side by side.

Hopefully, I can dress myself after the amputation. I imagine it would be easier with nothing there at all. I know the first few days, you were very nervous around it, but it will be gone soon. Then we don't have to worry about it anymore.

You remembered I was attached to it. It felt like everyone forgot that except for you.

Your brother,
Malachy Secundus

Note from J Bellamy

The amputation was completed on April 10, 1892. I put in the final suture at 6:56 in the evening. I removed all of the curse-affected epidermis and bone. I could not get all of the muscles. That would definitely have been overzealous and survivability would have been greatly reduced. I recommend that I am the one to change the bandages while your son is in this delicate state to improve the chances of healing with fewer complications. Also, I need to keep monitoring him so I can adjust the medications as necessary.

— J. B. B.

29 Aprilis 1892

I had the amputation on the 10th. I was unable to write in the journal until today because I was not well. I am still not well. J Bellamy removed not just the limb attached to me, but also my shoulder. I look very different now. I have been taking many things for the pain.

The pain is so immense at now and everything remains tight. That tightness was what I really wanted relief from, but it appears I am stuck with it. I can't adjust anything like I did before to help release some of the tension. I never noticed how much I moved that appendage to help with that until he had cut it off so completely.

Before, I hoped that the curse could be undone and I could go back to how I was at priori the morn of 16 Martius when my arm changed. I see that is not going to happen.

Father is clumsy with his help. He sometimes does too much, even though he remains hands off. I noticed he is around me more now that I'm fully human again with no bestial parts. Maybe it was like a gangrene that we had to stop before it poisoned all of me for him. He looks at me more even though I think I am very hard to look at. He seems relieved that it's been taken care of. He always says we'll get through this, but he isn't the one who is mutilated.

Elysia also does too much. She is a doting sister. She always fixes my hair because I cannot brush it well anymore and it's getting long, but we cannot cut it until I am more healed. We cannot risk the hairs coming into the wounds as it may cause infection. She keeps me company even when my head feels so confused from all the medicine. I can feel her nearby often, like an angel even when I can barely open my eyes. I know she is not there when J Bellamy changes the bandages. She was once, but she cried too hard to see what my body looked like at now. I didn't need that.

I believe she preferred me the other way. Right now, I think I do, too. But maybe I'll get used to me like this when I am healed.

J Bellamy is good company somehow even though he's odd. I think it's because he chats to me as if I were any other seventeen year old. He still teaches me like usual. But sometimes the pain comes in a wave and it's more than I can stand. He waits while I breathe through the worst of it. When it passes, his blue eyes look over me. He seems to know when I can think again because he continues right where he left off. "I took too much off," he says. "Next time I won't take so much off."

I don't like the way he says next time, but it's to be expected. Most men who study magic too long tend to have a scattered mind. J Bellamy is no exception. I think a lot of the reason why most of mankind has left wizardry behind is because we prefer when our thoughts make sense instead of getting mixed up by magic.

Sometimes, he gives me a candied orange he cooked in the kitchen. People tell me he's a good cook. He winks and tells me they were his boy's favorite when he was still a child. I love sweets, so maybe I am still a child, too. I feel like one in any case, because everyone is taking care of me while I stay in bed.

Because I stay in bed, I have been practicing the pin to

pass the time. I am pleased that I finally figured out how to undo it on my own.

Aurelius comes home soon.

30 Aprilis 1892

I am a cracked bell that rings dolor, dolor, dolor. When the pain medicine starts to fade, I am not to take another dose because my body is not ready yet. Sometimes I lie and pretend it is time. Elysia tells me she hates when I take too much medicine. She can tell when I tricked the servants because my speech gets confused and sometimes, I even look half-dead, and I get so nauseous that all that I eat I vomit.

I'm between doses at now. I can feel that the pain relief is fading. I can tell because it's hard to concentrate on this writing and the pain is getting more wicked.

Overseas, they give their daughters the name Dolores sometimes. 'Dolor' is 'sorrow'. Traditionally, it is a Spanish name I think. Here, 'dolor' means 'severe pain' or 'suffering'. Specifically in Nyuskom, 'dolor' is the kind of pain that makes one regret every decision ever made leading up to it. I shouldn't have let my Father schedule the amputation. It was better for me before. I was only strange before. Presently, I'm strange et in dolor.

Chapter 4

Be Patient With Me

With the satchel hanging at her hip, Abigail moved through the curtained archway that led to the dining room and beyond that, the kitchen. The curtain was decorated with bells and beads, which chimed softly as she passed through. When she was in the dining room, she flicked the lights on, and their amber-tinged glow escaped between the drapes.

With Abigail out of the parlor, John relaxed his cramping shoulder and sat up straight. The right side of his duster filled out. Unlike the drumbeat in his head, the chronic pain never let up. When he was able to open up that joint, away from Abigail's eyes, he used movement to try to ease it into a dull ache. His exhale came out rougher than he expected.

"Sounds like that's hurting more than it used to," Cyrus said. He was still twitching in his seat, but his hands were no longer pressed tight against his chest. Instead, they laid in his lap like quiet moths.

"Don't fret over me. In comparison, your condition seems the more difficult one, ver."

"Ain't no point in comparing, John. Besides, look: My hands

are freeing up." Cyrus lifted them and wiggled his fingers. "The rest of it takes a while yet."

"I did this to you," John said hollowly.

"You'd never've done nothing like this to me. You'd've . . ." He rubbed his temples and leaned forward. "Sorry. Just be patient with me."

"How much pain are you in, at-now?"

Cyrus took a few deep breaths and then sat up. "Psh, it ain't nothing. It'll fade once I get through this part of the morning. I'm already feeling much better." His entire body was steadier. "I figure you're always in some kind of pain. I used to take care of you, remember?"

"Yes-yes, I remember," John replied.

"I reckon you'd be more comfortable if you took that coat of yours off."

"I would remove it if it were only you. But I don't know how your wife would react to see a thing like me."

"Aw, Lordy, John. She's met you at least a hundred times in the stories I've been telling her."

"What have you told her about me?"

The tinkling of bells announced Abigail returning to the parlor as she passed through the curtains of the archway. She still wore the satchel, and was now holding stacked bowls. "He told me that you're a silly goose, John," she said brightly, interrupting their conversation.

John's right shoulder moved forward and down, and his silhouette slimmed.

"So far, from what I've seen, he'd be perfectly right," she teased.

Cyrus laughed.

"How're you coming along, sweetheart?"

"Ahead of schedule!" He fanned out his fingers, gave a mischievous grin, and made an obscene gesture to demonstrate his new dexterity. One hand circled into an O; the other one thrust two fingers into that hole he made.

"Oh goodness, Rus!" Her dusky face reddened. "We have a guest over!"

"Abby! It's John! He already knows how I'll be. What's the point putting up airs for someone who already knows I'm a right fool?" Still, Cyrus dropped the vulgarity from his hands for his wife's sake. "John, you've gots to tell me if she's blushing."

"She is."

Abigail set the bowls on the low table, placing them down with some noise. "I guess you're right, Rus. It's not like we're entertaining royalty or nothing."

Cyrus listened for the wooden knock to pinpoint where she had put them. His fingers explored the rim of the bowls to understand how they were stacked before he separated them.

"I might be the prince of nowhere," John added, offhandedly.

"I found you half-dressed and drunk in a wagon full of moonshine, ya silly goose. That's as far from being a prince as you can be." Cyrus placed the bowls side-by-side in front of him, on the low table.

"Hm, you're not incorrect," John replied.

"Well, prince or pauper, we're glad to have you," Abigail said. She kissed her husband on the cheek. "Knife's to the right of the bowls."

Cyrus tapped along the edge of the table until he felt the handle of the knife. He picked it up, but then shook his head and set it back down. His hands were trembling again.

"How're you feeling, Rus?"

"The usual. I'm almost there. My eyes . . . They're still doing that stupid thing, ain't they?" When he opened his eyes, they kept darting back and forth involuntarily, almost violently. He shut them again, for some respite. "It feels like it. Gives me a damn headache when they do that."

"Do your eyes stop doing that?" John asked.

"'Course. Eventually," Cyrus said. "We're getting to the point where . . ." He lifted a finger to ask for a moment.

"Cyrus? Are you not well?"

"Oh, just give him a second, John. That's all he needs," Abigail explained.

Cyrus's lips quivered, and his breathing became ragged.

"What's happening to you?" John asked, concerned. "Are you unable to speak?"

"John! Quit talking to him," Abigail warned. "Like I said, give him a second."

"Well, tell me what's wrong with him!" He didn't mean to be so demanding, but he wanted to know because this had to be why he was drawn to come here in the first place.

"Look John, I'm fine. Just. Just . . ." Cyrus cleared his throat, then grimaced. "Shit. Just be patient with me." His voice was strained. He tried to lift a hand, but it didn't work anymore. "Just buh . . . paysh . . ." His words fell apart and then they were gone.

"Too much excitement, sweetheart?" Abigail's brows came together, and a worried wrinkle appeared on her forehead.

The sides of Cyrus's neck tightened as he tried to work his jaw, but all he managed was a grunt and whimper.

"Oh, Rus." Abigail pulled the satchel off of herself and pushed it into John's hand.

"What is this? We need to stop it!" He hopped to his feet, ready to help.

"Please sit back down," she said.

"Explain why he acts like this!"

"Please sit, John," she said again, with more authority despite not changing the volume of her voice. "Once he's to this point, there's no stopping it."

Obediently, John took his seat. He could only look on.

Cyrus grit his teeth in frustration. Each of his breaths was drawn with wet effort.

"I know, sweetheart. It has to run its course."

"Will he be well?" John asked.

"Yes, this happens sometimes," she said. "I need you to stay quiet when he's done with this. He'll explain it when he comes out of it. He always does. Then, he tells a story to give his mind a moment to catch up." She turned her attention to her husband. "You just got a bit excited, didn't you Rus?"

Cyrus gasped as he breathed unevenly, as if between sobs. His entire body tensed so much that his back arched. A yelp was forced out of his throat before he flopped, crumpled on the loveseat, with his limbs akimbo. After a moment, he straightened himself back up into a seated position with trembling, uncooperative arms. He kept trying to move his jaw to regain the ability to speak, but it made his teeth clack together over and over, which frothed his spittle into a foam that gathered on his bottom lip and close-trimmed beard.

Abigail plucked the handkerchief from her husband's vest pocket. She then sat beside Cyrus on the loveseat. The fabric of her skirt tucked under her thigh as she scooted closer to him. A tender hand alighted on his chest, and she traced the path she wanted his breath to take as it moved the air into and out of his lungs. He matched the rhythm she set for him, and he calmed down. He tilted his head and opened his eyes to peek at his wife. His vision steadied briefly only in those sidelong glances.

She smiled. "There you are, sweetheart. I see you." She gently closed his mouth and then wiped at the drool on his bottom lip and chin. "You're in the parlor. About to help me cut the vegetables. Your hands are back, and your eyes are on their way. You can talk, Rus. You just got confused for a second, but it'll come back like it always does."

"What ah, tuh, tuh . . . hmmm?" His mouth trembled.

"It's late morning," she said, knowing exactly what he was trying to say.

"Hmm . . ." Cyrus's fingers fluttered over his wife's blouse, up her slim neck, and then he felt her face. He grinned, recognizing her soft lips under his fingertips. "Ah, luh. Late morning . . . Abby." Then, he laughed, finally getting his words in order. "Oh, be patient with me, my love. I was losing my mind right then, weren't I? Getting confused and all."

"Well, yes, you do that sometimes, Rus." She folded the handkerchief and pushed it back into his vest pocket.

"Ah, I'm sorry."

"You do a fine job getting your bearings. You always tell me to be patient, but you ought to be patient with yourself."

"See, it gets hard when my eyes start to work. I think it's 'cause my eyes only half-work for a while, and that's what confuses me," he said.

"You say that almost every time."

"Oh, sorry."

"And then you apologize just like that, too. But it's fine. That's how I know you'll be alright, Rus. When you say all the same things you always say."

"Have I told you about my friend John?" Cyrus asked.

Abigail looked up to meet John's eyes and put a finger on her lips to remind him to be quiet.

"You have, sweetheart. But tell me anyway. I love hearing about him."

Cyrus smiled. He always liked telling stories. "When I's younger, I inherited this farm from my grandpappy after he'd died. I tried keeping it on my own, but I needed a farmhand. And wouldn't you know it? I found one in a wagon—a foreigner who was in bad shape. He only had one arm. The other one had been cut off of him. I saw he needed help, so I decided to take him in. And wouldn't you know it: 'bout a year later, it grew back, and it weren't an arm at all. Instead, it was a—" He gasped. "John's here, ain't he? I just remembered that."

"He is," Abigail confirmed.

Cyrus sighed. "Sorry you had to see that, ya silly goose."

"Does this happen often?" John asked.

"Oh, shucks, it ain't bad as it used to be. Now, I might could be fuzzy for a lil bit. But John, if I need a moment, kindly give it to me. Then, I can put myself back together right quick."

"Yes-yes, I can do that, no problem."

John knew that the magical force which fueled his wander-lust had seen this scenario play out so many times. He could feel its smugness in that parlor like a shrike impaling its grasshopper on a thorn to display it: *Look, John, what you've done to him.*

It just loved things like that.

3 Maius 1892

Today, I'm in a moment of having a clarity. It's a rare thing at now, so I am writing all I can before I lose this again. I think it is in between too much and too little medicine. It feels always one or the other.

Aurelius returned four days ago. I didn't go out to the shipyard to greet him. I'm still healing and the weather has been bad. When it is wet, everything hurts more. I've seen him visit me a few times, but he doesn't stay long and I am so tired and with so much medicine that it's hard to answer his questions. The last few days I felt like my mind was too far away. I think my words came out as if I were inebriated, but I'm not to have any alcohol while I take this medicine. J Bellamy said not to.

Elysia tried to encourage me to walk out of bed because it has been nearly a month since the surgery. It was hard to place my feet. She doesn't know how to hold me to keep me from stumbling because I am missing so much of myself, so the attempt was short.

Aurelius was there to watch J Bellamy change my bandages today. Unlike Elysia, he did not cry, but I could tell he wanted to. He asked me how it happened. I told him I woke up transformed in the middle of Martius without explanation. He thought my description was a fever-dream. Then, when Father and Elysia confirmed it, he said it was like some fairy tale curse.

I believe there's a story like it. But my head hurts and I can't think of it. Elysia reads many fairy tales to me, but they all mixed up in my head and sleep comes too fast or too slow. Or too heavy or too light. Nothing is consistent.

Except that Elysia keeps reading the fairy tales to me. She says when I'm fretful, it calms me.

I asked J Bellamy about which fairy tale is the most like me, but I don't think he understood my question. Instead, he informed me that magic loves the stories that people tell each other. Stories are the best way people can hope to know what happens when it comes to magic and how it tries to affect men. We use allegories and metaphors to understand. It likes the plots we come up with. So sometimes, when it finds a space where it can touch a man, it makes those stories true. Apparently, that is what has happened to me, according to J Bellamy. He seemed honest when he said so.

The English call this month May. In English, 'may' also expresses 'possibility' or 'permission' or 'hope'. To me, it's the wrong month to name 'May' because I don't see myself with any of those three things.

Note from J Bellamy

I reduced the potency of a few of the medications. The side effects were disrupting his coordination, circadian rhythm, speech, and mental acuity, but the issue should be resolved now. He appears to be healing well.

— J. B. B.

12 Maius 1892

It is getting easier to write with the left hand only and my penmanship is improving. Elysia knows when I write in my journal because I get ink on the side of my hand. The ink looks so dark on me. I've gotten paler than she from how long I stayed indoors during my strange affliction and the recovery from my amputation thereafter, which I am still in the midst of. Aurelius said I'm almost as pale as the majority in Albion. I'm glad my family are teasing me again like they used to.

Occasionally, my family catches me at a bad time when the pain is being difficult. I am sharper to them and I don't mean to be. I am not good company at then. When I notice my family is weary of me, I send them away so they can get a break from it. I wish I could get a break from myself.

Today, the pain is not so much. There are good and bad days. I'm glad for the good days as long as I don't think too much about how I was before.

Elysia helps me on the good days. She walks slowly beside me and helps me to find a chair. I like to sit in the sunshine with her. We read books side by side because I cannot do much else yet. She pretends I'm not missing so much of my body.

The bad days are hard though. On those days, I can only grit my teeth and breathe. I feel like I am tethered to the dolor and it is bigger than me. My mind is locked up. Holding still hurts, but moving hurts, so I don't know how to be.

When J Bellamy undoes my bandages, he leaves it for some time before he redresses it. He says the air is good for wounds. That they need to breathe the way anything alive needs to. He can look at me steady when that horrible concave is exposed. I can't even look at myself there. It makes me nauseous, so I keep my eyes away.

J Bellamy told me again that he took too many bones from me. He said, "Next time I won't take as many from you."

Because my head was more clear this time, I asked, "What do you mean 'next time?'"

He explained to me, "It's a curse. It will come back. Tomorrow is Friday the 13th and superstition marks that day on every calendar, so probably then."

If I do get it back, I hope people will stop making a big excitement out of it. They have so many questions and I get overwhelmed easily, so I don't look forward to having it again. Sed, it is a condition better than the one I am in at now.

'May' could be a good name for the month depending on what happens tomorrow.

Chapter 5

Not a Morning Person

Once Cyrus was recovered, Abigail put the washed carrots and potatoes on the coffee table for her husband to get started with that chore. John's only job was to pass the vegetables to Cyrus. Abigail left the two of them alone to start preparing the other ingredients for the roast. Her departure was marked with the twinkle of bells and beads.

"The bells are new," John said.

"Yeah, I had them put up," Cyrus explained. "I can hear the difference whether folks're moving in or out. The sound's brighter when Abby's coming back into the parlor again."

"You seem to have adapted to being blind."

"I have for the most part. But it's a hell of a lot easier when my eyes work," Cyrus said as he peeled carrots. His fingers had become nimble enough to handle a knife. His eyes still wobbled back and forth, but it was nothing like the frantic movement before. Sometimes, he'd lift one of the vegetables close to his face to check his work.

"Is your vision improving?" John asked.

"I told you already. When I'm up for a while, I get better.

Damn arms have trouble listening to me yet, but they can be still when my hands're busy; so, c'mon now, gimme something else to cut."

John passed him a potato. Cyrus reached forward to grab it as soon as it was offered.

"How much can you see?"

He snorted. "I can see you're still wearing that ratty old coat. How 'bout we talk about what you're hiding underneath it?"

"You know what it is."

Cyrus continued cutting vegetables. "I wanna talk 'bout it anyways."

John grumbled. "Sed kware?"

"Well, now you ain't speaking English. But lemme see if I can remember. I know a bit of that language. Quarry . . . well, kwah-ray, that's your word for 'why,' ain't it?"

"It is." John passed a carrot to Cyrus.

His friend's sensitive fingers touched the carrot to understand the shape of it before he pushed thin peels from the vegetable, revealing the bright-orange of the root under the silver blade.

"Why must you talk of my accursed limb?"

"You never told me much about it, John. The last time you came over, you didn't stay long. That was before the war. Even before I married my Abby. All that time's passed, and it's there, same as ever. So, I wanna ask questions just in case I don't see you for another ten years. Does it still look the same?" With the lack of an answer, Cyrus asked another question. "Do you still need help with it?"

In the past, going quiet used to work, so John focused on the ribbons of vegetable skins filling the scrap bowl.

An annoyed snort puffed from Cyrus's nose. "I need you to answer *something*. Where'd you come from?"

It seemed staying quiet wasn't going to work this time. John simply said, "I'm from nowhere."

"Nowhere! Same answer as always, then. I'm gonna take a guess: Overseas?"

John shrugged.

"I ain't sure if you're nodding or shaking your head. I need you to use words. I'm *blind*, John. And you might could make me excited again. You can't do that, remember what happens?"

"It is unfair to use that as leverage."

Cyrus smiled. "Maybe a little. But if I'm gonna be like this a while, might as well use it. Let's try again: Where're you from? And you can't say 'nowhere' this time."

John rubbed at his aching shoulder under his duster. "Overseas is not incorrect."

"Ah! Now we're getting somewhere. Did you fly here?" Cyrus asked cheekily.

"No. I came on a ship like anyone else would. Can we stop talking of me?"

"You always hated talking 'bout yourself. Ends up, I don't know that much about you, John. Other than the fact that you have a—"

"Don't say it. She might be listening."

"She knows already," Cyrus said, amused.

"Even so. I don't like drawing attention to it. To anything about me that's odd."

"Fine, I can understand that. How many's I got left?"

John looked down at the vegetables on the coffee table. "Coupla. Almost done then. It's impressive how well you handle your knife. I'm envious."

"Oh, right. You can't cut worth shit on your own," Cyrus ribbed. "What about knots? Do I still need to tie them for you?"

"Well, I can *un*tie them," John said.

"So ya still can't tie a knot?"

"Not easily . . . Not very well," he admitted.

"And you said you was a handyman. How's that working out for you?"

"It's a job," John replied wearily. "Let's not talk of it. It's important that we don't."

"Interesting answer. Dodgy as ever."

"Yes-yes, I know. I'm more worried about you, Cyrus. You're not well."

"At least you're using words now. But I'll be fine, John. I can't stay dead. Didn't you hear the stories about me? That one really catchy song?" He laughed, but when John didn't join him, he just sighed. "I'm Cyrus, the Undying Soldier. People come over to visit me when it don't take half the day for me to see and walk again. They bring gifts. Sometimes, they bring stories, too.

"I've heard some stories what might be about you, John. There's a few of them about a one-armed wanderer, strong as hell. Like anyone else cursed, sometimes you're a devil but sometimes you're an angel, depending on who's telling the story. They say that maybe you're something like from those days when magic weren't so rare. I know you can do magic with those feathers of yours. That's what you did to me before you left that last time: Enchant me so I can't stay dead."

"I didn't know you would end up like this. I'm sorry, Cyrus."

"You know, I got to come home from that war because of you, John. Ain't that something?" He placed the knife and potato down on the low table carefully. He took a deep breath.

Guiltily, John said, "I wish I had known you were like this. I would have visited earlier, even with the drumbeat! But all I ever heard out there are the stories about how you kept getting up to continue to fight. How your perseverance helped win the war. I thought you were fine. I should have—"

Cyrus lifted a finger. He was struggling; his ability to speak was gone again.

"A moment," John interpreted.

His friend nodded. He put a hand up to hide what his mouth was doing.

"Should I get Abigail for you?"

Still behind his hand, Cyrus shook his head. He breathed little, moist breaths through a locked jaw.

John waited.

Then, Cyrus's breathing evened out. His hand tugged on the damp handkerchief in his pocket. He attempted to wipe his mouth, but during a spasm, he dropped the cloth onto his lap. His agitation with himself made his limbs too uncooperative when he tried searching for it with his fingers.

"I don't mind helping you if you let me," John said.

Cyrus took a long, pensive pause before he nodded, still mute.

John stood up and took the handkerchief from his friend's lap. He wiped the saliva from Cyrus's mouth, being mindful to be as gentle as possible. He didn't know how long Cyrus's life had been like this. But magic liked its plots, so years at least.

"I know it's not easy to need someone to do too many things for you."

Cyrus nodded again. He squinted his eyes and leaned in close. His face almost touched the coat to investigate it. His mouth was too loose, and a little bit of spittle touched the fabric.

"Sometimes words are hard for me, too."

A nod.

"At my moments when speech is being difficult, I'm not John, just John. But maybe something else, too. I have to find and gather those pieces of me. It is always easier to gather myself beside a friend who understands I'm not exactly human anymore. You always say I am crittery, at-then."

Cyrus smiled. "Jaw . . . nuh." He reached for John's hand and took the handkerchief from it. He wiped his own mouth this time and then tucked the cloth back into his pocket. "You're . . . huh. You're here. Sorry, give me a second. It takes a while. This happens when my eyes start working again. Have you gotten to meet my Abby yet? Sit and talk with her? I can't remember how you got here."

"How much do you forget when—"

"You have!" Cyrus interrupted John. "Sorry, my head gets fuzzy for a bit. Ah, Abby's wonderful! I wish you'd've met her before I ended up like this. I know just the night, too: I'd gone to town, she was there, we drank way too much, and we were dancing. It's easy to fall in love when you're dancing."

"You always danced ridiculous," John said, humoring his friend, not sure if he was all the way back.

"And you never did! Did you ever try dancing before you got cursed?"

John didn't answer.

"I know you're a real quiet feller and all, but I can't tell if you're nodding or shaking your . . ." Cyrus's easy smile faded like his words did. "Shit. I'm real sorry. I just remembered you already asked me to stop. I won't be like this all day, swear to God. I hope you stick around for when I'm able to do better."

John could feel magic's pressure on him to reassure his

friend. "Yes-yes, I will." Then, the next sentence flowed out of his mouth, unbidden: "I intend to stay the night."

"Oh, really now?"

"It's important that I do. It's for my job," he explained.

"You said you were a handyman."

"I did. A handyman *of a kind.*"

"Well, I guess I'll fix up the guest room later when I can manage the stairs again. You'll see that I'll be right as rain soon." He tapped the coffee table with the fingertips of his right hand. "Can you help me? I think maybe I was cutting vegetables earlier before I got all mixed up."

"You were." John picked up the knife and the potato one by one, passing each to his friend.

Cyrus felt the spud to figure out where he left off before he started cutting again. "How many do we have left? Ah, never-mind, I asked that one already. You said 'coupla.' Sometimes you say that when you mean there's a few."

"Yes-yes, that's right."

"Oh, where are you from that you say that? Coupla. And don't say 'nowhere' like you always do."

It felt like the conversation kept circling around. Move forward, back to start, ask questions. No answers. Apologies. One man liked to keep his nest of secrets; the other one, too confused to temper his curiosity.

Cyrus sighed. "I already asked that, too, didn't I?"

"You did."

"The last time you saw me, I was much different. But John, I'm fine. It's just that my eyes are trying to work again. I get confused sometimes when they're like this. It used to scare Abby. But we both got used to it. Please, try and relax. We have to enjoy the roast tonight." This time, he reached for his own potato, no longer needing John's help.

"You remember the roast."

"'Course. We're going to feast like kings!" Cyrus said. "Check on Abby for me and how the roast is coming along awhile. I usually wait till I look more presentable before I leave that room."

John used to send his family away, too. He understood what was happening, and he always hated when they seemed too eager to leave once he gave them permission to. So, he asked, "Are you sure you want me to go?"

"Yeah, I'm sure."

"Will it happen again?" John asked, his voice tight with worry.

"It might. Look, this is how I am right now."

"How is it for you?"

He gave a weary smile. "I ain't allowed to be a morning person no more. That's all."

13 Maius 1892

It came back. I have a shoulder again, which is nice. It hurts a lot less, but it still doesn't feel proper. I never know how to hold this thing my arm became because I don't think it belongs on my body. I know Elysia is soon to come to my room. It's so early now that I have to write by candlelight. In America, I'm told they have the new alchemic lights everywhere.

J Bellamy showed one of his lights to me before all of this mess. A small thing and the light was lilac. He explained last year that the light is a reaction of the potassium. It is brighter than my candle.

I am thankful that it's not too bright here. The darkness covers me enough so I don't have to look at it. I practiced moving it because I had nothing there for a month. But I can move that joint again and it helps when the muscles get tight on my right side of my back.

I took that cloak and I practiced putting it on. It took a long time and I had to look in the mirror. I don't really look at myself anymore, so it was hard. The shape of me in the mirror, in the clarscuro, is so uneven. One side is bigger than the other. It takes a long time for me to get it to drape right so it doesn't look too conspicuous. I was able to close the pin myself this time.

I know it will be a big excitement once Elysia sees me. So I probably won't be able to write more today. I know, at least, I'm more comfortable now. I know she will embrace me again because it will no longer hurt me when she does so.

25 Maius 1892

There is unease in our home since it has come back. My family is glad I'm out of pain. At the same time, there is a trepidation because how I am means that magic has marked me, and there's no true freedom from it if the amputation is temporary. It's not right for someone marked by magic to be in a leadership position. Magic is alive, and it's a fickle thing.

Father is hiring some diviners to tell my fortune late next month for us to know which direction to go. I have to stay on the grounds until Father knows what to do with me.

Aurelius said that people are asking about where I am. It has been over two months since our people outside of the grounds have seen me.

I walk the halls at times even with guests around. I'm allowed to as long as I keep the cloak on to cover it. The servants help to take care of it for me. Elysia has involved herself in matters of its care and hygiene, which I appreciate because she maintains discretion and sensitivity about it. I believe we are very close bonded because we are very close in age. She used to sing the songs when I played piano. I only have the left hand, so I don't really play songs on piano anymore. She keeps encouraging me to try, but every time I do, it reminds me that I'm not correct.

Instead, I am trying to find new hobbies. Mostly I watch the help. I think I was always too busy before that I never noticed the skills of these people. I was surprised to see J Bellamy in the kitchen working with the same virtuosity as the cooks. He told me that he was a cook once. I swear he's been everything at least one time. I wanted to try and he wanted to teach me but I found there's no good way to cut the vegetables with just the left hand. I got frustrated. He encouraged me to stay and watch.

It gets too hot in the kitchen, so I stayed for a short while only before I had to leave because I'm not to remove the cloak. It's getting too warm outside. I am Aestus-born, and I can feel Ver preparing to change to Aestus, and I love my season. I used to stand bare-chested by the ocean and play in the waters. I used to ride horses, but none of them like how I became. I used to do many things, but I can't do them anymore. I can still read and study at least.

My studies have switched to anatomy because that is J Bellamy's interest at now. In my opinion, he is too eager about the second amputation Father has already scheduled.

He said he won't take as many bones this time. Maybe it won't be as bad. I don't want it, but Father wants my fortune told after the amputation in case it changes the circumstances for the better. I think he envisions a future where I can still inherit Nyuskom with regular amputations. Does he not understand how horrifying that is?

'May' expresses possibility. I may be able to secure my birthright.

'May' also is for permission. May I please forfeit my birthright? I just wanted to play piano, travel, and come home for Aestus because it is my favorite season here. But now it's too warm because I am required to wear a cloak.

'May' also expresses a wish. May it not be so hot tomorrow when I watch the sea.

Tomorrow is the last day of May.

I realized I've had the months in the wrong language. Meya kulpa, I am just so used to writing it that way.

31 May 1892

Elysia took me to the shore. It was not too hot today
because there was a zephyr. There is a Greek god of the
West wind called Zephyrus. The West wind is the most
gentle of the winds. Today, the island is in the middle of
the ocean. Through the mist, I don't see the shape of any
other lands. I studied geography because I meant to travel
one day. I used to point out what all the lands were to
Elysia when we watched the shore together before all of
this.

I am still worried about the heat. Normally, I take off
my shirt and let the sunlight make my tan skin darker. I'm
the palest I've ever been because I'm not to leave my room
often. When I do, I'm not to remove this cloak.

These days, only Elysia will come with me. I cannot go
far because I cannot ride anymore. I make the horses too
nervous. I noticed people are also uneasy around me, even
when my right side is well hidden. I asked Elysia if she ever
felt uneasy. She said it's not conspicuous at first, but after a
time, when she is next to me, her body has an alarm that I
might be something not quite human.

I apologized to her for it. I don't want my sister to feel
that way.

She said, "You can't help it and it takes a long time
before I notice it too much. And by the time I notice it, I'm
used to it. So it doesn't matter."

I asked her, "Do you feel it at now?"

"Ita-ita, frater. It's not bad. I'm accustomed to it" is
what she told to me. Her English is not as good as mine is,

but I can tell she has been practicing. I've always been the best between us for languages.

We decided to enjoy walking where the shore touches the sea instead of worrying about what I might have become.

Aurelius says in other lands, the water runs up and down the shoreline and follows the moon. Nyuskom is supposed to be more tuned to its magic than other countries are, but what he describes sounds more incredible to me. Here, the water along the shore is always so still.

Chapter 6

Abigail Cooks

The curtain jingled as John passed through the archway, moving from the parlor to the dining room. The light overhead was bright with an amber cast. John's hand ran along the top of the table in the center of the room. It was the same table from before, when he worked as a farmhand here. His fingers found two small holes at one end—where he used to sit. Pegs used to be stuck in them that Cyrus would slot a special cutting board into so John could cut his own food at the table.

Two new matching liquor cabinets were side-by-side against the long wall of the dining room. Glasses of all kinds were on display. Wax-sealed bottles of wine rested in racks. He distracted himself by perusing the alcohol until he felt a small twinge in his head. Magic telling him to get back to work. He sighed and pushed through the swinging, saloon-style doors between the dining room and kitchen.

The pine cabinets had knots on them which made the doors look like maps, and the tile counters were a lighter color than the wood. An iron stove stood apart from everything. The fire was already going strong within its belly, warming the kitchen and heating up a single, large pot which sat on the stovetop.

Abigail's back was turned to him while she was preparing supper at the counter. Her knifework was fast enough that the biting scent of the onion didn't sting her eyes. She wore a mustard colored apron with flowers embroidered around the bib, and the waist-ties wrapped around her twice. She nodded to him in greeting before saying, cheerfully, "It's always a treat to be cooking with such fresh ingredients. That witch's satchel is such a thoughtful gift, John. We live out so far from town."

"Yes-yes. It's not as useful to me. I don't cook much, obviously." He lifted his hand.

"Rus said you helped him out in the kitchen sometimes. He showed me a few of the gadgets the two of you made when you lived here."

"Gadgets, like the curtain you have for Cyrus. Does he have other ones for the rest of it?"

"He does. I wish he'd let me bring him out in his chair. I worry about him falling."

"Chair?"

"He has a wheelchair he can use. He doesn't like using it if he can walk. But I guess his stubbornness is what's made him so famous anyways." Abigail sighed. "Well, you better be staying for supper at least, John."

"Yes-yes. More than that, actually. I'm staying the night. Cyrus said he'd prepare my room when he can manage the stairs. I can't imagine him suddenly being well enough to do all that on his own."

Abigail laughed. "Oh, once he can see again, it all comes back pretty quick after that. Two, three hour tops, I'd say. I usually keep him company to pass the time."

John thought of how Cyrus sent him away instead. "I used to send my sister away many times. But eventually, I let her remain at my side. It was better when she did. Time passed more evenly."

"What's your sister's name?"

"Elysia Pulkara, but let's not talk of me," John insisted, changing the subject quickly. "Cyrus also had another moment like the one you took care of. This time, I didn't make it worse."

Abigail slid all the onions from the wooden cutting board into a bowl with the back of her sharp knife. "Thanks for that John. It's not so bad when he doesn't completely . . . well, you saw how it was." She smiled. "Did you know? You're one of his favorite stories that he tells. He almost always talks about you when he comes out of those episodes of his. Sometimes, he likes to add little things to make his stories more interesting or nicer to listen to. I thought yours was something like that. Since you won't take that coat off, I'm going to guess that part of your story is true, as impossible as it is."

He tensed up.

"Goodness, John. I wish you knew how you are exactly"— she wiped the cutting board and her knife—"yes, exactly like Rus said you were. But the stories they tell about my husband, they are nothing like him!"

John relaxed a little bit. "Yes-yes, he has always said he's just a good man looking for a good time. That's all he is, really."

"That's right! See, you know how Rus is. But those stories everyone tells . . . Oh, they make him out to be this big, grand hero who loves his country and is selfless. And they even have a song about the battles he's been through! Though, I must admit, that one *is* catchy." She surprised John because she immediately burst into song, singing the chorus. Her voice was full and beautiful like an angel's: "What a soldier, true and tough, they cut him down and cut him up! Oh, he dusted off and then stood up, he carried on, carried on, carried on . . ." She stopped singing and asked, "Were you a soldier in the war, too?"

"Oh no, not exactly. I was a mercenary sometimes if the pay was right. I've gotten very good at killing people."

"You say that too candidly for someone my husband speaks so highly of."

"I'm sorry."

"It's fine. I like listening to you. Your voice sounds nice. You have an interesting accent."

"I try to hide it."

"My husband's name trips you up. He always tried to explain the accent to me. It's a lot prettier than how he made it sound. Where are you really from, John?"

"I told you. Nowhere."

"Tch, you also told me you're a handyman." Abigail put the flat side of her knife against the clove of garlic and smacked the blade with the palm of her hand. She rolled the clove free of its skin. The knife rocked rhythmically as she minced the garlic.

Abigail went to the sink. The enchanted faucet turned on as her hand neared it. Next, she approached the stove. Droplets flicked from her fingertips to the pot, where they danced to announce it was hot enough to sear the meat. The well-seasoned beef sizzled as soon as it touched the metal. She used tongs to turn it, browning it on all sides. Then, she added the onions and garlic. The delicious aroma filled the room as the alliums cooked beside the meat in the fond at the bottom. She deglazed it with a dry red wine. She tied herbs in cheesecloth and placed the wrapped bouquet with the roast.

Her proficiency surprised John. He wiped at his perspiring

forehead. "I used to watch the help sometimes when I was feeling well enough. You cook with refinement and technique," he noted.

"Well, my mother worked for the governor, so I was raised in his home, cleaning and cooking and all. One year, there was a cook who was very good, better than anyone else. His name was Joe Breckenridge. He taught me all about the small details that add up to a fine meal. But he was a very strange man."

"He is," John replied. "I've met him. He's odd but polite."

"Oh! Then you *have* met him. That's surprising; this is a large country, John."

"Odd characters tend to attract other odd ones."

"Are you saying you're odd then?"

Her probing curiosity was a lot less direct than Cyrus was when trying to get information out of him, which he was thankful for. "Yes-yes, I suppose I am odd. But mostly I'm plain."

The food was boiling. The kitchen's heat caused the hair at her crown to frizz up. Her hazel eyes studied his right side.

He cleared his throat and turned himself slightly away to hide it.

At that, she refocused on cooking and moved the pot to a cooler part of the stove so it could cook low and slow.

"Rus should be able to see by now. That means you don't have to worry about him getting excited no more. It's too warm for you in here anyways, John."

4 June 1892

J Bellamy has been teaching me much about anatomy. Not just about people, but also about different animals. I guess it makes sense given how I look presently. Today he showed me how most animals are very similar to humans underneath their flesh.

It was interesting especially when he compared the skeleton of the brachial limb. He showed me via the diagrams he had drawn, parts of skeletons he had in his possession, and demonstrated with his own arm how it all worked. Horses actually run on their nails, which is now a hoof. Their long legs are mostly a hand with one long finger. What is their knee is actually what would be a wrist for a person.

Dogs and cats and the other pad-footed beasts are similar except they are all on their tiptoes actually. The dew claw is their thumb but it is up the leg because disuse has made it small and out of the way since it is more important that they run and walk on all fours than have thumbs. But I know I've seen hounds use their small dew claws to try to hold bones when tossed some to chew.

Birds are very interesting. He showed me how the end of the wing is a hand and fingers. There is even a little thumb that he showed to me.

He asked me, "Are you curious about your anatomy now? You should explore the parts of it to see how it matches the parts of your human arm."

Instead, I tucked it closer against me underneath my cloak. I don't see the point if it will be amputated again soon.

I asked him if he ever had the uneasy feeling around me.

He laughed and said it's nothing really to him. He likes being around me because it feels like he can see the connection between men and magic a little easier when I'm near. That connection, unfortunately, is why Father is so insistent on the amputation.

When I asked J Bellamy when the surgery will be, he said next week. He says my muscles are configured differently now because of my transformation. He says last surgery, he did a vivisection to explore my body and had gained an understanding of how me and my curse are knit together. He got a bit too eager and that's why he took so much of me. He said he has a better idea what to do this time and promised again not to take so many bones.

He can be a frightening man at times.

10 June 1892

Elysia joins me on the balcony after my baths. She makes sure to stand between me and the world. We were always close, but I think this situation has made us closer.

It takes the limb a long time to dry after my bath. I feel almost too exposed with my shirt off because she can see how I'm put together then. I try not to look at it. I lay it open on the chair next to me and the vernal sun and the zephyr feels best on it. Better than it does on my human parts if I can be honest. I don't like how that makes me to feel as an animal sometimes. It's even hard to talk when I'm like that.

We read books side by side out in the sunshine. I sit at her right side, and I am her right hand man then. I like learning about the words that echo through many cultures. 'Right-hand man' is one of those. It means the one who supports you the most and is your best helper. I am sitting on the incorrect side. I don't see how I am in that role for her when she has been that for me through this strange Ver. In comparison, I am very useless when I am like this.

Once the limb is dry again, I put my cloak back on, and I fix the pin. Both of us remembered when she had to do so much for me. It is still too much that she has to do. I have gotten good at using my left hand. My penmanship is still awful, but it's legible. Even Elysia can read it if she wanted to. She never tries to. She said I need some privacy because I have very little of it. It is true. So much of my life at now, I am dependent on others.

I find it fascinating the things I can notice. When a man is so different-formed, he becomes an outsider. I sit apart from everyone. Even at the dining table, I have to turn my body so that everything fits. Father corrects me when he can see the tip of it out from the bottom of my cloak. Even the servants who aren't allowed to know are aware of what's underneath. Something beastly. Too many small mistakes have been adding up, and the rumors are flying around Nyuskom, according to Aurelius.

I never noticed the servants before. They were always there, making things convenient for us. But now I recognize their faces because I rely too much on them. They have to help me with my baths, with dressing myself, and with cutting my food. I feel they are better than Father is about it. They don't make it a big deal, but I think I am something uncanny at now. Sets them on edge. Even Father. Maybe that's why his hands shake. I know it's why the horses and the hounds do not like me.

Tomorrow is my second amputation.

Aurelius came to ask me how I felt about that. He stares at it, so I kept my cloak on. I told him I don't really have a choice. Father has already decided on it. Magic has already decided I'm to have one arm. I'm just a seventeen year old against forces stronger than me.

I asked him, "Why can't you take Nyuskom?"

He answered, "Because I have the wrong mother."

I said, "Sometimes it feels like Father loves you more."

He said, "No, no. He doesn't care enough about me to meddle in my affairs."

I told him he was very lucky.

Chapter 7

The Undying Soldier

Crossing the threshold by itself cooled John from the heat he had felt in the kitchen. He thought about how the bells and strings of beads were supposed to sound brighter entering the parlor than leaving it. The difference in the noise wasn't as discernible as John thought it would be based on what Cyrus had told him.

Cyrus was no longer on the loveseat. Instead, he stood at one of the windows, drawing the curtain open to allow morning's hope to beam into the dim room. The sunray lit the veteran's face and made his brown eyes almost gold enough to match his hair as he looked out through the glass panes. His strong jaw with his neat-trimmed beard carried his effortless smile well. The casual ease with which he leaned against the windowsill marked him a dreamer. He turned and waved to John as a gesture to indicate he was able to see clearly.

"Do you remember, John, how much I like stories? It's fun how many they have about me now. You know, they spoke about me on both sides of the war. On our side, I'm a legend, a hero.

I'd die and come back. Over and over. Relentless and tenacious, they love talking about how my perseverance won the war.

"But I heard what they said about me on the other side, too. In one of those stories, every time they killed me, I turned more and more into a worm. Now when they see a big worm, they split it in half just in case it's me so I don't come back. You know, they only killed me seven times in that story before I ended up a worm in the dirt. Seven times! Ha, I wish.

"Since I can't die, I was out there in the worst of it. All soldiers left pieces of themselves on the battlefield. Whether I'm a hero or a worm, I left a lot of pieces of myself, too. Perhaps more than most men. Lord knows how many arms and legs of mine there are scattered across America. But at the same time, I reckon I'm luckier than most men are. 'Cause soon, you won't be able to tell a thing as the day marches on. I'll just be a good-looking guy looking for a good time, like I always am."

John joined his friend near the window. Even though Abigail had said Cyrus wouldn't have another episode, he was still shy to ask difficult questions to test that. Instead, he said, "You seem more like yourself."

"Yeah, I feel more like myself," Cyrus said. "I wanna sit though. Mind helping me back to my seat?"

"How did you get to the window?"

"Lordy, John, it's like you forget what a right stubborn fool I am. Besides, being shameless is easy when there ain't nobody watching."

John noted the dust on Cyrus's knees and the way his clothes were crumpled on his body. "You crawled."

Cyrus grinned. "Like a worm."

"How do I help you?" John asked.

"Just follow me in case I mess up or something. I *can* walk, but it's, well, you'll see. And then it's hard for me—getting up on my own—if I do fall down."

John followed as Cyrus started walking slowly to the loveseat. He kept wobbling, still unsteady on his feet, but his legs were able to carry him. He moved with intention, splitting his focus between the furniture and watching his shoes. Only once did John touch him when he swayed a bit too much to one side, but Cyrus stayed upright the whole way to his seat. As soon as he made it, he plopped down on the cushion and leaned back with a sigh.

"You're moving better than earlier," John said.

"Yeah, I am. The rest'll come back soon. But look at you! Now that I can see clearly, that lil bit of gray looks nice in your dark hair."

John ran his hand through his loose curls, pushing it back away from his face and wiping sweat from his forehead.

"I knew you'd be getting warm in that coat of yours," Cyrus said.

"It's just from the kitchen."

"You might could open the windows up. Get a breeze going."

John moved around the room, drawing the thick curtains and extinguishing the candles as he passed them. The parlor brightened, seeming to grow larger as the sunshine came in. He then opened the windows, and the late morning air ran through the room. He wished it was cooler than it was, but spring was already threatening to bolt into a wild, furious summer.

John returned to the seating area. "The war ended a few years ago—"

"Six," Cyrus corrected.

"Six years ago. Have you been like this the whole time?"

"Yeah."

"I wasn't aware."

"'Course not. It wouldn't be good if everyone knew how their famous war hero woke up in the morning."

"Yes-yes, the stories they were telling were only ever about how you helped to win the war." John glanced at the coffee table with the two bowls on it. "None of them mentioned that you learned how to cut vegetables while blind. That it takes you until noon to see and to walk."

"Oh, don't count what I just did as walking yet. My balance is off. It's all on account of . . . I've been shot in the head too many times," he said the last part too flippantly.

"How many times is that?"

"A bit direct there, ain't ya?" Cyrus snapped.

"Sorry."

"Naw, it's fine. I weren't meaning to say it like that." He took a moment to gather himself. "Truth is, I don't really know anymore. It's been so many times that I've lost count." He clapped his hands together, and when he spoke again, his voice was lighter. "Well, no more dying, I hope, until I die of old age after a life well lived. If I recall correctly, that's the only way I can die and stay dead." Though he was smiling, it didn't reach his eyes.

"I'm sorry for that."

"Oh, not this again. I won't accept your apology, John. Because of you, I's able to come home after the war. As long as I have my Abby, I'll be fine. She got me through the worst of it. It ain't so bad no more."

Cyrus leaned forward to stack the bowls on the coffee table, placing the prepped vegetables on top of the peelings so John could pick up both in his only hand. He put the knife on the carrots and potatoes. "Look, I've finished cutting these. Can you take these to my wife?"

"Yes-yes," John said. "I can do that, no problem."

* * *

ABIGAIL WAS in a chair she had taken from the dining room. The kitchen was so warm the small hairs that poked from the front of her french braid were sweat-slicked against her temples. Frizz haloed her head in the humid warmth of the kitchen. Her mouth moved as she followed the dialogue between the characters in the book she was reading.

Right outside the kitchen, John rolled his right shoulder to get some relief before he tucked it down and hunched forward. The ache in his back intensified when he did that, forcing a pained sigh from him.

Abigail looked up and through the slotted saloon-style doors. "Well, come on in, John. You're bringing the vegetables, aren't you?"

"Yes-yes, I am." He entered the kitchen. "I didn't expect you to be reading." He placed the bowls upon the tile counter.

She finished the page she was on.

John continued to explain, in case he had offended her. "Usually, commonfolk aren't literate in this part of the country. At least, not enough to read novels."

"Yes, that's true. Reading is rare in the heartlands," she said. "Rus taught me, but he told me that you were the one who taught him how to read. So, in a way, it's all because of you that I can." She placed a bookmark made of lace over pressed flowers and shut the novel.

"Why are you hiding in the kitchen?" John asked.

"I keep hoping if I stay away, you'll finally let yourself get comfortable."

"I'm comfortable enough."

"Okay, John, if you say so."

She picked up the root vegetables and carried them to the stove top. Her brown hand lifted the lid of the pot. Hot steam rose up, but Abigail was impervious to it in the way kitchen experience always seemed to make cooks heat-resistant. The fragrance filled the room, promising a beautiful feast in a few hours. She dumped the vegetables in, mixed them around in the unfinished sauce, and then covered the pot again.

"Can I say something, John? It might help you be more comfortable."

"What is it?"

"When I was learning to read, I ended up reading a lot of fairy tales. There's one about a princess whose brothers were all turned into swans by a wicked witch. The princess had to turn them back by making shirts out of nettles that grew in grave-yards. I like that one a lot. It sticks with me because of how self-less she was. The princess, I mean. I can imagine her fingers working with those stinging nettles. Getting red and sore, but she kept going. For years. If she said a word, all of it would have been for nothing—that was part of it, too. I could see why she did it. A sense of duty. Because she loved them, she was just supposed to do it."

John recognized the story as one Elysia had read to him many times when he was recovering. "I know that one, too. Magic likes playing the same plots. There's stories similar to that one in many countries."

"She ran out of time; she didn't finish the last shirt."

"Yes-yes, in most versions, she never finishes that shirt, but she's still a good princess even if she was not able to fix everything."

"Well?" Abigail prompted.

John finally relaxed his shoulder in front of her, letting the shape fill underneath the duster. "There. I'm a little more comfortable. I don't want you to feel like you need to hide away."

She hurried to one of the cabinets and pulled out a silver tea tray. "Oh! Let's have some tea and bread all together. That should pad out the time for Rus until he can walk again. You know, he didn't always take so long."

"Did something happen recently?" John asked.

"Oh goodness. Just a month or so ago, we had a very rude guest."

"What did the guest do?"

"Actually, I think that story would sound better over tea, John."

Letter to Elysia (Translated)

Elysia,

I am about to go through another amputation. J Bellamy promises it won't be as drastic. Still, I am afraid because of how poorly the first one went. You've been by my side through all of this. I can't believe I stopped being nervous about you seeing the thing. Father sees it as the end of his legacy here in Nyuskom, Aurelius can't help but stare, J Bellamy looks at me as if I am a specimen for his study, but you see me, dear sister.

You told me once you thought it was very pretty when I stretched the stiffness from it. I thought you were lying, but I laid on my bed and opened it like a fan in front of my face and the sunlight filtered through it. Maybe I could see what you meant when you said that.

I hope this surgery goes better and I do recover eventually. Father and J Bellamy seem to be of the opinion they can cut off a limb as regularly as one would trim hair.

Thank you, dear sister, for arranging for the barber to come into my room yesterday. As the barber cut my hair, I thought of one of the fairy tales you told me when I was sick and in bed. It was the one about the barber who had to keep the secret the king had donkey-ears that he kept hidden underneath a hat.

I think I'd have preferred that story be my reality. Though, the part with rumors flying around anyway at the end is true. Aurelius told me some people think I have a beast's claw under my cloak. I think I'd rather have something like that. It would be more useful.

I asked Father when it's gone, if I could walk around again without the cloak. He said yes, I could. So maybe we will get to celebrate my birthday next month as normal.

Your brother,
Malachy Secundus

Note from J Bellamy

The second amputation was completed yesterday on June 11, 1892. I put in the final suture at 3:23 in the afternoon. I did not take as many bones this time from your son, as requested. I only amputated the following: the digits, carpo-metacarpus, alula, and the radio-ulnar bones of his right brachial limb.

I left the scapula and the humerus this time. If you are unhappy with the result, I can always take more the next time.

—J. B. B.

15 June 1892

I am not going to write a lot because I am in too much pain again. I'm told the operation went fine. Father is unhappy because enough is left that you can tell I'm cursed between the bandage changes. Once it is covered, it looks like it was just an arm.

Elysia reads to me while I recover in bed. She read the fairy tale that reminds her of us. She has tried to read it to me a few times, but it is hard for me to follow the story to the end of it. The pain medicine is very strong when it hits.

21 June 1892

The Aestival Solstice is today. You can tell who is noble born here. We still call it Aestus, but the common-folk call it 'sommer' now because more sailors say it that way rather than 'Aestus'.

I think things will be better. The bandages cover up the stump well enough, so wearing a cloak at now is no longer necessary. It is a relief because I was worried I'd be too hot for my favorite season.

I'm still dazed and in much pain, but this is not as bad as the last amputation.

J Bellamy says this time, he amputated the limb at what would be the elbow based on the comparative anatomy lessons he had given me. It's strange because the limb is much longer than my left arm when it is whole, but the humerus appears to be shorter than the left side by several centimeters.

It is easier to look at when it is bandaged up like this because I can pretend it was just an arm before the amputation. I think everyone is pretending the same thing at now, too.

J Bellamy says today is a high risk day for it to grow back because of the solstice, but as long as we stay up all night and don't let magic sneak up on me, then it will be fine. Magic loves the night the best. It's a mysterious time, and magic loves to play in clarscuro.

'Clarscuro' is a word here I don't think has a counter-part in English. It is the place where light and shadow dance and shift around.

I'll stay up tonight with my family. We'll brighten up

the night so much there will be no clarscuro for magic to hide in. It's nice because this is what we do anyway for the Aestival Solstice.

I hope it doesn't grow back. I don't want any more surgeries.

22 June 1892

It did not grow back.

Father joined us in our festivities last night. We were
on the shore with a great fire. Father and Aurelius drank a
lot of wine. J Bellamy said I could not because I am still
taking too many pain relief medications and alcohol is bad
to mix with them. Elysia drank juice with me, which I was
thankful for. I felt less like I was put aside then.

When it came to eating the feast at the pavilion, Elysia
cut my food for me. Our people could see me again, and I
think they put to rest the odd rumors of how I turned into a
monster. They saw me as a young man who had suffered a
great misfortune when they saw my sister cutting my food
for me.

I did play some piano, but it doesn't sound good
enough with only my left hand and I kept fumbling the
notes because the medicine makes my head to swim and
my fingers to be clumsy.

Everyone pretended nothing was wrong with me.
They sang the traditional Aestival songs to welcome the
season even though my playing was poor. Even Father
sang. He has the worst voice out of all of us, but it's my
favorite to listen to. When he sings, it means things are
well.

This time, the pain is much better because I can still
roll that shoulder when I feel too tight on my back, which
was something I couldn't do the last amputation.

Also, I think I discovered something. I am very strong. I
never noticed before because nobody ever allowed me to
do anything for myself since my arm's transformation.

I saw the servants were setting up the table and getting the outdoor seating prepared at the pavilion. There was only one more chair left, and it seemed a waste for them to make two trips. I wanted to be useful given what I had become. When I picked up the chair, it was not heavy at all. In fact, it had hardly any weight to it. Father corrected me. He said I'm not to move things, and I have to focus on healing instead.

My father has the diviners scheduled to come into town soon and we will visit each one in turn. I am very nervous about it.

Chapter 8

The Rude Guest

Abigail joined the men in the parlor after setting the tea tray out for all of them. John brought the cup to his lips and let the drink breathe its warm dew under his nose before he sipped it. The purple tea tasted earthy, sweet, and floral all at the same time. The room's atmosphere suited the drink. May's white sunshine beamed in, laying bright patches like rugs before the open windows. The fresh breeze blew straight through the house, keeping John from getting too hot for now.

Abigail stirred sugar in her tea. "Our guests always come bearing gifts. We get important men and their wives and sometimes their children, too. Mostly, everyone just brings us nice things to drink."

"Rare teas, fine wines, and liquor," Cyrus said.

"I picked this one to match your eyes, John." She sipped her tea. Her manners were elegant, well-practiced. "It's also delicious."

"Yes-yes, it's nice." John moved the limb he hid under his coat.

"You good?" Cyrus asked.

"The silly thing gets stiff," he said. "Abigail mentioned that your last guest was very rude."

Cyrus snorted. "Geez, that's an understatement."

"Will you tell me what happened?"

"Well, most of the folks who come and sit in this parlor are just happy to listen to my stories and have a drink with us. Usually alcohol, but sometimes tea." He lifted his teacup and then took a gulp. "Hm, tasty."

He continued, "Some's curious about whether it's true or not—that I can't die. They ask a lot of questions all about it. I kindly do my best to answer. And unfortunately, we've even had a few come in here and test it for themselves. We had one of those last month. He's the guest Abby was telling you about."

He made his hand into a gun, extending his index and middle fingers out with his thumb up. He touched his forehead. "Bang!" His brown eyes sparkled as he told this part of his story. "He shot me right in the head. Just blasted my skull open! Got my brains all over the place. Son of a bitch was squeamish, too. So it was blood and brains and vomit all over me, all over the rug. It always takes a couple minutes before I come to again. I's all a mess, but Abby's rug? That there was the real tragedy."

Abigail puffed out her cheeks. "Oh, I'm getting so mad thinking about it! He ruined the rug."

"Abby loved that rug. We had to throw it out."

"It was my favorite one!" As Abigail spoke, she got more impassioned until her voice's sweetness became vibrant and sharp. "I made that idiot clean up my whole house at gunpoint because I sure as hell wasn't gonna clean up after him! He went to jail for shooting my dear Rus, but it wasn't for very long. Apparently, murder only counts if it's permanent."

"Ah, I love it when you're feisty, Abby!" Cyrus clapped his hands.

"Oh, goodness Rus, you always get me all riled up." She blushed as she tucked some of the hair which had escaped her braid behind her ear. "Anyways, he got off easy since he was the son of someone important. I wouldn't have wanted him hung or nothing. But just three days in jail for killing my Rus? I know he doesn't stay dead, but he *was* dead!"

"Cyrus, what's it like to die?" John asked.

"Hmm. Well, dying hurts a lot," Cyrus said as pulled the bread plate closer to himself. "And when you come back, um, you've definitely . . ." He got quiet as he sawed the knife smoothly into the loaf. Bits of crust gathered like dust on the tray. "You've definitely lost some crumbs."

Abigail laughed. "Crumbs! Well, isn't that a way to put it, Rus!"

He smiled. "Yeah, you know, like when the crumbs come off of the bread, you can't stick them back on. But it's still bread. It just lost a few crumbs." He picked up a spoon, dipped it in the apple butter, smeared it over the slice, and then ate it.

"Well, there goes your metaphor." Abigail touched the tray. "You should try some metaphor, John. It's delicious."

"I'd love some."

She reached forward to cut the bread but paused. "Did you want me to get you your cutting board? It's no trouble at all."

"If you would cut it for any other guest, then that won't be necessary, ver."

At that, she cut the slice and placed it on his plate.

Spreading the apple butter wasn't simple for John. The bread wanted to slide around on the snack plate atop the low table as he smoothed the sweet, brown spread with the back of a spoon. His ears were burning when it took a little longer than he'd like, and he wondered if he was making a spectacle of himself.

When he finally tried the apple butter, it was like taking a bite of autumn.

"What do you think of it?" Abigail asked, as if he hadn't spent a minute on something that would take anyone else a brief moment.

"I think," John smiled, then ribbed, "three days in jail is not enough time for someone who shot your husband in the head et ruined your favorite rug."

"Oh goodness, now you're teasing me, you silly goose! I meant the apple butter!"

"I love it," he answered. "Yes-yes, it's very nice."

As they shared in chit-chat and enjoyed their purple tea, John could sense the magic in the rambling breeze moving through the room. Its enjoyment floated in the air like a feather. He preferred it when it was in this mood because it seemed like it wanted all three of them to be together.

Which was good because that was what he wanted, too.

4 July 1892

According to J Bellamy, this day is very important to Americans. I asked him if it was important to him. He said it probably was, and it probably will be once he returns to America. He changed my bandages like usual. He said it's healing well. He asked me about how the pain has been ever since he reduced my doses.

I told him it's better than the last surgery.

After he took care of me, he showed me a feather that gleams gold in the sunlight.

"How did you get the feather to do that?" I asked.

He told me, "It wants to be magic now. That's all there is to it."

When he sticks to science, he makes more sense.

He told me my English is improving. I agree because these journal entries are much quicker to write. My penmanship is neater, and it's not as bad seeing it on the pages. I will say though, the edge of my left hand is almost always dark with ink. Father tells me to wash it because it's unbecoming for someone like me to show up with an ink stained hand.

I try to grind the side of my hand against the soap, but sometimes, the soap slips away. I'm annoyed Father just orders someone to wash my hand for me rather than get something to make the soap still. I want to do it myself. I'm tired of everything being done for me. It makes me to feel like I'm a passenger of my life.

Elysia and I have been experimenting with my strength. It appears there is no such thing as anything heavy for me. Sometimes things are too big to carry, and they are unwieldy to hold, but they are not heavy. If I have grip and can lift it, I can carry it. When we were in the library together, I held my hand flat out for her, and she stacked books upon it. It was comical how many books she had stacked. It reminded me of the game we played when we stack the blocks. And like the game, the stack toppled. Nobody else knows how strong I am. Just Elysia. I think I want to keep it that way.

Tomorrow, I begin to visit the diviners. J Bellamy said he can be a diviner too, it's not hard, and he wrote a note on a piece of paper. He folded it up small, then tucked it into my breast pocket, and patted it when it was put away.

"Don't open it yet," he told me.

I asked, "When can I open it?"

"After it grows back again. Yes-yes, I think that's a good time" is what he said.

J Bellamy is always polite. Even though he's a foreigner, he knows to say 'yes' twice especially when you are lesser in the social standing or fond of the person. It softens the agreement without making it sound unsure.

We say it, 'ita-ita', in our language for that, a polite agreement. But it felt right when I heard him say it like 'yes-yes', and it made me to feel like maybe I am still myself.

5 July 1892

I'm tired. I saw three different diviners today. The first one was a chirologist, which means she reads my palm. She was very incorrect. But she gave good news to Father, and it pleased him. She told him I was fine to inherit my birthright because I appear normal except for missing my arm.

The second one was also a chirologist. This time, when she looked at my palm, she said she could tell I was cursed. Tears filled her eyes because she could see in the lines of my left hand how my first amputation went. She said it was not right for Father and J Bellamy to have done that. She also said it was in vain because even if all of it is cut off, I am still cursed. She said I'm meant for something else. Father did not like that news, but he admitted she seemed more attuned to fortune-telling.

The third one was an old man, and he used a crystal ball to scry. I liked his fortune-telling because I could see the pictures of my future in his glass orb. It was like looking at a dream. I traveled in that dream, which was what I always wanted to do. Also, there was no ocean in sight, which meant I had to be in a different country.

But what I saw and what the old man said he saw were very different. He told my father that it would be fine for me to follow the path drawn for me since I was born and that I could stay in Nyuskom. When my father asked about the amputation, the old man's fingers danced around the crystal ball.

"Yes-yes, how much of the right arm remains is fine for your son," is what he said, roughly translated.

I think my father liked the news so much, he didn't realize the man had called it an arm. It hasn't been an arm for a long time.

J Bellamy said tomorrow we need to keep an eye because there's a blood moon that night. It will make the atmosphere thinner between men and magic. Everything is more sensitive then.

Note from J Bellamy

I know that you typically don't like tea, but you need to share a cup with my friend. Since I know you like learning new words and seeing how they come about, her brand of fortune-telling is known as tasseomancy. It comes from the French for cup and the Greek for divination. Go ahead and look in your books for that.

— J. B. B.

7 July 1892

As J Bellamy predicted, it came back. And as his note predicted, that woman came as well. I received her outside at morn. I was wearing my cloak to cover it, but she knew what it was already.

She looked like one born on this island, and she was very beautiful. Her skin was a rich tan, her eyes were violet, and her hair was dark. She offered a gift to me, a carnation. She said it was my flower because my birthday was very soon, which is true. I asked her what her name was. She said names don't come natural to her, and this is the first time she tried being like this.

Elysia had the note J Bellamy wrote for me, and she had given it to Father at that morn. It was why he allowed the mysterious woman into our home and made a room for her on such short notice. She had many demands on how to set up her room.

She knew the date exactly the first time my arm changed. She knew the date exactly the first time it grew back. And that it had come back again yesterday.

My father asked her about my fortune. She said later today because magic loves the night.

I had the feeling that she was magic herself.

Chapter 9

Tasseomancy

They had all finished their tea. By then, the spring breeze blowing in one window and out to the ones across the parlor wasn't enough to cool the room against the roast simmering in the kitchen. John's forehead glistened with sweat. He lifted his shoulder up a little to see if that could free up the knot in his back. It would help if he had more range of motion than what he could manage with his duster on. He stopped when he saw Abigail's curiosity—she was trying to figure out what exactly was underneath his coat.

"It's been bugging you for a while," Cyrus noted.

"I'm fine, at-now. I swear it."

"If you say so."

Abigail looked down at the last bit of tea in her cup. "After we drink tea, me and Rus like to see what shapes are left behind in the leaves. We heard that they do it in countries overseas. It's popular there."

"Yes-yes," John said. "It's known as tasseomancy. A woman who did that read my fortune not long after I lost my arm. Nothing else worked to fix it, so why not try fortune-telling?"

Abigail perked up. "Oh, when we do it, it's just a silly game. I never met anyone who got a bona fide fortune before. What was it like?"

"She made it so that it was only her and me in one of the guest rooms, which was set up particularly for her. She brewed me some tea and invited me to have some with her. We chatted about whatever it was I wanted to chat about, which was nice because all of the conversations I had with any professionals until I went to her were about . . ." He glanced at his right shoulder. His story petered out as he got nervous again.

"Please, go on about the tea lady," Abigail said encouragingly. "I love hearing you talk, John."

"Of course." He started swirling his cup of tea. Dark violet eyes were dreamy in the memory he found himself in. "She asked me to do like this, move the last bit of tea all around so that it had every opportunity to settle where it wanted to. Then, she had me turn it upside down on a little dish." He inverted the cup over his saucer. "She told me to push my intention into it, impart myself so that the soul could move the leaves and give a more honest review of my fate for her to interpret." He put his hand over the upside-down teacup.

"Well?" Cyrus prompted. "What's a real fortune like then?"

"It's just a game for you, ver. It's the same, even for most professional fortune tellers. They don't really tell the future. They tell you things that will always be true. They tell you what you are meant to hear but are hard for people to tell it to you plainly. They give you advice that would make anybody's life better if they found themselves in your circumstances. The good ones know exactly what to say at the right time, and there's magic in the art of the right thing at the right time. The one who did my tea leaves felt real to me—a good one, better than everyone else."

He turned his cup right side up and leaned forward from his seat on the piano bench. Abigail and Cyrus also leaned forward, anticipating the precipitation of some obvious shape at the bottom of the teacup.

"Her special cups had a pattern on the interior. It gave her more things to say about the way in which the tea leaves settled: The shape, how they lay on the lines, and the symbols . . . she used all of that to give me my fortune."

"What did she tell you?" Cyrus asked.

John looked at the soggy leaves in the warm-toned cup. A grouping clung to the edge furthest away from him, a blobby sort of shape with points sticking out of it. A scattering across the center. He imagined the pattern she had in the bottom of the cup, with the zodiac symbols and the elements in the array. He wondered what that fortune-teller would say about him today. Back then, he still had a little bit of hope that he could change back; these days, he knew he was stuck like this.

When John thought of what she had said, it was in the language of that island, and he had to translate what he remembered: "Hmm, she told me that I was strong enough to endure what happened to me. She said that sometimes, odd things happen to people for no reason because there is a force bigger and more wise than anything you can understand."

He had received that fortune so long ago, but even then, he knew she had a connection to the magic of his homeland in a way that was richer and deeper than what most people had.

John continued, "She said, as I am, I was not fit for my birthright because I was no longer a man. She said I didn't belong on the island anymore and that I was an unlucky thing for my father to keep. That my father had to choose between everything or me. Of course, he didn't choose me. Thus, I was put on a ship to America. Exiled."

The air got serious between the three of them. John was surprised that, even after so many years, he still missed his father and his homeland.

Maybe it was just that it was almost summer.

But it was more likely that he was wishing for a life without the chronic pain of a body that was put together wrong, without the wanderlust that ate at his sanity when it started its drums in his skull, without the realization that he had become something that was no longer just a man.

It was Abigail who broke the tense silence. "I think I prefer it the way me and Rus do it. It's all for fun and doesn't mean anything except you had tea with some people you liked. Look John, I see a fish here. See? These are the fins."

John could definitely see the blob as a fish. He managed the ghost of a smile for her.

"I can actually tell the future. Do you know what a fish means, John?" Cyrus said. "It means that the roast this evening is gonna be delicious."

John definitely preferred their kind of tasseomancy.

12 July 1892

The aestival sun sparkles on the sea as dawn warms the sky. Through the mist, I can faintly see the marsh islands on America's east coast. It has been a long time since Nyuskom has been so close to America.

Father had more diviners come to town since that woman came. I could tell which ones were genuine and which ones were frauds. Father could tell, too.

The ones who are truly able to read fortunes agree with that woman. I am something in-between a man and magic, and I was made this way because I happened to be where the threads of wild magic converged and the world was thin there and it touched me.

I can tell he doesn't wish to send me away, but he has a responsibility to Nyuskom. It's one of the last places where people still can make or change enchanted objects. If he chooses me, maybe the island would become like everywhere else.

Maybe the mist would fade. Maybe the water would run up and down the shoreline here and follow the moon the way Aurelius said it does overseas.

Note from J Bellamy

Because I am familiar with magic, I advise following the recommendations from the various divinations you've received. I know one thing for certain: Nyuskom desires to give your son as a gift to America. It behooves you not to deny its wishes. You can say I am personally acquainted with such things.

I can accompany your son safely to America. I only require a gun.

—J. B. B.

Chapter 10

No Trouble At All

Abigail left to clean up the tea and wash the dishes, leaving the men alone again. If it wasn't for her, John probably would've abandoned his story as soon as he had gotten nervous. Now that he had calmed down, he could tell that he was supposed to have shared what he did. The feeling of satisfaction hanging in the parlor was magic keeping its eye on them.

"I can see why you're fond of her," John said.

Cyrus grinned. "I fell in love with her at the bar, not too long after you left that last time. There's a piano there. Anyone's allowed to play, and you could hardly keep her off it. I went there over and over, and when she played, I danced. That's how we fell for each other."

"She said you got that piano for her right before the war." John's gaze went to the baby grand in the corner of the parlor. "It's been a long time since I heard good piano-playing. How proficient is she?"

"Ah, she's got a real talent for it!" Cyrus got up, smoothly walking around the coffee table to the bench where John sat. "She said she started learning it from when the governor tried to get his son to play. She'd listen to the boy's instructor as she worked. And it just made sense to her. She'd always try practicing . . ."

John's surprised expression distracted him mid-story.

"What?"

"You are able to walk, Cyrus!"

"Yeah, about time, right?" He said with a chuckle. "Well, scoot off the bench. We'll have to put it back where it goes if you wanna hear my wife play."

John stood up, lifted the bench, and repositioned it in front of the piano.

"It's always incredible seeing how strong you are," Cyrus remarked.

"That's what everyone says."

"Now, it feels rude not having a seat for you. And I bet you can manage one of these chairs"—he touched the reading chairs where the guests normally sat—"if you took off that ratty old coat."

John readjusted the limb underneath his duster. Sweat dripped from his forehead; it filled a drop at the tip of his nose before splashing onto the floor of the parlor.

"I know you said it's fine, but I can see it's hurting you real bad now, and you're too damn hot, ya silly goose."

John tucked his left hand into the duster to hold up his hidden limb by the joint that was most like an elbow. He didn't say anything.

"You know, when it was just us, you didn't need to hide it," Cyrus noted.

The bells and strings of beads twinkled, and Abigail stood at the threshold of the room. "I can go, if you need some privacy to take your coat off, get it moving, whatever you need, John. You can come and get me once you're feeling better," she suggested.

John considered it because he was in so much pain, but then he said, "I wouldn't want to force you out of your own home."

"I promise I won't mind," she said.

"It makes a bit of a mess at times."

"Oh goodness, sweeping up is easy enough."

"And it can't be a worse mess than my brains blown across Abby's favorite rug," Cyrus added.

John bristled at his friend making light of his own death again. "You didn't really tell me what it's like when you die. You just told me about crumbs, like it was a joke. You keep talking about it like it's a joke, but it's not a joke, Cyrus. You've died. And you've died so many times you can't even tell me how many times it's been. The sight of you at this morn."

Cyrus ruffled a hand through his hair. He paced. Now that he could walk, it was hard for him to sit still. "You're right. I don't like talking 'bout how I came home from the war. How I wake up *every* morning."

Abigail cleared her throat. "Actually, I have a few things I need to do outside."

"Are you sure?" John asked.

"It's no trouble at all."

"Yes-yes, I can see that."

Instinct told John that he was supposed to stay and she was supposed to go. At least for now. It was just like yesterday when he felt compelled to shop for the ingredients to make a roast, but when it came to the vegetables, he knew he wasn't supposed to buy any turnips.

20 July 1892

I am on a small, celeritous ship carrying some rare, enchanted things in its cargo, destined for America. I suppose I am one of those enchanted things. Nyuskom is near enough to America that when we break through the mist, we could see the Eastmost islands clearly not too long after we set off on the trip.

J Bellamy is aboard the ship as well. I am thankful there is someone familiar, but now that I am on the ship, the closer we push to America, the more I feel an unease that surrounds J Bellamy. I wonder if that's what Elysia felt. If it is, it is like she says. An alarm that informs me that he might be something not-quite-human.

I keep the cloak tight against me as the wind pushes on me and tugs at the hem. When I look behind me, Nyuskom is already gone before I know it. I just see the sunlight. I see now why new visitors are rare to our island.

The ship's captain asks why I do not remove my cloak. Whenever anyone on this ship asks, I consider the repercussions of undoing the pin and letting the cloak fly away. There's an instinct that thrums through me, telling me to open it wide because it wants the wind to blow over it.

J Bellamy tells me that America is so wide and vast there are places you can find where nobody else is around except for America's wild magic, and he says it's waiting for me.

Letter to Elysia (Translated)

Elysia,

I hope this letter finds you. America is very beautiful in some places. The waves run up and down the shore in the way Aurelius said it would. In other places, the notions of industry that much of Europe has been toying with are here, making the air foul to breathe. The streets are crowded, and people walk very close together. I am not fond of how dirty it is in those places.

Also, whoever said Americans have alchemic lights everywhere was dishonest. They are in many places, especially the cities, but most use lamps and candles here just like we do.

J Bellamy purchased a narrow covered wagon and a mule. He tells me that mules are better than horses because they are braver around things like us. He said they, too, are in-between things.

Now that we are here, I think J Bellamy is marked by America's magic the way I'm marked by Nyuskom's. I never realized how he is like a magpie until I saw him collect many things into the cart. Whatever we pass, if it is interesting, he places it in the wagon in a crate or a box. He even has enchanted the boxes so food stays fresh within them. He cooks beautiful meals.

I always thought he was off-putting because he was American, but I see the other Americans are also wary of him. You told me that there's an air about me that feels strange. I think I feel a similar strangeness from him.

I think I still have that air about me, too. But it takes a while for people to be unsettled by me in that way because I am a foreigner. They assume the oddness is because I'm not born here, and my spoken English is still poor.

People here cannot even guess what I hide under my cloak. They don't usually ask about it because they assume it is an injury or a deformity rather than a curse. Usually men don't have monstrous pieces replacing parts of their bodies. I still think if I had a claw, it would be more useful. I don't even have anything close to fingers now on my right.

When I think about it, maybe I do. In the comparative anatomy lessons J Bellamy had taught, the last joint is what used to be my hand and fingers. I even twitch it when I'm nervous the same as I used to. I think they remember being fingers, and they still dream of piano.

I miss you, Elysia, because J Bellamy often refuses to help me with it. He keeps telling me about his friend's wife and how she adapted fine enough with a three-toed foot and a shorter leg. I am confused because I could have sworn that when he told me the story in Spring, he spoke about his son. But I know time slips around for those who know magic too well. So maybe he is just confused.

My name is strange here, and people have trouble under-standing it, especially with my spoken English as bad as it is. J Bellamy told me that he advises I change it. I asked him what I should change it to. He told me he was not good with names. For example, it is because of him that the name of the mule is Muley. He said I'm a plain man for the most part, so he suggested John.

I liked that he called me plain. I realized that I never wanted to be remarkable. I just wanted to play piano, travel, and be home for summer. I can't do the first or last, really. I guess I'll have to settle on traveling.

Luckily, America is very big.

Your brother,
Malachy Secundus
John

10 August 1892

J Bellamy is better company some days than others. I can see his mind is not put all the way together. I feel bad for him sometimes. It is from too much magic filling his head. I also have too much magic, but it is easier to see its effect on me because of what my right arm became.

J Bellamy told me, "Once touched by magic, you become a playing piece for magic's grand schemes." I suppose that is why I'm not to inherit the throne in Nyuskom.

J Bellamy knows far too much about the magic of America. Though he seemed familiar with the amenities of our palace when he lived in Nyuskom with us, he is certainly more at ease deep in the wilds of America.

He simply has to look at the wide sky, and he knows how the weather will turn. America is very tumultuous in the weather at times. Some days, the sun beats down on us. Other days, it is sudden torrents of rain and when it stops just as abruptly, the road shines like the sea. The lightning breaks the sky open. He says sometimes, the wind whips up so strong it turns itself into a funnel that sucks mankind's progress up and wrecks it down. He says the people here just brush it off and rebuild as if a force of nature hadn't tell them not to.

But the weather isn't all bad.

Some days, it is a zephyr with gentle sunlight. I get to take off my cloak then, and I'm shirtless and you can see me open it wide. The wind feels good over the feathers.

Chapter 11

Unique Anatomy

"Can I take your coat?" Cyrus asked in the same way he'd ask any other guest.

"Yes-yes, I suppose." John put his hand at the front of the duster. His fingers undid the buttons, but he kept the coat pinched closed. Deep breath. He tugged the right side open, revealing the bird wing he had kept hidden all day. With a smooth movement, he pulled the coat off of his left arm with the same hand. John was self-conscious about the large wing which had replaced his right arm over sixteen years ago.

Cyrus took the duster. The fabric draped shapelessly as down feathers and dust sprinkled onto the floor. "I'm gonna shake this outside before I hang it on up."

John only nodded. He hated what a mess it made.

Once Cyrus left, John opened the gray-brown wing with a wince. Everything was stiff from trying to keep it forced in a bad position against his body all day. The feathers were raggedy from being stuck under the cloth for so long. Arthritic and weak from disuse, the wing trembled as he tried to lift it using its own strength. The limb frustrated him; he was unable to move it well enough to get relief for the human parts of him until he warmed it up.

He needed to use his left hand to support the wing to allow his aching shoulder and back muscles to rest. J Bellamy's lessons on anatomy always sprang up into the forefront of his mind anytime he articulated the parts which corresponded to a wrist and hand, moving the longest feathers.

Still using his left hand to hold it, he started moving it from the elbow. This stretched open the wing until he pulled it back to close it. The motion was deliberate, and soon enough, it was freer in the joints. He was finally able to fully open it and flapped it a few times, which felt nice and got the blood flowing.

John folded the wing. This time, he didn't try to force the shape to be tight and narrow against his ribcage. Instead, he let it take as much space as it needed while propping it up with his only hand.

Cyrus returned to the parlor. He approached John to get a closer look at his shirt. It made sense; he had never seen John wear any kind of clothing that fit well after the wing came back. The shirt was made just for him, with snaps below his wing. Something John could put on and remove one-handed that also accommodated his unique anatomy.

"I's worried when you left that you ain't got nobody to help you with all the little things. But I see you got yourself a tailor who keeps those things in mind for you."

"Yes-yes, I have."

"Can I take a look?"

John lifted his wing so that his friend could see how the metal snaps came together under it. There was a fabric tab John could hold in his teeth to keep that seam pulled together, and then it was simple for him to push the snaps shut. The tab folded in half and was pinned to the shirt with a handsome, wooden toggle closure to keep it from dangling around when he didn't need to use it.

"Your tailor's very good. All's this easy one-handed?"

"It is. And it's nice to have clothes that fit well. I didn't have the luxury before." John looked around. "Though this seems hardly a luxury compared to the riches you have at-now."

"All this luxury came after they saw how I'd come home from . . ." Cyrus took a deep breath. "When you left, John, I still did a lot of things for you. I's worried about whether you could take care of yourself or not. And when you came on in today, I didn't know if you'd still need some help. Now I've my own thing to deal with, and I reckon I don't got it in me no more to help you the way I used to. But it looks like you got it all figured out; I'm glad."

"I missed when I lived here. You had made little gadgets for me. Some worked; some didn't. But you made me feel very plain, and that's what I needed at the time. I'd have liked to stay, I think. But then I got this job."

"Are you a handyman in the same way you're from nowhere?" Cyrus asked.

"I believe so. Both are true, at least." John was still trying to rub the pain out of his right shoulder. "It's not easy, lugging around this old thing."

"Here, hold still." Cyrus put his hands on his friend's aching body. There was a knot on the right side of his back, as usual. He rubbed on it while John stopped moving, eyes shut, stuck between the pain of the thumbs working on him and the tightness finally being released. Once the tense muscles of his back relaxed, John let out a shuddering breath. It had been a long time since he had anyone touching him like that.

"Feel any better?" Cyrus asked.

John nodded.

"It ain't strong as I remember it."

"I don't have a use for it, so it's atrophied a bit." John used his hand again to support his wing so his back and shoulder could rest. Though he was more comfortable, the ache never fully left him.

"You used to hold it like that after we was done working. It hurts worse now, don't it?"

"It does. Arthritis."

"Is it on account of you keeping it under that damn coat?"

"No-no . . . Maybe a little. But mostly it's because every way I hold it hurts eventually," John explained. "The way I've been cobbled together. It doesn't work very well." As soon as he said that, magic encouraged him to continue. Experimentally, he did. "This happened to me when I was seventeen. It didn't hurt then, but it still felt wrong."

"What do you mean by that?" Cyrus asked.

"Put your hand here." John patted his upper back. He was in between a man and a bird there.

Cyrus did so, placing his hand against the cotton fabric, pressing into his friend's strangely-shaped scapula.

John always described it as instinct, but everyone familiar with magic mentioned threads or strings when explaining it. He understood why; it felt like Cyrus's hand was tied tightly against him, maybe even finished with a little bow. He was meant to be here, showing his friend how his body was put together.

Because John had a bird-wing, he imagined this just-right feeling was similar to the migratory instinct that had pulled him to America's shoreline when he was on that boat long ago. It was a thread that brought his hand forward to select the potatoes and the carrots yesterday at the market. Maybe he kept calling it instinct because too much of him was an animal sometimes.

If it were threads, then he was a foreigner being woven into America's grand tapestry. He wasn't aware of the design, but he remembered that the beautiful tapestries hanging in the hallways back in Nyuskom always had stories on them.

John knew it was time to share his.

"I've had this thing for half my life." He moved his wing up, forward, and out over and over. "Do you feel it? The bones and the muscles—there's something off." Every time John slowly flapped that wing, his muscles protested the bones they were not made for.

"Yeah, I feel it," Cyrus said. "There's a hitch there or something."

"That's right. And when I rest it . . ." John folded the wing. Most of it was in front of him because of the way the appendage was attached to his body. "Because a man was never meant to support such a thing, there's nothing for it to rest upon. It pulls on the parts of me, still a man. I'm told I'm missing a bone birds are meant to have. Thus, my whole life, holding it and moving it is, um—thinking the word—ah, 'compensate.'"

John's back and shoulder had to work in concert to keep the wing from slipping down the side of his body. That meant, when the wing was at rest, his shoulder and back muscles were forced to be active. The only time they weren't was when he propped it on something—like how he put his left hand under it to support its weight.

"John, has it always been like this?"

"Yes-yes, since first it came. It's too big to allow it to do what it wants. Because it is very long, I have to keep it up. Sometimes, I do let it to drag when I am very tired of it. I try not to. It pulls

at me, et it makes it to look dirty after a little while. I have a difficult time to keep it all clean as is."

Cyrus took his hand off of John's back. "I can tell you've
been taking care of it, even if it's a bit rough-looking right now. I
used to have to do some of it back in the day."

Curiously, Cyrus stroked his friend's wing. John allowed
him to explore the difference between the contour feathers and
the long, stiff flight feathers.

"It's not easy by myself. I am able to do it for the most part,
at-now. Better than the last time you saw me."

"Well, it's awful nice to finally get to know a lil bit more
about that wing of yours." Cyrus brushed the wing's powder
from his hands.

"Yes-yes, it was time to tell. My work is mostly about the art
of the right thing at the right time, ver."

"I thought you said you was a handyman, John."

"I am. A handyman of a kind. Let's not talk too much about
it. It's important that we don't."

"You ever gonna explain what you mean by being a
handyman?"

"I will later, I promise. But first, can you explain how dying
makes a man to lose his crumbs?"

28 August 1892

I am getting accustomed to the care of this strange
limb, but I still need help with bathing it. It's embarrassing,
but the main problem is that I like bathing it too much,
especially when I wash it in the wild streams. My mind
feels like it's not human at then. It happens every time.
J Bellamy sees me splashing in the water with it. He
doesn't help me out of the trance like the servants used to
or like Elysia used to. He simply watches me make a fool of
myself.

This time last year, I could play in the water at the
shoreline back home and not have to worry about slipping
into the instinct of some animal. I'm upset that he lets the
behavior to carry on without a thought to interrupt me.

I have figured out the drying of it. I hold it open like I
did back home, but it's not easy to use a towel. Instead, I
shake it off, and I can fluff up the feathers. It's strange to
move it in that way because there's no equivalent of those
movements on my human side really. It makes me wonder
if I am still human.

I've gotten used to keeping these feathers neat, too. I
found a soft brush to use, but sometimes I use just my
fingers to align everything. This is another place where I
feel maybe I'm not quite human. I know which ones need
to be fixed and which ones are fine. My fingers work
quickly, reminding me of the weavers on the loom. They
are so sure of where everything is to go and work with
hands that think faster than even their own minds.

When I preen the feathers, it's like that for me. I find a
space where my head empties out and I just do what feels

proper. Still, I like it too much. After I do it, it's hard to think in words.

J Bellamy tells me he's glad I'm finally getting to know my strange body. He had been wanting me to do that for a long time.

Note from J Bellamy

Please return my friend John.

— J. B. B.

Note from J Bellamy

I regret to inform you that the bodies of four men are in this box. They are unidentifiable. I've made sure of that. I'd like you to be aware of the fact that the only reason I've chosen to entertain offering them to you is because my friend insisted that they get the chance to be put to rest with their families.

—J. B. B.

Note from Dr. Willard Cross

The bodies of four men were brought to my office on September 12, 1892 at approximately 11:20 am in an enchanted chest and with a note plastered on top. Whoever wrote such a note is mentally unwell and dangerous.

Their faces had been completely destroyed, as if crushed. There was one bullet per corpse, and each one had gone directly through the heart in the exact same manner. The wound suggests the shots were made from a distance. The bodies were cut apart, separated into several small pieces, and then tossed together into the chest.

Somehow, the corpses do not rot while in this chest. This allows me to take some time to process this information before I begin this endeavor.

If I begin this endeavor.

Letter to Elysia (Translated)

Dear Elysia,

I have been having many adventures in America. It is a beautiful country. Everything here is vast. I feel like, in Nyuskom, only the sea is vast. I miss you, but I want you to know and understand that I am doing fine. Nothing bad has happened to me since arriving in America.

J Bellamy is taking care of me. He is not bad at it. He has raised his own child before, and he's surprisingly gentle. He is gentle to his mule as well. So, of course, he is gentle to me. He is a remarkable cook. The food he makes over the campfire always tastes as if he has a full kitchen to work in.

If you ever see me again, I had the thing amputated for convenience. J Bellamy says that the magic in America won't make it come back so soon. Maybe I will look like a plain man when you see me next.

Your brother,
Malachy Secundus
John

29 September 1892

J Bellamy performed another amputation on me two weeks ago. He amputated me to my shoulder, but he left a little bit that can move.

The wing was broken two places, and he said the way it was would have made it difficult to heal. He explained that even if it mended with the splint, it would heal badly, and there would be a chronic pain on me. He said cutting it all off to give it a chance to come back anew would probably be less painful in the end. I was still leery, but he didn't give me much choice. I wanted to try the splint.

I think he is too happy to cut off pieces of me. I am not sure anymore if he is a man with too much magic in his head or if he is something else. It was too easy for him to kill men and then to cut apart their corpses.

I'll try to recount what happened.

J Bellamy killed four men. I had never seen him use a gun before, but he was so efficient that it seemed impossible he was just a man.

I was captive for three days total in a cellar. They didn't give me food and I was kept tied up the whole time. The way they handled me and tied me up, I don't think they understood how it was attached to me or how it moved. There was much swelling and much pain.

The first day, a note was nailed to the cellar door. I told them I could read, and I read the note aloud. It was J Bellamy's note asking them to please return me. That's how they learned of my name, but they said the name was too plain for something like me.

On the third day, J Bellamy opened the cellar door.

The four men looked up and drew their weapons. They surrounded me. He raised his own gun and it felt like he moved it directly where it would shoot the men through the heart. He simply pointed the weapon and aimed true.

Despite not informing him of my strength, he had asked me to crush the bones of their faces so that they could no longer be identified. I didn't want to, but J Bellamy's prowess with his weapon was so frightening that I did it. It was easy when I put my mind to it, like crushing pastries because it was crisp and then like jam inside. I was horrified by how effortless it was to do that.

He said he could tell I was upset, even though he was here to free me. I told him that we can't leave them in the cellar like this and that they needed a proper burial. He took a chest from the cellar and used magic to enchant it. A golden feather that he placed on the box. He put the four men in it after he cut them up, and they all fit even though the box should be too small. He said he'll make sure they will get to their respective families.

He said he had a friend who always tried to explain how to be good to him, but it does not come naturally to him. He said he knew I was better than him on matters of good and evil, and it was for that reason he took my suggestion on returning them. But the manner in which he did so was sickening. So removed from humanity.

I remember when I was in the cellar, very much in pain, and he passed me a bottle of moonshine after he took a drink from it. He told me it is lucky there is a lot of nice alcohol in this cellar. When I took a drink, it was not nice.

That moment with the moonshine is what I always think of first when I think of that day he came to save me from the cellar. More than how much my broken bones hurt. More than how quickly he killed those men. Or how easily he cut them up. Or how their faces looked crushed in my hand. Or the amputation that came soon after once he cleaned up the wagon enough to perform a surgery.

When I think of 12 September 1982, I see him drink from the glass bottle and then pass it to me and the alcohol is not nice at all.

It's funny the things you remember the most.

Chapter 12

On Losing Crumbs

Cyrus brought a bottle of brandy over. When he poured the alcohol into intricate crystal glasses, the geometric designs filled with topaz. John finally got himself into one of the reading chairs. To fit, his wing had to be open, draped over the arm. The tips of his feathers barely touched the floor of the parlor in that position until he bent the wing and hooked the part that was most like a wrist on the edge of the arm.

"You're comfortable like that?" Cyrus asked as he picked up a glass.

"Yes-yes, it stretches my back in a way that feels nice." John nervously wiggled the tip, which bobbled the pinion feathers. He was itching to preen the wing, but he knew if he started, he'd get lost in the task. "You're staring at it."

"Well, John, it's a lot to look at. Besides, I'm sure you stared at me earlier. Back when nothing really worked."

"Fair point, ver."

Cyrus held out the glass. "Here. Take it. You're less fidgety when you're a little drunk."

John picked it up from the bottom and sat back, relaxing in

his seat. The brandy was cradled in his only hand. "I'm finally cooled down, and you're to warm me back up with some alcohol."

"You asking me to take the brandy from you?" Cyrus asked with a smirk.

John moved the drink closer to his body to protect it from being snatched away. "No. I think this suits me more than tea. Besides, you're delaying it—explaining how you wake up."

Cyrus stayed standing as he picked up his own drink. "I am. Just like you don't like talking 'bout that wing of yours, I don't like talking 'bout how many crumbs I've actually lost."

John enjoyed the drink. The perfume of the brandy near his lips prepared him for its mellow and sweet taste. It was like fruits and flowers underneath the oakiness and bite of the well-aged alcohol.

Magic was filling his senses, urging him onward. It was gentle this time, though. No drums or a twinge of pain. It held the same soft-hearted desire John held. In the warmth and peace of the parlor, it was the right time to ask the Undying Soldier to bare his soul and talk about the dark things he kept chasing away with his jokes about worms, crumbs, and dirty rugs.

Maybe even Cyrus felt the pull. "It weren't easy for you talking 'bout that wing, was it?"

"It's never easy to explain it."

"Alrighty then. It's only fair if I talk 'bout these damn crumbs. But how'm I gonna start?"

"You can begin with something you've told me before: You said you were shot in the head too many times," John prompted.

Cyrus took a swig to embolden himself before he began. "Why yes I was! I'd say getting shot in the head is definitely the worst for losing crumbs. I hadn't even noticed I was losing crumbs the first few deaths. I think it was when they'd tortured me, cut off my hands, and gouged out my eyes before finally killing me . . ." Then, it was as if the fun swagger he tried to bring to his words wimped away because he accidentally remembered they were true.

"Yeah, that's when I started noticing it. I woke up in the morning, and my hands felt stiffer, and I's having trouble with my eyes. 'Twas blurry for a short while, a few blinks really is all. Those were the first crumbs I noticed. Maybe there were other signs before then, but I just weren't aware yet." His words lost their momentum.

"The more I died, the worse it got. See, if I don't die a while, it don't take as long to feel like myself again. It's just the hardest for me when I wake up in the morning." He took a deep breath. "Every morning."

"Can you tell me how it is when you wake up?" John asked, curious.

There was a pause for Cyrus to gather himself again. Then, he set his drink on the low table before he continued his explanation. He needed his feet to be moving to keep his words moving, so he paced the room as he spoke. "When I first wake up, my thoughts are in a jumble. Nothing works. I can't even talk when I wake up. I can only make noise. Can't even sit up on my own. And I'm blind. Well, I reckon you saw that bit. Abby says my eyes keep moving. What's that look like to you?"

John could see Cyrus was using it as a brief moment to take a break. He answered, "As she said, your eyes dart around, like you're trying to follow something that bounces to and fro all around the room."

"That right?"

"Yes-yes. Why was the parlor so dark when I first came at-morn?"

"If the light's too bright, sometimes I get a headache. It makes me aware something ain't coming together quite right." His fingers laced together to demonstrate. "Things get confused as I try making sense of it. Then everything just"—he pulled his hands apart suddenly—"gets away from me. I reckon maybe it's too much all at once, and I forget how to do damn near everything.

"It can take a long while for me to set myself right after a fit like you saw this morning, 'specially if I've died recent and 'specially if I try to rush myself through it. But I've gotten better getting my bearings. It really ain't too bad now. It was worse right after the war."

"How so?" John asked.

"See, at the tail end of the war, I's captured and imprisoned by the other side. I's tortured and shot in the head, over and over and over again. They saw how the morning was for me, and I reckon maybe they believed that meant I's getting closer to death, inch by inch. So they killed me more times. Hundreds of times. Maybe more than that. It's hard to say. By the time my men found me, I weren't really myself. I was unable to move or speak or see. I could barely even think. Everything hurt. They couldn't kill me to end my misery, so they brought me on home."

Cyrus paused. His brown eyes were wet, shining in the afternoon sunshine. He cleared his throat.

"I need you to continue," John pressed. He wanted to give his friend a break, but there was something in the room bigger than both of them, and it wanted Cyrus to continue. John was more sensitive to it, and its desire was crushing him.

"It ain't a pretty story, John."

"Neither is my story. Please, I need you to tell me the worst of it. It's why I'm here: I'm on business, Mr. Cyrus Cooper. My work is important."

"What is it that you do, John?"

"I told you, I'm—"

"A handyman. But what the hell do you mean by that?"

John was desperate because he needed today's job to come together, and he was afraid that he couldn't get Cyrus to do what he was supposed to. A leap of faith, that's all he needed from his friend. Just trust him. "Please."

"Well, if it's really that important to you . . ." Cyrus took another swig of brandy before setting it back on the coffee table. "Ask your questions. I'll answer them best I can."

John sighed as the pressure in his skull relaxed again. "Grasi. How were you faring when you came home from the war?"

"The first few weeks, I barely felt like a man. That story they tell on the other side, about me turning into a worm . . . Honestly, it's not that far off, really. The military had the new room built down the hall so it'd be easier for everybody taking care of my needs." He added, "I'm not gonna show you that room."

"You don't have to show me the room, but can you tell me how they took care of you?"

"Lordy, well, my body was twisted up on that bed. And there were nurses who lived in, helping with my care. I couldn't talk. So, they had a schedule they followed, make sure all my needs were accounted for. I was a job for them. I reckon they thought I was just a body they kept alive. But somehow, Abby . . . she saw me."

"What do you mean she saw you?"

"Well, she just talked to me. And she listened what she could. And she figured something out so I could tell her things. Even though her husband didn't have control of his body most of the time. And she had to feed him. And comb his hair. And she'd have to change him because he'd soil himself. And then wash him up like he was a . . ." Cyrus corrected himself. "Like *I* was a baby. She saw it was me.

"It did get better after a while. It got a lot better once I could talk again. Once I could, I asked her why the hell she stuck around. You know what she told me?"

John shook his head.

"She told me she read fairy tales to practice reading—see, I started teaching her before I left for the war. Anyways, there's one about a princess who had to make these nettle shirts to turn her brothers back into princes. She said she understood why she did it even though it was hard and it hurt. My head was still mixed up a bit when she was telling me all this. So I didn't mean to . . . But I told her I met the youngest prince in that story. I reckon you always reminded me of him, with his unfinished shirt at the end what left him with one bird-wing. And then I started telling her about you. I think she thought I was just telling my own version of the fairy tale. I didn't mean to tell her, John. But once I did, it felt right to."

"I don't mind, Cyrus. She's been kind about it. The story probably isn't unrelated. Magic likes to play the same plots. And it likes to hear the stories men tell. So it all comes back around. And I wonder, what came first? The prince with a bird-wing or the story of a prince with a bird-wing."

"Which one you reckon came first?"

"The latter. Man is more creative than magic is."

"My wife picked a good story, didn't she?" Cyrus's mood was brightening again.

"Yes-yes. She did." John rolled the last bit of brandy around the bottom of his glass. "And you're lucky to have her. I'm envious. I'm not allowed to hold still long enough to fall in love."

"That just means you have to fall in love faster, ya silly goose."

John chuckled. "I suppose you're not incorrect. I'll have to take lessons from you."

"Yeah, now that I can walk again, I can definitely teach you how to dance."

"I don't want to learn how to dance like you. You dance like you're mad."

"Suit yourself," Cyrus said as he leaned over the back of the loveseat. "But I am the one who managed to get himself a wife."

"You sure it wasn't a miracle?" John asked, cheekily.

Cyrus smirked. "Miracle or not, dancing helped."

John finished his glass and placed it on the coffee table. "How long did it take before you were able to dance again after the war?"

"It's been six years since I come home. 'Cause all those deaths had just happened, it took a long, long while. I came home in early Spring that year. Yeah that sounds right, I remember feeling a soft rain falling over me when I was being moved from the battlefield, and the men were talking about starting their gardens. It was summer when I was in a wheelchair. By the fall, I walked unsteady, but I could walk. I remember that's when we had the stone walkway built so I could be more surefooted. I know I could dance by Christmas. I'm sorry John, my memories from that time are fuzzy. I had a lot of days that first year when my eyes were in-between, and when they are in-between . . . you saw how I was. Yeah, I was like that for a long time."

"It must have been hard."

"It was, but I had my Abby. She made it bearable for me until I was better. When I haven't died for a good bit, it's only about two hours altogether that it takes me to come back to how I'm supposed to be. When that's all it takes, I don't mind it much at all.

"But sometimes, yeah, we have a rude guest who shoots me in the parlor, and then it takes me a while to be able to talk, to move, to see, to think. It takes until the afternoon right now for chrissakes. It took even longer a few weeks ago. But after another couple weeks, I'll be back to helping Abby make breakfast again. I don't want you worrying none about me 'cause . . . well, I found that I've gotten used to this, the way I am now. What about you, John?"

"I've adapted well enough. I find jobs here et there. As you know, I've found work as a handyman of a kind. I'm getting a bit good at it. It's only me most of the time."

Cyrus huffed, disappointed in that answer.

Defensively, John said. "It's easier for me to be alone. I don't have many people who know what I really look like. How I really am."

"You know, the only reason I'm allowed to see that wing of yours is 'cause you didn't have it when we first met."

"That's true." Before, he had always believed it was serendipity that Cyrus found him in that wagon half a lifetime ago, but now he knew it was what was supposed to happen. J Bellamy would have said it was his thread to follow.

Note from J Bellamy

I have to leave you now because I have a thread that I just have to follow. You have one that you have to follow as well. At this moment, we are meant to part. But we will meet again. Odd folks tend to keep bumping into each other in that way.

I took the mule and left you the wagon. I think that's a fair arrangement. You'll need the moonshine more than I do.

— J. B. B.

3 October 1892

J Bellamy removed the stitches in my arm the day before he left me. He left so early that the sun was not yet up and by the time I had awakened, the campfire had burned down to ashes. I am stranded here in the middle of America, but there is enough food and drink in the wagon for a few good days before I have to worry about it. I remember we passed a town to the East and I can see it like a speck on the horizon. I am not wanting to get up and walk because I am still in pain. I started drinking because there is no more pain medicine.

10 October 1892

A man has taken me into his home. His name is Cyrus Cooper. 'Cyrus' is a name that I have heard in Nyuskom. The origin and etymology of the name is convoluted, going through many cultures and lands.

Some say it comes from 'sun', and I can see this man with that meaning because his hair is blond. Others say it comes from a word that means 'to bestow care', and that's what he did for me as soon as he met me. He saw I was not well, and he attached his horse onto the wagon and walked alongside his beast, leading her to his farm. Another proposed origin of the name is that it means 'to do' or 'to accomplish' and I could see he was by himself on his farm. He explained that he had just inherited the property from his late grandfather.

When I asked him if his grandfather was always late, he laughed and told me that when Americans call someone 'late', sometimes it means they are dead. He asked me if my name was really John. I told him it is my American name and it suits me.

"When did that arm get cut off?" he asked me.

"Last month," I told him, but I knew he made the assumption that lacking an arm was new to me based on that answer. I didn't know how to explain that my arm transformed in the middle of March and that this was the third amputation of it. My spoken English was not good enough yet, and Cyrus could not read.

Because of my accent, he asked where I was from.

"Nowhere" is what I told him.

He laughed at that.

He told me he needed a farmhand. I was looking for something new to do anyways, and I told him that I'd like to try being a farmhand. He said I can try once I'm better.

12 October 1892

Cyrus did not want me to help him with the work today, but I watched him work yesterday, and I wanted to try. I informed him that I am actually very strong. He did not believe me until I showed him. When he saw how easily I could lift things, he asked me if I had been touched by magic. I said I was because that was the truth.

"That's why the air feels strange here now. Too much magic," he said.

I apologized for it.

He told me that he doesn't mind.

I told him I don't want to talk about it very much and that I just wanted to be a plain man named John. I only showed him because I wanted to help him on the farm and be a good farmhand.

It is very inconvenient to have one arm. I still am not very good at many things. Farmers tie many knots actually, more than I thought. I also struggle with the use of a knife.

J Bellamy left enough of an arm that I can use it to hold things in my armpit and sometimes I can hold and grip things enough to work with the ropes and the tools. I use my mouth to hold things, too. For some things, I still need help. I haven't figured out how to do many things in life, but I'm learning.

I think sometimes this life of mine is unbecoming for a prince. But I am a farmhand now. To be a farmhand is not easy, but it passes the time and I don't feel so useless, which is nice.

Letter to Elysia (Translated)

Elysia,

As promised, I'm writing to you when things are going well for me. This has been the longest time an amputation has remained, and it has healed nicely. I watch for those days where the atmosphere is thinner and magic can affect men more easily. I go to the bar in Fairview those nights. There is an alchemic light which shines bright and chases away the strange shadowy places where magic likes to hide so it can't sneak up on me and ruin this nice life I have made with Mr. Cyrus Cooper.

Mr. Cyrus Cooper is a farmer who has taken me in not long after J Bellamy and I parted ways. He feels much older than me, but he is only five years older than I am. I think the reason he feels older is because he is relaxed, good-natured, and very good at being a farmer. I work as his farmhand now, and I'm bad at it. But I'm learning.

The animals still don't like me. I think they can sense how much of me is magic. I think Cyrus has a notion about it, too. Still, I pluck the feathers as they come in so that he doesn't discover how I really am. I think it's easier if he thinks of me just as John who has one arm and is learning life with one arm. I never figured out a last name, but I think I like this new name without one. It sounds even more plain to be John, just John.

Mr. Cyrus Cooper is a very clever man. He invents tools for me to use so that I can manage and be independent. I have been teaching him how to read in return. It's remarkable how clever men are, even without literacy.

I think you'd be surprised to know that I can cut my own food now! Cyrus has made me a cutting board. It has a wall on the back so I can put my food against it and it does not roll away easily. He put what is like tines on a part of it so I can skewer food to still it if need be. It is not perfect, but it is much better. He also has made other adaptations for me. The soap hangs steady for me, so it does not slip from my hand and I can wash my hand properly now. He said he can see I want to work hard and it's fun to figure out how to make things possible for me.

Your brother,
Malachy Secundus
John

25 November 1892

The Americans celebrate a Feast Holiday called Thanksgiving. That is what was done yesterday. It is nice, making such a big spread for the last of Autumn's harvest.

The English word 'Autumn' is very similar to Nyuskom's 'Autumnus'. They have the same etymology. There's a mountain not too far that is the color of fire because of the trees changing color and the leaves falling down. Cyrus said some Americans call the season 'Fall' for that reason. I think that is too simple, but maybe it is fine.

He tells me my spoken English has gotten a lot better. I still cannot handle the animals at all. They don't like me. When we go to town, I ride in the wagon J Bellamy had purchased. Cyrus always jokes that he got a free wagon by taking in the one-armed foreigner. Even when I'm not good at being his farmhand and I need his help taking care of myself, at least he got a nice wagon.

I like when we visit the shops in town. People also are nervous around me because of the magic that clings to me and makes me to be strange, but they assume it is because I am a foreigner and I have only one arm. So I guess that is convenient, at least. I am mostly shy because I am afraid that people might be like the men who put me in the cellar. And I remember moonshine and pastries.

Cyrus loves to dance, but he is too excitable when he dances, so it looks funny. He encouraged me to try to dance, but I was very nervous to join. He told me I can watch. So I watched.

Letter to Elysia (Translated)

Elysia,

I am writing to you after a fine year. I still look like a plain man with only one arm. Maybe this strange affliction of mine has lifted, and I will not regrow the wing. I suppose I still have to pluck the feathers.

Mr. Cyrus Cooper, like you, shows discretion about it. I never do it in front of him but I know he saw the feathers in the dustbin. He has asked me a few times, but I told him I don't want to answer. So he stopped asking.

I have been teaching him how to read. In the wagon, J Bellamy had left many books behind. Some are fairy tales, and some are the classic novels. I am using these books to teach Mr. Cyrus Cooper how to read. He is a quick student, but mostly because he is very stubborn.

He has been teaching me many small things, so I might need less help with taking care of myself. I am also getting much better at being a farmhand. Mr. Cyrus Cooper likes when something American is surprising to me. I still get amazed by the snow here.

Snow is rare in Nyuskom and when it fell there, it was very soft and light like a powder. I think the magic made the winters to be very mild for us. The snow here was heavy and deep. When there was a blizzard, it made the snow as deep as my knees.

We had to shovel the snow on the porch and a path to the barns. I did as much as I could. I have been getting better at being useful. I use the little bit of arm I have left to help me hold the shovel when I dig through the snow. Because I am very strong, I do a good job.

Your brother,
Malachy Secundus
John

Chapter 13

Donkey-Holey

J ohn bounced his wing-tip nervously, a leftover habit from when he used to have a hand there. His father would correct him for fidgeting and say it was unbecoming. He thought about how much he had to unbecome Malachy Secundus Valerio de Nyuskom in order to become John, just John.

The feathers were unkempt from being underneath the duster all day. Instinct begged him to preen the wing, but thankfully, he had enough control over himself to withstand the urge to comb through the feathers.

"I never minded when you had to fuss it," Cyrus said.

John looked away from his limb. "I'm going to try not to until later. A more private time, I think." He puffed up and shook his wing to calm his desire. It had to be good enough for now. "It is very inconvenient to lug around this thing, but I don't think I'd get it cut off again. I always fear it will be like the first amputation. That one was the worst one." He traced how much of his body had been removed with his index finger. "All this, gone."

Cyrus's eyes widened. "How the hell did you live through that, John!"

"I don't know. I barely did. When it grew back, not so much was taken ever again."

"How many damn times has your wing been cut off?"

"April, June, then September." He held his thumb, index, and middle fingers up as he named the months off. "Three times. Same year." John frowned.

Cyrus clenched his jaw. "How the hell could anyone do that to you, John? You was eighteen, but you acted brand spanking new to the world. If I was there, I'd've punched a few people upside the head for cutting off your wing."

"Maybe if you were there, I'd have not minded having it so much."

"I remember when you still had a nub, you had me stay up with you some nights. You said we had to keep that clare-skurro away. We went to the bar in Fairview, they had a bright alchemic lamp there, and you insisted we stay till early morning."

"Yes-yes. It kept it away for a year. I got comfortable being John, who was your farmhand. Maybe I thought that was the end, and I was free." He touched the lip of his crystal glass to ask for more alcohol. After Cyrus poured the brandy, John picked up his drink. "But then it grew back."

"One morning in October, out of the blue!"

John shook his head. "Not out of the blue. The night at-priori was Friday the thirteenth, October 1893. Magic likes to mark Friday the thirteenth on many calendars. I was vigilant the first one that year, in January. But I got comfortable here and forgot to check the calendar." He sipped the brandy and let its perfume fill his head. "Even still, for a full year, I had been plucking the feathers in secret. I know you found them a few times. You stopped asking about it very quickly."

"We were good enough friends that I figured it might be something you kept close to your chest for a reason. But then you grew that wing! Lordy, was I surprised!"

John chuckled. "You were frightened, and you came into the room with a hammer in hand and, if I recall correctly, a pot on your head."

"You was reading that *Donkey-Holey* with me. So, I reckon I had notions of being a Spanish knight."

"Don Quixote," John corrected. "And the point was that he wasn't a knight. His giants were windmills."

"Well, mine was you, all suddenly with a bird-wing instead of that little nubby you had all year. I ain't never seen nothing like it! But once you talked to me, I realized it was you. Just changed. I needed time getting used to it. If you'd've said something about it before, I might could've been fine from the second I laid eyes on it."

"Maybe," John admitted. "But you did better than most. Pater—Father—was upset when it came the first time. Elysia, my sister, she was frightened, but when she saw I was still her brother, she made herself brave to it. She was braver than me about it the first week. She told me it was normal for me to be nervous of it, since I was stuck to it." He glanced at his wing; he was still fidgeting the long feathers. "These days, I'm not scared anymore. Most times, I think of it as a part of me, and I don't mind it even though it aches my back; but sometimes, I am too aware how strange it is to have something like this. I think that's why I'm nervous for your wife to see it.

"You see me, Cyrus, all of me. Most of the time, I'm John, just John to you. But when people see it for the first time, it's like the first day. It always reminds me that . . . I'm not exactly a plain man. As much I want to be one." He finished his second glass of brandy. He was feeling the effects of the alcohol, but he knew it wouldn't last long. It never did. But for now, he was comfortably warm-headed.

"You know, my wife would be better than I was about that wing of yours."

John groaned. "I know she would. And I know she's kind. She's been too nice about it that I could tell pretty early on. She knows what it is."

"Of course she does; she's my wife. She knows everything I know about it, John. She even knows how funny you get when you fuss it. So, she knows what to expect."

"I don't like when it is someone new to see it. The initial shock is always hard for me."

"Well, your tailor must've seen it."

"He has," he admitted.

"How was it when he saw it the first time?"

"He insisted on making me clothes as payment because I had helped him and his son on one of my jobs. He and his boy were just odd enough for me to decide they'd be fine to know."

Cyrus laughed. "What about me? Am I odd?"

"At the time we first met, no. But now? Yes-yes, you're another one who's odd enough."

"Then, what do you mean by 'odd?'"

"What I mean is the odd ones already know magic and how we're all at the mercy of its whims when it happens to have access to the matters of men," he explained. "Not that we should concern ourselves with anything like that."

John returned to the original topic before Cyrus could ask questions. "I tried to have him take my measurements over my duster. He humored me to show me it wouldn't work. He said I had to take it off. I told him what was underneath and that I was afraid. I asked him not to make a big excitement over it."

"And did he?"

"Well, no. Not really. He's a very polite man, he always is. He's not really a tailor either, he's just good at tailoring. He's mostly a collector of enchanted items.

"When he took off my duster, I turned away so I didn't have to see my wing or how he would react to it. But still, I could hear his breathing change when he saw it. He said his favorite curses always change the configuration of a man."

"Oh, so he's an *odd* one."

"Yes-yes, that's what I said! He said he didn't know how to make a shirt for me, but he had some ideas he wanted to try because he saw I didn't really have a decent solution. When he had his questions, they were more about how I was put together, which wasn't bad really. He wanted to see the range of motion I had et what was easier or more difficult for me. He had made me shirts until we found what worked well. Whenever I see the two of them, I get my shirts mended. They cook me a meal, too." He felt the tipsiness already starting to clear up.

"That sounds real nice," Cyrus said. "I'd like to meet them one day."

"I can make that to happen," John said. "He would love to meet you, I think. Despite what a madman he is, his boy seems well-rounded. They are an interesting pair."

"What're their names?"

"Joseph Breckenridge, but he wants to be called Joby. His son is Lou."

"That name sounds familiar."

"It is. Abigail knows him."

"Oh! I remember now. Her cook! Then, definitely have them come on around sometime. It'd be a nice change from entertaining people like generals and politicians and rich businessmen." Cyrus peeked out the window to check the time. "I should be fixing to set up the guest room if you plan on spending the night. If you ever convince your friends to come, they can stay in my old bedroom. Right now, me and Abby have to use the new one down the hall. There ain't nothing wrong with it, but it's definitely a room built for a man who's lost too many crumbs."

By the end of the conversation, John was completely sober. Only a wagon full of moonshine had ever made him drunk long enough to even call himself drunk.

14 October 1893

It came back. I had a full year without it. I can't believe I forgot it was Friday the thirteenth yesterday night. I didn't insist on going out to the bar where they have that one alchemic light that shines so brightly it chases away all of the clarscuro. And overnight, the magic had come and snuck up on me and made me to have it again.

When I woke up, I noticed that I took too much space. I felt the blanket on it, pushing down the feathers. I remember sitting in that room and wishing it was a dream. I had forgotten what it was like to have something there, fully there. And looking at it, I thought it was the end of this comfortable and plain life I had built up for myself as Mr. Cyrus Cooper's farmhand, but still I had to compulsively sort the feathers that the blanket had put out of order.

When the door knocked, I remembered how much I dreaded my friend opening it and discovering what I was. He was very alarmed when he saw me with it. He shut the door immediately after he saw how I had changed. Then he came in later with a pot on his head and a hammer in his hand. He was very cautious coming in. He asked me if I was some devil or something.

"I'm John, just John," I told him. "I swear it." I think when I said that, he saw maybe it really was just me.

"What are you doing?" he asked to me because I was still trying to fix the feathers.

"I don't know" is what I said because I didn't know how to explain anything in spoken English in a way that made sense at then with my heart beating as fast as it was and my head full of nervousness. I was still picking through my feathers. One stuck out, and I pulled it, and it came out easily. I don't know why, but I saved it.

He told me my English is not easy to understand when I was talking so slowly. I didn't know I was talking so slowly. I think he knew I was as unnerved as he was. He said breakfast is ready but it might be cold now and went downstairs. I didn't come down. He came up with my food.

Through the door, he asked "Is it there for good?"

I said if he doesn't mind it too much, I don't want another amputation, please. He said I could keep it and he wouldn't mind.

Note from Cyrus Cooper

John —

I see you holin up in that room all shy but I need help for the fall garden.

The wing is a lot to look at so I mite stare but I don mind it all that much promiss.

You mite look funny but you still my farm hand and my frend.

I miss you readin donky hote cus I need to see what is gon happen.

16 October 1893

I stayed in the room for the entire weekend. Cyrus took care of me by leaving my food outside of my door and knocking on it to tell me it was there for me. I'd open it up and take the meal and then set out my plate again when I was done. We talked a little through the door, about mundane things, like the weather or the plans for the garden. One time I let him come in after I wrapped myself up in a quilt. Still, he knew what I had. I thought he was fine, but when I had to adjust the way it was underneath the blanket, he jumped a little.

At this morn, he left me a note that he slipped underneath my door. His spelling is atrocious. Especially the butchering of Don Quixote. I think that was what convinced me to leave the room and come downstairs sans blanket. I didn't have a shirt to fit how I am anymore, so I felt too exposed. His eyes wanted to stare at it, but he made an effort not to. I washed my hand while he got my cutting board so I could help him prepare breakfast in the normal fashion.

I had to figure out how to sit at the table again. After breakfast, he kept me at the table by having us play a card game. It was good for us. It was something to distract us.

He shuffles the cards very easily. When it's my turn to deal the cards, he lets me put them all face down and mix them with my hand and then square them up. I have to set the deck on the table and pull the cards one at a time to deal them, but he doesn't mind how I do it or that it takes me much longer than it does him. When we play, I can fan the cards, but I still pick the cards in my hand I want to discard with my mouth like I did before when I had nothing there.

But then I moved the limb without thinking. It flapped, and it made me to scatter most of the cards on the floor. I apologized for being like this. I was picking up them, very embarrassed and very scared.

He got out of his seat and gathered the cards next to me, like I wasn't strangely made. He didn't jump like before. "You can't help it, you silly goose" is what he told to me.

I wanted to protest that moniker, but I also didn't want to deter him from being friendly to me. So, I let it go. I hope it doesn't stick. I don't want people thinking I'm a goose when I am a plain man.

Letter to Elysia (Translated)

Elysia,

The wing has grown back, but Mr. Cyrus Cooper has gotten accustomed to it. It was a shock for him at first in the same manner that it was a shock for you. Like you, he helps me with it sometimes. It is not easy having something like this attached to me.

However, it is not as difficult to have it this time, if I'm honest. I never got the chance to exist with it in the open and to explore a life where I learn to use it. Having it makes it easier to do some chores. For example, when I use the broom, I can use the limb to have better leverage for sweeping. Mr. Cyrus Cooper was thankful when I opened my wing to give him shade when we were working together in the garden.

He calls this time of year 'Indian Summer' even though it is autumn. But I see what he means. It is hot and bright as if it is summer. In the autumn, we finish the last harvest, and we prepare the plot for winter so it will be ready in the spring for planting. I am excited for next year because I will be more helpful to him.

I can't wear shirts anymore because we can't find any that fit me. I feel like a wild thing sometimes. The baths are still hard for me to not get lost in the trance. The same thing with the feathers. Mr. Cyrus Cooper helps me with the feathers the way you used to, but I am learning to help myself. Mostly now, he makes sure to talk to me, and he makes sure I have something sweet while I wait for my mind to come all the way back. It doesn't feel as bad as it used to.

I hope things are going well in Nyuskom. Autumn is your time the way summer is mine.

Your brother,

John

Malachy Secundus

4 January 1894

The moon is so dark at night. The snow is deep. Cyrus
has given me a big coat to wear as a gift for the holidays. I
told him it is easier now to move the snow than at last year
because I have more of a limb to maneuver the shovel. He
told me he is glad I have the wing then if it makes the task
easier for me. I'm still not sure if I'm glad to have it, but I'm
more comfortable now.

He told me that he was supposed to set up the farm
and then find a wife. But he doesn't mind to take life at a
slower pace. He said it's best that he finishes learning how
to read so that, by the time he gets to looking for a wife, it
would be easier to be a better and more attractive husband.
He is a handsome man. His hair is the color of the wheat
fields in late summer and he has wide hands that look like
they can hold the whole world in them.

I find it interesting that I am Aestus born and Aestus is
my season. Cyrus is Hibernus born, but he hates this
season. He says it's too dark and cold. It's called 'Winter' in
English. Cyrus says he likes the way I say it. I make the
middle of the word sound sharp as an icicle. He makes it
sound like 'winner' almost but the hint of the 't' is there.
He says he hasn't heard someone pronounce their 't' as I
much as I do.

Sometimes, it is very isolated in the winter. It is also
very cold. My wing is very warm, and he doesn't mind it
when I wrap him up in it. He keeps saying, now that he's
used to it, he prefers me with the wing than without.

I think secrets make people fonder to each other,

maybe. Because I know I look strange with it, more strange than when it was just a bit of arm left.

I never got the opportunity to look for a wife or have relations with anyone because I became like this before I got the chance to try it. I am afraid that wrapping my wing around Cyrus may be the closest I'll be to having a love because of the way I ended up.

That thought makes me feel so lonesome.

22 March 1894

It was a full moon yesterday and it was also the Vernal equinox. America felt almost as magic-heavy as Nyuskom that day. It reminded me to write in my journal because I remember when I was very nervous about keeping the clarscuro away. Now, I am not worried. I know I have a good place with Cyrus.

He tells me my English is getting better. I think so, too. It is not difficult to write a journal anymore but I also find that it feels different to write in my journals now. I think I was using them as a way to cope with everything that was happening to me and my feelings about it. I still have only one hand, and I admit it does make things to be harder for me sometimes. Usually, it is fine though. Cyrus doesn't mind when it takes me longer to do something, and he doesn't mind to help me if I ask for it.

As Spring wakes up the farm, there is a lot to do. I like that I am busy now and that I am useful. The ground still has a lot of snow covering. The animals remain wary of me, but they just give me space when I put their food in the trough, and then they gather around once I'm gone away. It feels too long ago when animals used to not be so wary like this. I feel like I was just a boy when that was still true.

I help with preparing the garden. This year, Cyrus wants to make it a little bit bigger so we can have more crops and then maybe we can sell the extra that we don't eat.

It's still nice and cool outside, so it's fine to wear the big coat he got for me. We head into town sometimes like I used to. The people in Fairview smile and wave as if I were the same as always. I don't know if they'd be as friendly if they knew what I hid underneath my coat, but I know Cyrus is and that's enough.

Chapter 14

Can I Say It Out Loud?

J ohn had put his coat back on to go out and look for Abigail while Cyrus set up the guest bedroom. He stood on the porch for a moment and scanned the fields. The cattle were lying down in the pasture, relaxed. He felt bad, knowing that approaching them would disturb their languid peace.

He walked down the steps. The right side of his body felt far too large for him because he wasn't forcing the wing tightly against his side. He wasn't twisting his shoulder forward and down or hunching his back anymore. Despite that, he was in pain. He was always in pain. When it was bad, he missed those strong medications J Bellamy used to give him. But sometimes, they didn't do very much, and they just made him feel sick in addition to everything else.

He followed the stone walkway. Now that he knew why it was built, it looked very different to him than it did when he followed it this morning. It was a gadget like the beaded curtain—a road to every important part of the farm—and it helped Cyrus when he wasn't able to walk easily. There were low ramps rather than steps for the slight changes of elevation;

John didn't notice them before. The decorative fences were for his friend to grasp if he needed extra support or to brace his body.

The cattle stood up. They lowed as they made their distance, nervous and flighty. Animals were always suspicious of him. They could smell that he wasn't really human anymore; he didn't fit anything they could understand.

The half-weeded garden looked the same as this morning, which meant Abigail hadn't worked on it. Next, John checked near the coop, and that was where he found her feeding the chickens. Immediately, the chickens hurried away at his approach as if he were a predator.

Abigail watched them go as they flapped away urgently. Then, she turned to face John, the source of their alarm. Her braid was looser than it was this morning, and the hair that had gotten free framed her brown face in frizzy curls. Her hazel eyes showed concern for him. "Does everything scatter like that?"

"Yes-yes, for the most part."

"It makes your horse seem even more incredible. I took care of her for you. She's a lovely animal."

"I still had to get her accustomed to me."

"How'd you manage that?"

"There's a few animals who are more curious than afraid. Lucky was one of them. Also, there were treats involved."

Abigail laughed. "Of course there were. But Lucky? I'd think it would be in your taste to name her something else. Like a mythical horse or a heroine from an old story. Something like that."

"She came with the name. It seemed a bad idea to change a name like that."

"You're right. You'd be inviting bad luck, then."

"That was my thought as well," John said. "I think you're more like Lucky than your chickens."

"I'll take it as a compliment. She *is* a nice horse."

"Yes-yes. I'm sorry for making you feel like you had to leave."

"I had to take care of the chickens anyway." Abigail eyed his bulky right side. "Is it feeling better?"

"A little." He lowered his eyes.

"I'm glad. I can imagine it gets cramped under there."

Anxiety gripped his throat, and his heart pounded.

"Why don't we head back inside, John? You always relax when Rus is near."

Together, they walked toward the house. Abigail led the way and John followed a few feet behind. Occasionally, she checked over her shoulder at him. At first, John read unease in her eyes, but by the time the two of them made it to the front porch, he realized she was only curious.

"Mahne, Abigail."

She stopped at the foot of the steps. "Something wrong?"

"Before we enter your home again, I wanted to say you were correct. At the beginning, you said the house would get too warm for me to continue to wear my coat inside. You've been very gracious to me even though I haven't always been a good guest."

"You've been fine, John," she said. "I know you're sensitive about it. Rus told me that much at least."

He considered for a moment to open up the coat and spread that wing to show her what a strange thing he was. Trusting Abigail should be easy; she was kind. And he wanted to do it. In preparation, a deep, deliberate breath filled his lungs. His left hand gripped the front of his duster. "Sometimes, the sight of something strange makes people to behave cruelly. I learned that odd ones tend to accept it easier. You are a very nice woman—and very smart. Maybe it would be fine to . . ." He couldn't do it. Not yet. "My mind . . . I worry it's a little beastly at times. In this case, I think it's my instinct that stays my hand and makes it not to remove my coat." He let go of the fabric.

"Oh goodness, John. I don't think it's any sort of animal instinct. It's just that you had a whole slew of bad experiences about it. I think I'd be the same way. You know, Rus was similar after the war."

"At-posteri the war, Cyrus told me how he was. That you had to take care of everything for him. At the beginning, it sounded more like mother et infant than wife et husband."

"Ah, so he did tell you all of it," she said.

A breeze fluttered by, playing with the hem of Abigail's skirt and pulling at John's duster. It seemed to come from nowhere. It brought a down feather out and stuck it to the front of her cream-colored blouse. She plucked it from off of her breast to study it. "I've noticed since you've come around there's a feeling in the air. Like the way it feels before a storm but look how blue that sky is; it's been getting more noticeable the longer the day has worn on. Is this what the chickens felt?"

"Yes-yes, I believe so."

"Then, is this one of yours?" She showed him the small down feather pinched between her long fingers.

"Maybe it belongs to a chicken," he answered glibly.

"Oh goodness! I know it's yours, John."

"Then why ask?"

"Good question." She let go of it, letting it flutter down to the stone walkway under her boots. "If I said it aloud, what you're hiding under there, I think it might help."

"I don't see how it would."

"It helped Rus. If I told you why saying it aloud helped him, would you change your mind about keeping your coat on?"

"I may reconsider."

Abigail smiled. "Good because I just want you to feel comfortable enough to enjoy the rest of the evening, and I think it's worth it to try."

"Fine. Try."

She took a deep breath. "Rus came home in the March of '02. I told him I knew he couldn't really say much yet, but I was listening. I left him space to answer however he might, and he would by making some noise or moving around . . . I knew he was there. I told him I could see him. I think he couldn't even see himself.

"He was very frustrated with how his body worked back then. I said it out loud. I said I could see he was worried about shaving his beard or that his hair was a mess, but I'd make sure he would look nice and neat. I told him I just needed to wipe his chin up sometimes, and I didn't mind it because he was doing better eating.

"Yeah, he needed a lot of help the first few months. When he started talking again, it was much easier. At first, he couldn't make words like you or me. But he made noises shaped like words. I listened real well and figured out what he might be saying.

"I still do it for him when he has trouble with it. We learned quickly he was always gonna go back to how he was after the war early in the mornings and late at night—"

"He didn't say anything about the night," John interrupted.

"Oh, that's because it's better than the mornings," Abigail explained. "See, he usually turns in for the night before it gets bad. He came together earlier than usual today, so I expect him to fall apart sooner this evening."

John's stomach tightened with guilt. Magic kept taking crumbs from Cyrus because John dared to exert his will upon it ten years ago. "I apologize for making your husband to be like this."

"Oh goodness, John. You're looking at it the wrong way. Because of your miracle, my dear Rus got to come home. What a gift that is."

"Cyrus said the same thing about it."

"Of course he would." She gave John a once-over. "Please, can I say out loud what it is you're trying to hide?"

"Let's try it." He braced himself.

Abigail reached for his left hand, and he let her take it. Her small calluses were sharp against his skin. His heart thundered in his chest. She squeezed his hand with both of hers and said plainly, "You have a wing where your right arm ought to be."

It wasn't as bad as he thought it was going to be to hear her say it, but he still didn't understand how it was supposed to help him.

"So? How do you feel?" she asked.

"I'm not sure."

"We tried at least. For what it's worth, John, I hope you change your mind about keeping that ratty old coat on once we get inside." She smiled, then hurried up the steps.

John followed.

When they entered the house, Abigail waited at the threshold between the entryway and the parlor. John stood near the coat rack. The empty peg beside his hat made him want to try again.

"You've never seen anything like it," he warned, gripping his duster on the right side.

"I doubt there's another man like you in America, John."

"You're not incorrect," he replied thoughtfully. "If there were someone else like me, I'd have bumped into him by now. Odd characters tend to attract other odd characters." He didn't move to unveil the wing, suddenly feeling like he was drawing too much attention to it.

But then, Abigail helped him by treating him like he could've been any other guest. "Would you like to take off your coat?" she asked in exactly the same way she did the first time they entered the house that morning.

"Yes-yes, I think I will this time." He started removing his coat on the wing-side the way he always did. Then, he used his left hand to peel the duster off of the same arm in a smooth, practiced movement.

Abigail held her hands out to receive his coat. Though he kept his right side away from her, his long gray-brown feathers folded across the front of his body where she would be able to see them. He passed the duster to her, and she hung it on the coat rack next to his hat.

"You have a wing where your right arm should be," she said again, quietly.

John was surprised that her saying it out loud really did help him this time now that it was out in the open.

He smiled. "Do I? I haven't noticed."

"Oh John, you really are a silly goose. Just like Rus says."

Note from Cyrus Cooper

John —

Today is your birthday and I got you some root beer since you like it.

Also some new books.

I think you told me twenty but you seem younger to me.

Cus you are bad at many things but you learn fast so I dont mind it one bit.

You been a good farmhand and strong as hell even if you got one arm.

Anyways enjoy the books maybe they will be as good as donkey hote.

18 July 1894

Yesterday was my birthday. I know I haven't written in this journal for a long time, but I find that I don't need to anymore. We have already harvested many summer vegetables. Because of how I look, when Cyrus goes into town to sell the vegetables, I am to stay home.

He asks me about my home. I tell him, this is my home.

Then he asks me where I am from, and I tell him that I am from nowhere. I know that answer frustrates him. I don't want him to know I am anyone other than John, just John, who is a plain man except for the fact I have a bird wing instead of a right arm.

Cyrus still tries to figure out how I can wear shirts. He has tried making some for me, but they are not well made and fall apart quickly. I am too shy to try a tailor. Cyrus is putting an effort because I miss wearing a shirt. I feel too uncivilized when I am shirtless.

Alone on the farm, I almost forget that I am strange sometimes. I do many things to keep me busy so I don't think too hard about what I am at now. I weed in the garden, and I collect the vegetables that are to be collected. I check the fences to make sure they are not in disrepair. If they are, I will fix them. I am very strong, and I can push the nails right into the wood without a hammer even. That makes the work quick. Cyrus has gotten me a small wagon that I can tug along because I cannot handle a wheelbarrow very well. I put my tools and supplies in it when I do my work.

I don't think too much about how I get left behind when Cyrus goes into town. I was definitely left behind a lot when I was still in Nyuskom. I think the difference is that, when Cyrus returns, I can tell he's thought of me. He tells me how he helps people by reading things to them sometimes. He brings me new, sweet things to give to me for when I'm a little bit not myself. He tells me that he wants to give me the full American experience.

I like the gifts he got me for my birthday but I like that I'm allowed to live here even more.

31 December 1894

The good thing about the winter months is that it is not strange to wear a coat everywhere at all. Because I am quiet, sometimes people in Fairview think perhaps I am not intelligent. I find the way I am, it always will make rumors fly. My sleeve hangs empty on the right side. I like that it suggests an arm was once there or is meant to be there. I find people don't ask questions a lot.

There is talk sometimes about me and Cyrus. It is just the two of us on his farm most times other than the visitors he invites in, usually women. I can see how that would be strange.

When the guests meet me, they see how I am and that I am not made right and I really don't talk much at all. I nod or shake my head so they don't hear my homeland in my voice. My English is much better but it is very apparent I am a foreigner.

I like when Cyrus's friends come over and they make room for me at the table. If they are curious about why I wear a coat inside, Cyrus tells them to stop asking questions. I like when he makes everyone stop and remember I just want to exist. Once I am more comfortable, I talk a little. When I see they do not mind me, I am happy. I dream that maybe I would have people to love me the way they love Cyrus.

Sometimes, I do go out, but always with Cyrus. I am nervous to go out by myself. I think it was when the men took me into that cellar that made me afraid of being by myself around people. I haven't told him about that. It was complicated before to explain it.

I'd have to explain J Bellamy and how he was the man who amputated my wing thrice. How he might not be a man, actually. How magic works. How it doesn't work. How I came to America. How I'm an exiled prince who is cursed.

How maybe the curse was my fault because I was quietly hoping for a way out while being too obedient and agreeable to stop walking the path Father set for me. Maybe the curse was Father's fault because he wanted me to stop spending so much time on piano and pretending I could just travel and play piano in other countries. Maybe magic was listening and gave us both what we asked for and what neither of us wanted.

But too much time has passed and it feels like explaining everything isn't worth it anymore because that was the past. And this is the present, and the present is nice.

Letter to Elysia (Translated)

Elysia,

I'm not sure if the letters in America are getting to you. But in case they are, I am writing again. I don't think the timing will coincide, but this letter is meant for your birthday. Here, October also has a haunting quality to it. The trees are all ablaze, and the garden is starting to be too old and will need hacking down soon with the sickle.

I think you would like it here, at least to visit. You would like to see how I am figuring out what I want out of life, and there is one person at least who doesn't mind the way I look. If this is how it will be, I think I'd like to keep the wing this time. I wish more people didn't mind it.

I was afraid to admit it to you before, but it feels good when the sunlight plays on it. I spread the wing open wide and let the wind blow through its feathers. It feels like for a moment I am perfectly made because it feels nice. But the rest of it, no. At the end of the day, my shoulder and my back ache. I have to hold it up with my left hand. Cyrus worries about it then, asks if it hurts me. It doesn't hurt as badly as my first amputation. I think I will always compare any pain to that hell.

Compared to that, these days are bright and happy. When it's cold enough, I don my coat, and I join Cyrus in town when he goes to the bar to dance. He's not a great dancer, but he's fun to watch.

More than a few times, he brings a beautiful woman home. We sit in the back of the wagon together because I cannot drive the horse. Mostly she stays on her side and I stay on mine, but sometimes, she chats with me to pass the time. My English is getting very good.

Your brother,
John
Malachy Secundus

10 March 1896

I injured his horse. I didn't mean to, but I am so strong. Sometimes, I forget how odd I am when I stay here on the farm. I need to stop pretending I am still human.

He keeps telling me he is not angry with me, but I can feel it seething under his skin. The horse's mouth will take a long time to recover and it might not, but this is why I don't drive or ride the horses. I can't do it anymore and he encouraged me to try. I think that's why he doesn't say he's angry, but I think we both learned that sometimes, there are things I am just not to do anymore.

Malachy Secundus rode horses, played piano, and loved the summer.

That is not me anymore.

Note from Cyrus Cooper

John —
I dont know how you fixed up Rosie but I know it was you.

19 March 1896

Cyrus is in a better mood ever since I helped his horse. She is doing fine at now. I used one of my feathers the way J Bellamy used his. But I think his was mine the whole time.

I remember when the wing came back a few years ago, one of my feathers stuck out more than the rest, like it was bigger and wanted to be selected. It came easily into my fingers. I don't like to admit it, but after I preen the feathers, my mind isn't all mine.

What happened yesterday night was that the moon was a crescent. It lit the world up enough so there was clarscuro everywhere. That instinct I have sometimes, what J Bellamy might call a thread and what suggests I'm something that isn't only John, told me that it was time.

I opened up the top drawer of the dresser where I kept that feather next to the little brush I use to groom my wing. And I saw it shimmering gold. Years ago, J Bellamy showed me a feather like it, shining gold the same way. He said it did that because it wanted to.

It wanted me to use it.

I walked out of my room and then outside and I went to the horse with her injured mouth. I made a wish and it came true. Rosie wasn't hurt anymore.

Chapter 15

All Jitters

Abigail had gone to the bathroom while Cyrus and John got comfortable in the parlor again. For Cyrus, that meant he leaned over the back of the loveseat, gesturing wildly as he spoke, as if he couldn't help but exercise the freedom he had to use his legs and arms as he pleased. Meanwhile, John was sitting in the nearest reading chair to Cyrus. His wing was propped up on the arm again. He kept looking at the feathers slightly out of place, and it set him on edge. Usually he could wait, but he couldn't anymore. Magic was pushing on him again.

"You're all jitters, John," Cyrus noted.

"The instinct is strong. I keep wanting to . . ." His left hand hovered over his wing, as if asking permission to touch it. He was afraid to say it aloud. "I've been wanting to."

"Yeah, I noticed you was holding off on it. Well, go on ahead with that. I ain't stopping you."

"Abigail is going to see me."

"I told you she'd be good with it. If she ain't, I'll take care of you."

John nodded. His feathers puffed up as his fingertips combed through them. The feeling was delightful, and it always made his scalp tingle. He didn't tear his eyes away nor pause the task when he said, "I will be stuck doing this. Until I'm done."

"I know that, too. You used to live with me. For years. I know you like it when I chat with you while you're fussing it."

Guided by instinct, John scratched at the powder down feathers to turn them into dust, which he wiped over the rest of the feathers. His replies were coming slower as his mind got less human. "I hate … how it makes. Makes me to feel … like an animal."

"Well, you ain't an animal. I'll tell you that."

John didn't answer, too preoccupied by his wing. He tilted his head with a blank expression. Down and dust collected on the floor as he continued preening.

"You're my friend. Just a plain man from nowhere. Sometimes, you get a little crittery is all."

He shifted his wing to get access to another part of it.

Cyrus took a deep breath. "Hey John, listen."

John forced himself to answer even though complete sentences had become impossible. "Listen. I know … don't … I don't. Look like. Hard t'talk … like this."

"That's alright. I know that; I'm just making sure. Well, I'm gonna go get the root beer from the cellar. You want some?"

He didn't look up. "Get root beer."

"Well, I'll get you some. I know you feel a bit funny after you do this."

"Funny," he repeated. It was the best he could do for now. Words kept getting harder.

"That's right, John," Cyrus said gently. "Now, Abby won't mind you like this either, so don't worry none 'bout that. But I'm the man of the house, and I ought to be the one carrying the crate up from the cellar."

The bathroom door opened and then closed. Abigail was done then. Her steps came lightly up the hall. She stood in the yawn of the archway, getting an eyeful of John. Her scrutiny made him self-conscious.

"Abby." Cyrus stood straight up. "I'm fixing to get the root beer here for John. He prefers it if someone's talking with him while he's fussing his wing."

John's fingers were busy in his feathers.

Abigail went to sit on the loveseat. She kept her movement controlled around John, which meant Cyrus must have told her how easily he startled when he was like this. Once settled in, she watched him. Her eyes were soft on him while his were transfixed on his cursed limb.

"Rus always told me you can't even look away when you fuss your wing."

John didn't respond at all.

"I wonder if maybe it's like reading a real good book," Abigail said. "The kind that makes you leave the lamp on all night. Then, it's like there's a magic comes by to visit, and it spins the story around in your head until it all comes alive, and you don't sleep at all. Then, the morning light comes, and it's like you danced with something ancient all night and drank your fill from its cup, and you feel only halfway back."

When John heard her say that, he paused from his task. He wanted to lift his eyes and answer her, but it was too difficult; he couldn't even think in words. Instead, he moved his wing again to reposition it, this time focusing on the part closest to his right shoulder.

"Don't you worry John, I know you're listening," she reassured him.

He was relieved she understood that much at least.

Cyrus took the relief as a sign that John would be okay. He stepped out of the room and left the house. The root beer was kept in the cellar to stay cool.

John's feathers flattened when the front door shut. He was tense, and his left hand was trembling, stuck where it was.

"You're just fussing your feathers. That's all," Abigail said. "It's easy for me to chat away. I'm already used to it. See, Rus had a long time when he couldn't talk either, and he liked when I was chatting at him, too."

Comforted by her words, he fluffed the feathers up again and continued. His movements had a twittery quality to them, reminiscent of the songbirds that searched for worms at dawn.

"My Rus. When he was starting to see again, he'd have days where that's the best he got. He gets to his best and stays like that for a couple hours. So, for a long time, he was confused more often than not. He got into the habit of telling stories until his mind caught up again. We both loved that fairy tale: 'The Six Swans.' And he mixed up your story and that one. I see why now that you're here.

"When you first showed up on the doorstep, I wasn't sure if you were exactly like how Rus said you were. But I saw you were bashful, and you were sensitive about your right side, so I just decided it might be true. I spent all day trying to imagine it, but it really is just like Rus said it was. I know you don't have a choice about this part of it. He told me that, too. He said during and after, it's like your mind goes crittery. I hope it's not too embarrassing for you."

John had just one more section to do. When he finally set

the last feather right, he was freed. He could lift his gaze. Still nervous, the tip of his wing wiggled.

Abigail's eyes followed the way his long feathers twitched. "Are you feeling okay?" she asked.

"I'm all jit-ters." His *t*'s were always a little over-pronounced, but they had become sticky, hard to talk past smoothly.

"That you are." She crossed her legs.

John spooked in the way wild animals did when people moved too suddenly. He didn't mean to behave that way, but he felt more wild and magic than man at the moment.

"Sorry, John. I don't mean to make you jump."

"I know . . . crit-ter. It. Is not." He shook his head. Rather than continue trying, he gave up.

He played with the toggle closure on the front of his shirt, running his fingers over its smooth wood in search of some movement to help direct the tense energy he was feeling—one that didn't involve the tip of his wing.

"I noticed your shirt fits you very well," Abigail said.

He nodded and lifted his wing to show her the snaps.

"See, I was wondering because there weren't any buttons on the front. It looks nice on you."

Another nod.

"That means you must have a tailor."

"Ita-ita. Meus tailor . . . Joseph Breckenridge nomen est."

The pause when Abigail had to think through John's mixed up speech made him too aware he wasn't speaking English. He was about to apologize and try it again, but she figured out what he meant.

"Oh! My cook was Joseph Breckenridge. And I know you

aren't fibbing at me. So, are you saying your tailor and my cook are the same person?"

John nodded. He was thankful she was smart and that she didn't assume he wasn't when he was like this.

She continued speaking. "Joe came around the last year I worked at the governor's right before I turned nineteen. It was in '97 I think. He said he needed to make sure I was learning how to cook right because he saw I had potential. He put the seed in my head that I should move out. I followed him out of that big house, and then he disappeared on me in Fairview in the middle of me on the piano at the bar. I was allowed to stay upstairs if I cleaned. So I just did the same job except it weren't as fancy as the governor's home, but I got to play piano as much as I wanted. It was nice."

"Piano . . . is nice."

"Oh! Actually, you said it so perfectly this morning. Remember? You said piano is good company sometimes." She kept talking to him as if he were speaking normally; he liked that.

"Good company," he repeated.

"Well, thanks for the compliment."

"Thanks for . . ." John realized what he was doing. "Sorry."

"There's nothing to be sorry for. I'm having a nice conversation with you, my husband's good friend John. A plain man," she said pleasantly.

It was enough to have him smile. He looked at his wing and then back at her.

"Goodness John. It's just a wing. And sometimes you have to—"

He perked up and angled his head, adjusting with jittery avian movements to interpret why the feeling in the room changed ever so slightly. He could say it was instinct, but really it was magic telling him what was coming. Maybe magic was what told all the secrets to all the animals.

"Something wrong, John?"

He pointed towards the entryway. "Cyrus is here."

She stood up. "Well then, I best open the door for him."

3 April 1896

Cyrus wants to talk about the miracle I performed. I'm nervous about it because I wasn't completely myself when I did it. My thoughts were different, like the way they are after I have to mind my wing. I don't like talking about how I am during those times. I did find another feather I wanted to save, but it was not golden. The first one didn't start shining gold until later. So maybe it will be the same.

I don't think I understand how magic works. I just know of my brushes with it. J Bellamy was probably the closest thing America has had to a wizard in recent years. Then, there was the nameless woman who told my fortune with her tasseomancy. This curse of mine, of course, which makes me have this ridiculous bird wing attached to me in lieu of an arm.

I have had it for four years.

Having it on this farm isn't too bad really. But I realize I don't do anything I used to want to do. I wanted to play piano and travel and come home for Aestus. Cyrus doesn't even know I used to play. It doesn't seem important to tell him. It is one of those things I am not to have anymore.

I have told him a little bit about Elysia. And a little bit about my half-brother. It's hard to talk about Father because I don't want him to sound awful. Before all of this happened to me, I was Father's favorite. He noted my aptitudes and developed them and was proud of me. But I think when I was getting closer to being a man and showed none of the ambitions he wanted me to have, he was worried. He saw my temperament was to be as I am right now. Except I wanted to play piano.

Now I am a farmhand. I don't think I will have this limb cut off again. It's easier to work with it than not. I'd rather be a good farmhand than look like a plain man with one arm. I believe that's what I want to be, as useful a farmhand as I can be.

I asked Cyrus what he wants to be. He said he wants to be a good looking man looking for a good time. He is delightful sometimes with his words.

Notes From Cyrus

John —
It's like you cant hear me.
Its different from when you fuss your feathers.
When you fuss your feathers you still can hear me.
You just have trouble talking sometimes.
Can you read this note?

What do you mean by a drum?

How long has this been going on?

Let's just turn around and head on home.
I don't want you going crazy.

You sure you can still work on unloading the wagon?

Fine but right after we heading home

18 August 1896

The drumbeat is gone now, thankfully.

Before today, when we went into town, there was a noise that pounded like a drum in my head. It wasn't so loud before. I didn't pay it any mind when it started in April because then, it was easy to stop it, and it was not as loud.

I'm trying to understand the rules because I normally don't hear the drumbeat. It stops when I walk around because it wants me to keep moving when I'm not on the farm. But during summer, it's too warm for me to walk around outside of the wagon.

Normally, I stay on Cyrus's farm to escape the sound of the drumbeat. It was not this bad the last time I came to town in May, so I came along because my strength would have been convenient to help move some of the supplies off of the cart.

I couldn't even hear him talk to me because it was so loud. I felt thankful that I taught him how to read and write. He passed me some notes, and I was able to answer him. I still could help him to do the work he needed of me, but my head was pounding, and I could hardly stand it then.

He asked me many more questions once we got home. I answered them as best as I could. Because I thought it had to do with the second feather I saved, I showed it to him. It was gleaming gold at then. I don't understand why I saved it. But I told him when it gleamed gold like this, it can make a miracle.

He asked me to show him. I did so by making it so that

the soap never ran out again. He laughed and told me that if it really worked, then that would be a fine miracle to witness.

Whenever I used up the feather, there was no more drumbeat to worry about.

11 October 1896

I got another feather, and I've had it for several weeks. I don't know what to use it for, but whatever I need to use it for, I have to be careful. I just know I have to. When I go into town, I hear the drums, but it is not too loud yet. I can still hear what Cyrus tells me and what the townsfolk tell me.

I know the drumbeat will get worse. I have already decided that when it gets too bad, I'll just stay at the farm. I like living here anyways.

Cyrus and I have lived together for four years. He is twenty seven years old now and has yet to take a wife. When I ask him about how he told me he was supposed to look for a wife, he laughs and tells me that maybe being a bachelor makes more sense for him at now.

Last night, he asked me if I ever laid with a woman. I got shy and shook my head.

Virgin, he called me. He smiled and told me that it makes sense an angel would be a virgin.

It was a funny thing to say. I don't feel like an angel at all. I have one wing where my arm should be, and no matter how I move it, it feels like it doesn't belong. I'd like to think an angel would be better made than I am. When the work day is long, my back and my shoulder hurts. I think it's been too many years that I'm in the wrong shape.

Sometimes, I explore myself and then pleasure myself when Cyrus goes into town and leaves me alone on this farm. I know he is finding pleasure for himself there. He is charming and sometimes brings a woman home. Not last night. Last night he stayed home with me, we drank root beers and he talked about how much he's gained since learning to read. We played some poker, and I won almost every hand. He said I'm lucky.

I almost told him my name used to be Malachy. It is a nice name but you could think of it as 'mal' which means 'bad'. And 'lachy' is pronounced the same as 'lucky', and I thought about how I was an unlucky thing for my Father to keep. Maybe I'm a good luck charm for Cyrus because my name is no longer Malachy.

Cyrus is very handsome. He has hair the color of wheat in late summer, and he dances shamelessly and laughs easily. Of course everyone falls in love with him. Of course he's not a virgin.

Summer. I just noticed I say summer instead of aestus. I wonder when that changed.

23 January 1897

The pounding in my head has gotten so loud and terrible off the farm that I'm stuck at home. The snow is so deep that Cyrus is stuck in here, too. He is always excited to show me the snow because I'm still not used to how much snow falls here in America.

He said that he's happy I taught him how to read and write because it makes the time pass by easier in the coldest, deadest parts of winter. He said the winter is always hard for him because it is dark, and the darkness lasts too long. He asked me if I liked the winter.

I told him it's not that bad, but it's just too white and it hurts my eyes sometimes.

I didn't want to tell him that my favorite part of winter is that he's stuck in the house with me and that he is more likely to touch me. That he can tuck underneath my wing for warmth and I'm happy he doesn't mind it and I'm also happy that I don't mind it either.

I asked him what kind of a wife he wanted.

He said he needs someone who is curious. Who asks questions and is so bright she can light up the room. Someone who will blush when he's being inappropriate to let him know when he goes too far, but who loves him anyways. He said he wants a woman who is strong but soft.

I told him he needs to find a wife who cooks just as good as my tutor at least. I told him he cooks the best food in the world. He said well, I can agree to that.

Then, he said whoever she is, she has to be able to make good music so he can dance to it. I laughed and told him his dancing is ridiculous, and she'd have to be able to play ridiculous to accommodate him. He said the most important thing was for his wife to be nice to me. If she wasn't, he'd leave her immediately.

Then, he asked who I wanted as a wife. I only thought of what my favorite things about him were. I told him I wanted someone who was kind and talked to me when I was stuck fussing my wing and didn't mind it if I sometimes got a drumbeat in my head. Someone who was honest and maybe a little bit too shameless most of all.

He knew who I was talking about and he laughed. He said "John, we're not going to get married. We're good friends, and you're too plain to be my wife. You just need to find yourself someone to fall in love with."

I asked, "Don't you mean someone to fall in love with me?"

He said, "That ain't gonna be a problem for you because you're actually very easy to fall in love with, you silly goose."

Chapter 16

Odd Ones

While Abigail was letting Cyrus into the house, John used the small moment to fully stretch his wing in order to work some of the stiffness out of it before he propped it up on the chair's arm again. The married couple chatted fondly to each other and then entered the room.

John flinched as Abigail passed by. His violet eyes stayed low in an effort to remain calm. He hated how twitchy he got right after preening, when he was still not quite himself. The hem of her skirt fluttered about the laces of her boots. Cyrus followed his wife into the parlor. Glass bottles clinked together in the wooden crate he was holding. He set it on the floor near where Abigail took her place on the loveseat. Her legs crossed at the ankle; one foot tucked neatly behind the other.

Cyrus selected a bottle. "Abby surprised me by opening the door at the right time, but it was nice because my hands were all full. She said you knew I was right outside. Are you telling the future now, John? You weren't doing that before."

"I learned it . . . from my new . . . work."

"A handyman." Cyrus opened the cap and passed the drink to John. "Here. This ought to help you talk right again."

John took it and was thankful to have something to fill his hand. He brought the brown bottle to his lips. The carbonated drink sparkled on his tongue with the flavors of wintergreen and sassafras. It had been a long time since he had root beer. He felt that it always had such an interesting taste, unlike anything he ever had back in Nyuskom. It always filled his senses up. Every sip, his mind felt a little more human and a little less something else. "Meya kulpa. Fakule non est . . ." John paused to switch out of Nyuskom's creole. ". . . to speak in English."

"Fah-cool-lay means 'easy' in your language," Cyrus prompted.

John brightened up. "Yes-yes. In English . . . 'faculty' has. Has the same roots as 'fakule.' Both come from Latin 'facile' which means 'easy.' From 'facere' meaning 'to do.'"

Abigail smiled. "Rus always said you liked words, John."

"I do. I like to find new ones. Know where they come from." His speech remained stilted. He thought of what she had said earlier about drinking his fill from the cup of something ancient. Maybe it really was like that. If that were the case, he'd rather have root beer than whatever heady thing magic gave him when he preened his wing.

Abigail picked at the small fluffy feathers that had collected on the hem of her skirt before flicking them onto the floor with the rest of the mess John had made.

He blushed. "Sorry for the chaos."

"Goodness John, this ain't a 'chaos.' I don't mind it at all. Besides, we can sweep it up later easy enough."

"I can sweep up . . . non later." He had to pick up some of

the words she spoke to form his sentence. His embarrassment made his words awkward to find again.

Abigail kept her voice light. "You're our guest, you shouldn't—"

Cyrus patted his wife's knee. "Broom's in the same place as always," he said to his old friend.

At that, John set his half-finished drink on the coffee table, stood up, folded his wing, and walked over to the closet under the steps to retrieve the broom. He started to clean up his mess. The bend of his wing wrapped around the end, and his left hand powered the sweeping somewhere in the middle of the broom handle.

A plain man wouldn't hold a broom like this.

"I take it that the chickens were fine?" Cyrus asked his wife as John swept the feathers up.

"Of course. The garden still needs weeding, though. I also took care of John's horse for him while I was out there. Goodness, Rus, you need to get out there and see her. I've never seen such a well-trained animal. She's marvelous."

"John? With a horse? Animals tend to be nervous around him."

John had swept up his little pile. The busywork was helping him calm down.

"Yeah. Last I remembered, horses got real nervy around you. You always had to ride in the back of the wagon or walk alongside," Cyrus said. "But it wasn't like you ought to be handling horses back then anyhow. We tried once, remember?"

"I remember Rosie . . ."

"It's alright, John. You fixed her right up."

John nodded. He squatted on the floor with the dustpan and

hand broom. The bend of his wing braced the dustpan while he swept up the pile of dirt.

"I like that dust pan," Abigail remarked. "It doesn't leave that pesky line on the floor like all the other ones I've ever used do."

"Hmmm. I made it . . . no more . . . pesky lines." He put the feathers in the dust bin at the edge of the room.

"Hey, finish your drink, John," Cyrus said. "I don't mind it too bad when your head's a bit crittery, but I miss chatting with you."

John sat down again, feeling much better now that the mess had been cleaned up and his wing was back to being propped up. He finished the rest of his root beer and set the now-empty bottle on the coffee table. The carbonation made him hiccup several times, but it was exactly what he needed for his words to flow again.

"So, you have a horse now. How's that even possible?" Cyrus asked.

"I had to take a lot of time for Lucky to become accustomed to me. She is trained well because I had a woman to help me."

Cyrus grinned suggestively at that. "Oh? A *woman?*"

"Yes-yes, her name is Marguerite Blanchard. She prefers to be called Margie. Like how it was with my tailor, I helped her, and she wished to return the favor. She noticed I could not ride, and she decided she had to teach me. She had to adjust how she taught things since I only have the left arm to use, and I had picked up many bad riding habits because of this old thing." He lifted the feathers on the end of his wing to indicate it before letting them flop down again. "Also, I'm stronger than I ought to be. I could be hard on the horses if I wasn't careful. At first, I was only allowed to adjust how the reins laid in my hand. She told me that horses aren't meant to be ridden."

"Well, if horses aren't meant to be ridden, what are they meant to be then?" Abigail asked.

"Horses are meant to be horses. That's all. And that's how I learned to ride. Margie explained how the way I am affected the way the horses moved, and I was being selfish to ride as if I weren't like this. That's what she looks for: how the horses move, how the people move, and how they are moving together. She was interested in the way I was put together, too. She has seen this wing. The first thing she told to me once she saw it was that the way it is attached to me doesn't make much sense. She said I was 'sigogglin.'"

"Sigogglin? Well, that wasn't very nice," Abigail said.

"It's not incorrect." John glanced at his feathers. "Margie was the only one who took one look at how it is attached to me and could see how much it aches." He recalled the way her fingers investigated the shape of his wing, then cued the movement of it to explore its range of motion. She was able to explain, in detail, how poorly made he was in a way he could understand. "Her honesty is refreshing. I like working alongside her. Being next to her often makes it easier to hold still."

"Do you work with her often?" Abigail asked.

"I do. A few times a year, usually when the air is crisp because I can wear my coat. Sometimes, she moves horses. Usually between the ranches at Oaks Bend and the Holler. The ranches are a day apart, and they send an escort of hired guns with her. If I'm around, they hire me as a mercenary because I have gotten good at it. But mostly because I get along with Margie.

"She's odd, and people don't know how to take her. But I do.

I chat with her, and I'm as odd as she is. I let her talk as much as she wants about the anatomy and movement of whatever it is that catches her fancy. Usually, the horses, but sometimes, it is me."

"You sound real fond of her," Cyrus said.

John smiled. "I am."

"You ought to bring her around some time."

"She isn't the type to leave her routine or her work, but I'm sure you'll meet her someday. Like I said, she's an odd one. Et you are as well, Cyrus."

"Am I an odd one?" Abigail asked, curious.

"You must be a little odd because you've met Joby, then you've married Cyrus et took care of him at-posteri the war. Then, you've met me. That's not a coincidence. Yes-yes, I believe we're all odd ones here."

25 February 1897

The feather has been gold for a while. I'm not eager to use it. But maybe I should soon. I can hear the drums again when I am at the edge of the property. As if my world where my head can be quiet is shrinking. When the drumbeat starts, it's been getting louder. I try to push past it when I am working on the fences, but it's getting harder to. Cyrus has noticed it because I'm much slower now to do the farmwork. When he comes out with me, there is no drumbeat.

I think I'm to use it on him, but I'm not sure what miracle he needs.

After I preen my feathers or bathe my wing, I'm not really just a man anymore. It frightens me. My mind makes room for all of the things magic wants to tell me. Sometimes what it tells me is like a premonition of what's to come. The land is preparing its part in something.

America's wild magic is wearing the smile of a gambler who knows he has the winning hand, and everybody's already thrown their money in the pot. And I know I'm at the table. I think it wants me to be the dealer.

I know magic is tricky, and I'm afraid of using my feather to make a miracle on him. Cyrus is not a horse with an injured mouth, and he's not the soap which never runs out. He's a man, and I don't want to ruin his life the way magic has ruined mine. But at the same time, if magic hadn't changed my life the way it has, I never would have met Cyrus.

Tomorrow is his birthday. I couldn't buy him a gift

because I can't go into town anymore with this drumbeat in my head. I wrote a poem for him instead.

It is thanks to him I feel like I might be allowed to be happy and content. At least for a little while.

John's Poem

How can one winterborn be so summer touched
In the late-wheat of your hair et in how much
The world seems to behold you
As worthy et fold you
In the warmth that goldens your
Eyes in squinting smile
Makes me to swear that I'll
Dust down
Thistle down
Feather down
Won't let you down
Here, just here
A moment now
We share root beer
Post fuss
Just us
John et Cyrus
Between Aestus et Hibernus
Between salwayed et farewell bade
Both of us, summermade
For me, you await
Until my state
Become
Unburdened
Unbirded
"Come be
John, just John"
You say to me
Cyrus, grasi

27 February 1897

Yesterday, I recited my poem for him. He told me I have a way with words. He was gentle to tell me I will always be a precious friend to him. He will always be one to me.

He then told me he could tell the drumbeat was starting to harm me.

I told him respite was rare.

He said he'd like me to try a miracle on him.

I told him not till tomorrow because I don't want to ruin his birthday. Just like in the poem, we had root beer after I preened my feathers.

So, today I used the feather the way he wanted. I think Cyrus is safe because he does not look or feel any different. The animals don't seem apprehensive about him, so I don't know if the miracle took. But the feather disappeared in a bright yellow reaction like the last two did. And he said he believed that my wish for him will come true.

I told him I wanted him to find a beautiful wife who could play music he could dance to and who could cook delicious meals. Who would accept me the way he can. Who would love him no matter what even if he turned out to be something as strange as me because of this stupid gold shine feather. I still don't trust magic.

The drumbeat was gone, and I didn't see his perfect wife materialize. Maybe I'm no good at miracles. At least I am not too bad at being a farmhand anymore.

21 March 1897

A new feather came on the first of this month. I was already starting to feel the drums filling my head every time I held still, and I used the feather as soon as I was able, on the fifth. Then the next feather came later that same day. I just enchant things I can. It's small things here and there.

I made it so that the faucet comes on by itself when you have your hand underneath, and the water is always the perfect temperature. I made it so that the dust pan never has the little line of dirt between it and the floor. I made the hammer that always hits the nail and never your finger a few times, and Cyrus sold some of those ones for enough money to buy an alchemic light for the dining room. It's a beautiful lamp that hangs above us. I made the mirror in the bathroom so it never fogs up.

I haven't gotten a new feather in a few days, which is a relief. Perhaps magic is giving me a break. I had wanted one for a while. I only want to be John, just John. A plain man who doesn't deal in miracles about twice a week. Instead, I am something odd who can feel magic pulling him by a thread to a destiny where he is the one who deals everyone's hand. Magic knows the outcome. It is the cheater who has put the deck in the order it wants. I don't want to be like this.

Because it wasn't too hot yet and I didn't have to worry about the drums in my skull, Cyrus took me into town to help him shop. Fairview remembered me, and many were happy to see me. We celebrated Spring in the bar when we were all done with errands.

I almost told Cyrus about moonshine and pastries, but today was a day when we didn't have to worry about much. I didn't want to ruin the day, and I didn't want to ruin the night. He danced, and I watched him dance.

I went to the piano to see how much I still remembered. I didn't commit enough to sit on the bench because I have to be careful how I sit with this thing attached to me. I stood at an angle and tried some songs, but I was out of practice and my playing was not very smooth. They kicked me off to let someone else with two hands play and who can sit properly at the piano.

I used to play better than the man who played. I think if I had a little more time, I'd remember it. I was surprised that five years is somehow not enough time to forget how to play piano and I think my body aches to play it more than my shoulder aches. I think if I could sit in front of it like I used to, the music could flow down my arm and my fingertips.

But alas, I've only one hand, and it's the left.

Cyrus let me drink as much as I wanted. He said I was 'three sheets to the wind' as he helped me into the back of the wagon. I was in a heap, but I remember most of the ride anyway because I never stay drunk for very long. 'Three sheets to the wind' is because I was unsteady like a ship with loose sails. I found it amusing that a man who has never been in the ocean would say such a thing. I used to live where there were many ships. I told him about where 'three sheets' came from and he said it sounds like I'm only 'one sheet to the wind' already.

Then, he said he was lucky to have met me. I really must have still had at least 'one sheet to the wind' because I told him my name. It was hard not to when 'lucky' sounds so much like 'Malachy'.

I said to him, "Before I was John, I was Malachy Secundus Valerio de Nyuskom."

He laughed and said that John, just John suits me much better.

I agreed with him.

17 July 1897

It's my birthday. I am turning twenty three. I have had this curse for more than five years now. I need to keep moving so the drums can stop. It's not easy being like this. Cyrus being near is not enough to stop it anymore, and he sees how it affects me. Even close to the house, I get drums. It always starts quiet and then grows in intensity every time I try to rest.

He is worried when I can't hear him very well. I can't figure it out, so I have to wait until it closes in and gets so loud and the only place in the whole world where I can't hear those infernal drums is right where I'm supposed to use this feather. I tried placing it on something, but I don't know what to wish for, and I don't know what it's supposed to do.

Before, it was easier. I just wanted to use the feather, and it made itself work for me and I had peace for a day or two, sometimes three. I don't have a lot of time in between feathers anymore. Sometimes, for peace, I walk the fence, looking for any holes.

Because of this, the fence is very well-maintained. It's quiet if I keep walking. Cyrus walks side by side with me sometimes so we can chat and I can hear him. We wanted today to be a day where I could be free of it. That's what he did today. Just walk the fenceline with me.

Even in the house, I hear it. I don't hear it when I bathe or when I groom my wing, but my head feels full of magic then. Because it was my birthday, Cyrus talked to me while I was bathing in the tub. It was what I wanted the most.

He poured the water over the wing. He watched my

feathers fluff up as they got wet and saw how I moved it in
the water. He told me he thinks it's precious that I do that.
He kept talking to me even though speaking is very hard
for me during that time. I became a little bit more animal
than usual. It wasn't frightening because Cyrus was there,
taking care of me.

When I was done, he wrapped me up in a towel. It
takes a while to dry, so the both of us went on to the porch
and we shared a cake until I could think and talk again.

When I was there on the porch, there was no drumbeat, but I could feel America's magic stirring through me
and telling me what it wanted from me because I was
fresh-bathed. Baptized into a strange creature half-man
and half-magic, I could see and hear what's to come next.

Every bite of cake I ate, I pushed it away until I
couldn't understand what it was saying anymore. The
drumbeat that came back was a gentle tapping in the back
of my mind. I knew to use my feather on a suitcase so it
could be like that chest J Bellamy made that he put the
bodies into. That's when I wondered if he cut off my wing
thrice so he could have my feathers to use.

Tomorrow, I'll try the suitcase. I know that after I make
it, I will have to leave. I think I'll stay next to Cyrus until
the drums get so loud and relentless that I can't even hear
him speak.

Letter to Cyrus

Cyrus,

I think you understand something is happening to me, and I cannot stay on your farm any longer. I decided to wait at least until the air cooled down so I could wear my duster comfortably in case someone might see me on my travels. I have a suitcase packed with everything I need. My boots can never wear all the way through, and my coat, as dingy as it is, can never become threadbare because I have a wing that sheds magic feathers. When I travel, the drumbeat in my head quiets. But when I hold still, it is like I'm being punished for daring to hold still.

If I could, I'd have loved to hold still next to you. My years living with you on your farm, I will always consider them my Halcyon Days, a memory like a dream when things, for me, were peaceful and bright. 'Halcyon' is a kingfisher. In many cultures, this bird represents peace and prosperity. But it is also a bird who dives headfirst into the water to catch fish. You are someone who is something like that for me.

I hope you find your wife. I feel bad that you put your life on hold so I could catch up and figure myself out. I think you understand that I have feelings for you, but you always handled me with grace and gentleness. I like that you let me to explore them, at least a little bit.

I liked that you kept people in and out of my life, bringing them into your farm to play cards with me or to chat with me. I liked that you would take me to town and drink and make sure everyone remembered I was just a plain man who was trying to live a good life. Fairview was a nice town for me to have ended up living near, and your farm was a good place for me to learn how to have a wing. I will always appreciate how you spoke to me when I was grooming my wing so I didn't feel too strange and how you waited for me to be myself again after I was done.

Don't worry too much about me because I am very strong, can deal miracles, am literate, and my spoken English is not so bad anymore.

Love,
John, just John

Chapter 17

Piano

On the road, it would take a long while for John to come back to being a plain man after his mind would stretch thin. During that time, he could see all of the magic in America and what it was trying to tell him. It was a lonely existence because it was rare for John to find kind spaces where he fit, just as himself, without having to adjust for other people. With his head still magic-drunk, he'd search for something to fill his hand or put a strong taste in his mouth to expedite the process of regaining his humanity.

Today was faster than usual because of Abigail talking to him when he was working on his wing and Cyrus offering a bottle of root beer right after. And that bottle of root beer did go through him pretty quickly.

When John went to use the bathroom, he found so many accommodations that made this part of his life effortless for once. The thick block of soap was mounted on a hook, and he knew it would never run out or change its shape as he rubbed his left hand into the familiar dip that gave the most surface area. Remembering the enchantment he had given it long ago, the faucet ran automatically at the perfect temperature when he needed it to.

It seemed strange that Cyrus and Abigail kept things the way they were until John recalled how his friend started that morning, with his hands tight and balled up. Six years after the end of the Enchanted War, Cyrus had woken up every morning using some of the gadgets John used to use.

He rinsed the sweat from his face and studied the mirror to see how well he had done. He cleaned his forehead again, rubbing at where the dust from outside had mixed with his perspiration. A few down feathers had gotten caught in his silver-touched dark hair; he picked them out. Satisfied, he scrubbed himself dry with a clean towel made of fine cloth.

Then, a bright, tinkering tune that frolicked up and down the keys of the piano romped from the parlor, down the hall, and called to him right outside the bathroom door. The song, which he recognized, was a classical piece. He placed his hand upon the edge of the bathroom sink and moved his fingers as if he were playing along—a progression of chords. His wingtip twitched; he could only imagine what his right hand would have done if he still had one.

* * *

WHEN JOHN ENTERED THE PARLOR, Abigail was still at the piano. The song had changed from that playful tune to a beautiful, rich, melancholic piece. He waited until she finished playing before he asked, "Where's Cyrus?"

"He went outside to weed the garden. Probably look at your horse, too."

John turned to leave, but then he reconsidered; he was curious and wanted to watch her. "Before I go, could you play some more piano for me, please?"

"Of course!" Abigail glowed with pride. "I take it you liked my playing?"

"I did."

He approached to stand with his left arm facing her. His violet eyes studied her hands as she played. Her fingers perched like tan birds upon the ivories. Her wrists were low, supple, and flexible in front of the keys. Feeling the music, she swayed with it. The song she picked was complicated and quick-running, delightfully dissonant in parts to build tension before it resolved itself in a satisfying turn. She was showing off.

John was impressed. "Ah, that song can be tricky to play smooth right there if you don't adjust your fingering in the way you did. Very good."

Abigail abruptly stopped in a discordant crash of the keys. She brightened up. "Goodness! I didn't know you played, John!"

"I used to very long ago. I was good. Some would even say a prodigy. But all of that was before my transformation."

"Rus never mentioned that you played."

"It was another thing I'm not to have anymore; it wasn't worth mentioning." John had his wing folded in front of his chest while he held it up with his left arm.

"Well, did you want to try playing?"

"It's been a long time. I just have the one hand—the left hand. Not many pieces sound good with just the left hand."

Abigail scooted to the very end of the piano bench. Her hazel eyes sparkled. "What if I played the right hand for you?"

John imagined himself playing side by side with Elysia. She

had always asked him, and he always denied her when he was winged. Just like back then, he looked at the space that was made for him. He couldn't imagine fitting there next to Abigail without pushing her off of her seat. The wing was attached to his shoulder wrong, wanting to lay in front of him every time he folded it up. He'd have to hold it open behind him to be able to sit close enough to play the way he wanted if she were to join him. But he couldn't even do that because he had let the damn thing atrophy from years of disuse. It would definitely end up touching her, and he couldn't bear that.

"No, I don't think so," John said.

Abigail centered herself on the bench again. "Doesn't the roast smell wonderful?"

"It does."

"Go get Rus. Even if he's not done in the garden, tell him to come on in and wash up."

John inhaled. The scent permeating the parlor was glorious. "Is the roast ready?"

"Not yet, but it's been a long time since Rus has had the opportunity to dance. Oh, he just loves it, John. And we finally have someone strong enough to move all the furniture for us, lickety-split." She started playing the highest notes, letting her fingers discover a twinkling melody.

"You're putting me to work?" he asked.

"Well, you *are* a handyman, aren't you?"

* * *

JOHN HAD GONE OUTSIDE to the garden. Cyrus squatted in the dirt, surrounded by the young vegetables. He pulled some weeds and tossed them aside so their roots could crisp up dry in the late afternoon sun on the stone walkway behind him.

The gentle breeze blew through John's feathers. Sometimes, when he traveled America's vastness on his own, he wouldn't see another human face for a few days, and he'd have his wing stretched open as much as he needed, and for a few days, it would hurt less. Until he remembered how much he longed for connection, he would enjoy the magnificent freedom of isolation.

But what John had right now was better:

He was standing at the edge of the garden with his wing unhidden, and he did not feel out of place as he watched his friend pulling at a thistle. Cyrus got most of the root, but like always, a little bit snapped off in the earth. In a few weeks, they'd battle again.

Grinning, Cyrus waved. "John! I took a gander at your horse before I started in the garden. She really is a nice, sensible horse."

"She is."

Cyrus tossed the thistle on top of the pile of discarded weeds. He removed his thick gloves and tucked them into his tool belt. "I'm surprised you didn't run out here as soon as you was done in the washroom. Normally, you stick to me like a burr. Not that I mind."

"Your wife is better company than you are."

"That is true," he agreed. "My Abby has the supernatural ability to make any guest feel right at home."

"Yes-yes. Her hospitality is a better talent than anything either of us can muster."

"Wait till you hear her play piano!"

"I have. She plays beautifully. How does a fool like you manage to find a treasure like her?"

"Ha! I keep telling you! The secret is . . . you have to learn to dance! Remember, John? I told you already that it's easy falling in love when you're dancing. And maybe a lil drunk. They go hand in hand when it comes to love. You ought to dance with Margie sometime."

John's face flushed. "I'm not much of a dancer, and I don't think Margie's the type to dance anyway."

"You never know until you try!"

"I suppose that's not incorrect—oh, speaking of dancing, Abigail sent me out here to get you because I'm to move all the furniture and set the room . . ." John's voice drifted because his friend had started humming and stomping his feet. "Cyrus, what are you doing?"

At that, Cyrus clapped his hands together, did an enthusiastic spin, and pointed straight at John. As his energy continued to rise, his humming got louder until he was scatting random syllables in some loose musical sense. He waved his arms while stepping out a few interesting moves with his feet, and then he thrust his groin several times.

"Must you always be indecent?" John lifted his wing, shielding his eyes with it so he didn't have to look directly at Cyrus. Somehow, he danced worse than he did over ten years ago.

"Aw, I missed when you'd hide your eyes with your wing, ya silly goose."

John spread the flight feathers slightly apart to peek through them. He saw Cyrus grinning, proud to have given him second-hand embarrassment.

"And that little peekaboo with your feathers! Once I got used to it, I always liked that wing of yours, John. It's fun seeing you use it."

"You're shameless, Cyrus."

"And don't you love it!"

10 October 1897

I had made it so my boots cannot give me blisters, which is a convenient thing when I walk this much. I have my suitcase, and I keep my coat in it usually when I travel because it is that time in October when suddenly the air gets very warm and feels like a slice of summer. I think this time of year makes me feel nostalgic.

Autumnus is Elysia's time of year, and this month is her month. Aestus is my time. Even though Cyrus is Winterborn, this is his time more than the rest of the year somehow. I miss him a lot, and I wish I could have stayed.

I think the worst thing about being the shape I am is that I don't have a shirt which fits me. I feel uncivilized without one. I think if I had a shirt, I'd feel more like a person. The ones Cyrus tried to make for me didn't last long. He wasn't a good enough tailor to execute the ideas we had. I know shirts can fit me because Father had some tailored for me in Nyuskom, but they were impossible for me to dress myself without assistance.

The problem is finding an American tailor, and I am still too shy about how I am. I just want a shirt that fits and I can put on by myself, but maybe that is too big a wish for something like me.

Sometimes, when there is nobody to behold me and I'm in the wilds, I can take off my coat and my left hand holds the wing up to ease my shoulder. Then I pretend I am just a man enjoying a very long walk.

Other times, I'm like an animal because I let my thoughts get empty and wide the way it does when I groom

my wing. When I get like that, I know things I can't understand and I understand things I can't know.

Most often, my mind is something in-between out here
in the lonely wilderness, and it reminds me of how my
shoulder is in-between.

These days, I can always know if someone is coming
up to me. I don my coat before they do, and they never get
to see how I really am. They just see a crooked man with
one side bigger than the other. If they have a large enough
cart, I can ask for a ride or if they don't, I walk alongside for
the company. Sometimes we set up camp together.

The moon has been very big these past few nights. I
found the moon being full makes everyone more romantic
and open. I can still feel that drumbeat, but when everyone
around me is succumbing a little bit to that kind of magic
that makes them tell stories around the campfire, my head
feels quieter. I showed them how I can light a match one-
handed. Most of the time, I am enough of a foreigner that
they don't want to interact with me.

I think I never considered how much Cyrus made it so
people would talk to me, and maybe I would have been
more sociable in Fairview if I knew how lonesome this traveling would be.

It is nice when everyone is under the lunar spell that
makes them open minded enough to include something
like me.

23 October 1897

Today, I believe I saved a young woman's life. I came across a kidnapping in progress. The woman was very precious to someone rich, and the three men were trying to do a ransom. The woman was all tied up and blindfolded in the little cart behind their horse. It made me remember when I was tied up and taken into the cellar. I wanted to make sure she was not going to be hurt.

I think they meant to kill me, but earlier that morn, while there was still frost on the blades of grass, I had preened my feathers, and I was still a little bit wild. It was as if I could see everything they were about to do. Because of this instinct, I knew how to move to keep them from hurting me. It was effortless. Their horse was nervous about me, and two of them were trying to keep the animal under control. The third one had the gun.

It was very easy to crush his arm that was holding the gun. At that moment, the wind picked up so they could see the wing a little bit. I think that's what caused them to pause. And I could taste in the air how they were afraid. Fear tastes as if I were hiding a coin in my mouth.

The two other men drew their weapons. But I was able to know where to aim the gun. It was as if I knew the exact place to point the gun before pressing the trigger, and it reminded me of how easy it was for J Bellamy to kill my captors years ago. I killed them all before they knew what was happening.

I made sure my coat was covering everything well before I undid the rope and the blindfold from the young woman. She calmed the horse down first, as if that was

more important than the fact that I had just killed three
men. I told her I wanted to bury the bodies. She said it
makes sense. We looked for a shovel in their cart together.
She found it and gave it to me.

She watched me pick up a dead man's body with one
hand and just remarked how very strong I am. I was
relieved that she didn't think I was frightening. She waited
not far away and watched me while I buried the bodies.
When I was done, she approached me.

"I'm Marguerite Blanchard," she said, "But please, call
me Margie."

"John," I said.

"What's your last name?" she asked.

I told her I didn't have one, that I was John, just John.

I only can shake with the wrong hand, so usually there
is an initial fumbling with someone not sure if they should
shake with the right or left. Or they offer their right hand to
where I have no hand. But Margie shook my hand,
reaching for it without that awkwardness.

She asked if I could help her get home because she was
very easy to kidnap. I told her she'd have to drive the horse
because I can't.

She said, "Well I can teach you how since you saved
my life."

I told her how I hurt a horse very badly once and I
never wanted to do anything like that again. I admitted to
her how I was very strong and I could remember poor
Rosie with her bleeding mouth and her wide eyes with the
whites showing and Cyrus's seething anger.

She laughed and told me, "You killed three men this
morning, but you're worried about the horse. I like that."

She drove the horse and we chatted along the way. She told me about what she meant about being very easy to kidnap. She said she couldn't recognize people by their faces or voices. She said the men claimed to have known her, and they probably did, because they told her that they had pancakes for her with all the fixings. She loved sweet things as much as I did. That's how she ended up kidnapped.

She said she could tell I was made wrong with one good arm and one hidden one that was not made right. She said she saw how strong I was, stronger than a man ought to be. She said my accent was strange and nobody else talked as I did. I was nervous and ready to run away, but then she said it all made me easy to tell apart from everyone else and that's why she liked me.

26 October 1897

The trip back to Margie's home was straightforward. She drove the cart. I stayed in the back of it for most of the trip. She talked so much about the movement of the horse she was driving and how his muscles worked. Her voice helped me because when my mind is partway magic, anybody talking at length to me brings me back until I can feel more like myself. By the time we got to a town called Oaks Bend, I was just me again. It was nice because I think I haven't been just me for too long.

There is a woman there, and she owns everything. She runs a successful venture breeding, training, and selling high quality horses. Her name is Elizabeth Bixler, but she goes by Bitty Bixler. Because I got Margie home safely, she is letting me stay in this room. I am holding still but I don't hear the drums anymore, and I haven't used the feather. I think I'm meant to be here.

Ms. Bitty Bixler sat me down and had a talk with me about Margie. She said that Margie is peculiar, but she is very good at caring for and training the horses. She told me not to take advantage of her. I told her I won't. I swore it.

She then asked me what I liked about Margie.

I told her that I liked how she was so easily happy. I liked that she talked to me even though sometimes speaking can be difficult for me at times. I told her that I liked her bluntness and how it was as if everyone was all the same to her eye. And everyone was worth trusting.

Ms. Bitty Bixler said she liked my reasons. She explained to me that Margie might seem simple at times, but she wasn't. That she was perhaps oblivious when it came to matters of the heart, and she was uninterested in uninteresting people.

She said she could see why Margie had taken a shine to me. I was very interesting.

I told her I didn't mean to be.

She thought I was funny and said there's always room in her home for funny men.

Letter to Elysia (Translated)

Elysia,

I apologize for not sending you a letter for so very long. Do not worry about me, dear sister, for I am well. A lot has happened since my last letter to you. I have moved out of Cyrus's home. I still have this wing of mine, and it's not as bad to have it anymore. I am getting used to it, I think. I've had it for a long time now. It's been almost six years. Sometimes it is inconvenient because I do have to keep it hidden. After all, it is unusual for a man to have a bird's wing instead of a right arm. Sometimes, people are not kind when someone is unusual.

I have met a friend named Margie. She talks to me like she talks to any other man. All she talks about is how things move, and she tells me I move poorly, which is not a lie. She has this remarkable inability to recognize faces. You'd think this would make her mistrustful or suspicious, but instead she is the most guileless person I have ever met. Sometimes, I am afraid for her because of how she is. I think you would like her because you are kind. Only kind people can like Margie because she sometimes requires some patience, but I think I've lived a life where I am used to being patient, so I don't mind.

I am staying right now in the home of an eccentric woman named Elizabeth Bixler, but she goes by Ms. Bitty Bixler. She is literate and rich, and her wealth comes from her entrepreneurship. She rents out the rooms of her large house. Margie and I are just two of the many lodgers here. I keep to myself because of how I am.

Margie is very good with the horses. She has told me that she can teach me how to ride, too. She is so optimistic about it that I believe her. The horses are still nervous around me, but I have noticed the horses here are less afraid than any other horses I have met.

Your brother,
John

Chapter 18

Let's Dance

John never liked to draw attention to his incredible strength. Such a rangy guy shouldn't be able to lift a chair, one-armed, as if it were made of paper. All three of the reading chairs touched the wall as the floor opened up in the middle of the room. The loveseat was too big to move in the same way—he had to pick it up by one end. It wasn't heavy, but it was unwieldy to manage with just his left hand. So, he'd lift it for a little and set it down to keep the movement under control, alternating where he held it and continuing to reposition it closer to the wall until it was also out of the way.

"Is nothing heavy for you?" Abigail asked.

John casually picked up the coffee table along the side, gripping it with his fingers, and leaned it against the wall to maximize the space in the parlor. "No, nothing is. Except for the wing." When he was done moving the furniture, he held his wing again with his left hand. His shoulder and back were aching.

"If you need, you can lay it on the loveseat, John."

"It might get messy."

"It's easy enough to clean," she insisted.

He sighed, but accepted her suggestion. He opened the wing and draped it over the loveseat, resting the part of it that corresponded to an elbow against the back of the furniture. The stretch across his back muscles felt nice. "This is better."

A chime of bells accompanied Cyrus's entrance through the archway between the dining room and the parlor. His face was blushing, and the glasses of wine he had in each hand matched his complexion. He walked over to his wife, kissed her, and handed her a glass. "My love, my love, my love," he sang.

"Oh goodness, Rus. How much have you drank already?"

"Well, I only have two hands. I had to drink mine up so I could bring some out for the two of you." Cyrus walked over to where John stood near the loveseat against the wall and passed him his glass.

"Yes, I see that." Abigail sipped her wine. "Oh, I love this one!"

John tried the rosé. It was sweet and juicy. He wasn't surprised she loved it.

Abigail placed her drink on an end table before she walked over to the baby grand piano and sat herself neatly at the bench. She got into her playing posture and turned toward her husband, waiting for him to begin. His foot tapped out the tempo. Her head nodded to the beat he was setting. Then she played, matching his steps.

The melody was unassuming at first, but then the two of them exchanged a mischievous grin. Abigail's song became a carnival tune as playful as Cyrus was. Her music emboldened her husband as he swayed and jumped and spun.

Abigail crashed her hands onto the piano keys. At that noise, Cyrus stopped moving and stood with his legs together.

He straightened his arms out, spreading them wide, and let his hands hang down loosely, as if he were a scarecrow.

Abigail pressed down a pedal and quieted the piano, then created a thumping rhythm, ever so slightly discordant. Cyrus hopped in time to it, matching the strange, tense energy of the music. His hands limply flapped, and his head nodded in time with his small toe-hops. Then, a brief pause. Suddenly, he lifted his head and made big movements again, windmilling his arms. Abigail played wildly as he did so; she rocked at her bench like a woman possessed, grinning with delight as her hands blazed over the keys.

The two of them were free, expressive, not caring about how ridiculous their song or dance were. Just feeling the music to create a spontaneous masterpiece.

John could see the love story right there in that moment. Cyrus's dancing had always been too much for most traditional songs, and Abigail looked joyful in discovering a way to make the piano match his unique energy. He pushed her piano skills to their limit, and she let him look like he might actually be a good dancer.

After that performance, Cyrus and Abigail traded places. The veteran's playing was nowhere near as good as his wife's. Sometimes, he'd hit a sour note that clashed against the other, mistakes that he just kept playing through until the melody smoothed out, and he figured out the even, easy waltz with only three chords.

Instead of dancing on her own, Abigail approached John and held out her hand. "Do you dance?"

"I've never tried."

"Do you want to try?" Her voice was gentle.

Magic pushed on John until he said, "I do . . ." Sometimes it was frightening when it spoke for him. Eyes low, he added his own words to reclaim a bit of free will: "But I don't know how."

"I'll teach you," she offered.

"I don't want to dance like Cyrus."

Abigail laughed. "I can teach you how to dance sensibly. No one else should dance like my Rus."

He remained reluctant; he had only ever watched before.

"John! Could you please just dance with my wife already!" Cyrus howled from the piano.

"Fine," John said. He moved away from the wall, following Abigail to the middle of the room.

She turned to face him. John held his left hand out, unsure of what he was supposed to do with it. Then, there was the matter of his wing. He tried tightening it up, folding it as small as he could, pushing his right shoulder down and forward in order to tuck it up as tightly as possible. Because of how it was attached to him, the wing ended up between them. He didn't want to take up too much room, but he also didn't want to accidentally bump her; they stood too far apart.

"I think you'll have to move your wing out of the way, John," she said. "We need to be a little closer together in order to dance."

"I don't know if I can."

"Please try."

He opened his wing and carefully moved it so that it was over her back, but not touching her. She glanced over at the trembling wing to gauge the size and position of it. "Okay, John. That works."

He stayed silent, afraid that he'd do or say the wrong thing.

"I'll take this one." Abigail took his left hand in her right hand. "And I can't have my other hand flopping around with nowhere to go. So, it will go here." She placed it on his right shoulder. He stiffened under her touch. Her fingers were light on the fabric of his shirt. "You're okay. I know you're nervous. It's just my hand touching your shoulder."

He nodded.

Her explaining it made it easier for him to accept. She waited for him to get accustomed to her. The tension relaxed, then she started to sway; he followed her motion as Cyrus played a slow song for them.

John continued to loosen up in her arms as they danced, but his wing was struggling to stay up. Soon, it dropped and touched her back.

"I'm sorry." John tried to lift it up to keep it off of her, but was unable to. It needed a break. "We can stop."

"Please, let's continue until the end of Cyrus's song at least. I'm having fun."

He moved the wing again, but, this time, he placed it across her back to prop it up. "Sorry." It stopped trembling from fatigue, resting against her.

"It's perfect like that, John."

He studied her face to try to catch her in a lie, but she remained encouraging and sweet. Her hazel eyes had a lot of green in them now that he was close enough to see it. Her french braid had steadily been coming undone throughout the day, and pieces of curled hair framed her dusky face. The wine had warmed her cheeks. He could see what Cyrus meant about drinking and dancing.

John got the hang of the three-beat rhythm. He wished the song was just a little longer when the music stopped.

"You better remember this for when you find your own

lover!" Cyrus teased. "You aren't allowed to fall in love with my Abby! She's mine!"

"Well, you heard my husband." Abigail undid her arms from around John. She switched places with Cyrus on the piano. Her playing was much better than his. She chose a jaunty song from the mountains which was easy to dance to.

Cyrus galloped around the room. Then, he grabbed John by his hand and led him around, dragging him into a formless dance that left them both breathless.

10 November 1897

Margie keeps peppermints for me in her pocket
because she knows how I get sometimes. When words are
harder for me to say, she gives one to me. She said I remind
her of a horse when I'm like that. She likes horses, so I take
it as a compliment.

She helps me to clean up my feathers by hiding them
in the middle of her trash, and she keeps watch at the door
when I take my baths. When some time passes, she will
knock on the door for me to ensure I don't spend too long.

She doesn't ask how I am put together or why I molt
feathers, but I feel like she might have an idea because of
the way she makes sure I have space for it. She's just more
interested in how I move than the fact I have feathers.

I hold it more loosely when I'm around her, and it's
been a little more comfortable for me lately. Not as much
pain as usual. She has, so far, not minded that I don't talk to
her about it.

Some things are still difficult for me with one hand
only, and I miss how easy it was to use things in Cyrus's
house. While Bitty and Margie are patient with me when
things take longer for me to do, I've noticed some lodgers
tell me "never mind" or they just do things for me.

The main thing better about this place is that there is a
piano set up in the dining hall to entertain the guests. I
miss piano so much.

When Ms. Bitty Bixler invited guests over, she had
what she called a soiree. 'Soiree' comes from the French for
'evening activity', and Nyuskom has a word that sounds
similar. It is 'sirre' except it means 'an enjoyable evening

with friends'. Margie and I didn't attend the soiree. Instead, we had a sirre in one of the sitting rooms by ourselves.

We played cards. She used her mouth to pull the cards from her hand for discard. When I asked her why, she said it was because that's what I did. I told her I do that because I only have one hand. She said it wasn't fair if she played with two hands, and I played with only one. I told her that's true. She asked me if I didn't go to the soiree because of her. I told her maybe a little, but only because I was scared, too. Then, I told her about my friend Cyrus who I used to go to the bar with sometimes.

I like Margie, but she isn't strong the way Cyrus is. When she's upset, she goes quiet. I told her I can't imagine going to a soiree or a bar with her. She told me that it makes sense. She doesn't like when there's too many people around.

Margie has me accompany her to mind her horses. They were very afraid of me at first, but she rewarded them for staying calm. I am able to feed and water them without them showing fear towards me, which is a big change. The horses here are very brave compared to other horses I have met. When I asked her why, she said it's because Ms. Bitty Bixler needs them to be brave.

12 November 1897

Ms. Bitty Bixler informed me that she breeds and trains sensible and brave horses because there's a war coming soon. I wondered what she meant by soon and I had a lot of questions. She said she had a friend named J Bellamy who was telling her all about it. So she could probably make a lot of money with her horses. Wars are good for making money. I wouldn't know, but it sounded correct.

I asked her questions about J Bellamy.

She said, "Oh, he's dead now."

I asked when this happened.

Last year sometime, he admitted to killing four men and cutting them up, putting them in a box, delivering them to a surgeon, and was hanged for it. That's how she got to be good friends with Dr. Willard Cross. He was the surgeon who received the box, and he had to sort through the bodies. She said the two of them sat side by side at the hanging.

She also said she had seen J Bellamy die before, and it never really sticks.

I was worried about that.

"Do you know him?" she asked me.

I told her he was the one who brought me to America but he left me in a wagon full of moonshine after taking the mule for himself.

She laughed and said, "Well, that sounds like him. He's a piece of shit sometimes. But if he likes you, he won't kill you. You and I are still around, so I guess we're on the good side of an immortal madman. He's probably America's last wizard."

I agreed with her about him being a piece of shit, not killing those on his good side, and being America's last wizard. She gave me a shot of whiskey. "Better than moonshine?" she asked me.

I told her it was.

I like Bitty Bixler. She's forthright and unabashedly herself. Her left eye changes color. She changes it to match her outfits. She wore a violet dress, thus she had a violet left eye. It matched the color of my eyes, and when she wears that one, she tells me we match. She said once upon a time, she used to try to match the eyes and hide that her left eye wasn't real, but after Margie, she makes sure it's a different color so that Margie can always recognize her.

I asked her if she always shares such things so readily.

She said she doesn't usually share and that there's a feeling about me that reminds her of J Bellamy. Except she can tell I'm a good person. She can't tell if J Bellamy is a good person, but she notices each time he comes around, he feels a little more human.

I admitted to her I was not entirely human and underneath my coat, I look different, but I was shy to show her.

She was gentle and said, "You don't have to show me a thing. I've seen and been with impossible things. Oh, I even had sex with a man cursed to have an ass's head. Granted, he had a man's head at the time. And a very handsome face. His name is Nick."

"Nick Bottom?" I asked.

She said, "I see you're a man of culture somehow. Well,

the thing about magic is that it likes to play the same plots. That's something J Bellamy told me."

He told me something similar too. It made me think of the fairy tales Elysia used to read to me as well as the ones I used to read to Cyrus. I love stories.

I even love the one that Elysia and Cyrus said sound like me at the end. That one is called 'The Six Swans' or 'The Wild Swans'. It depends which book you're reading it from. You never really know what became of the prince with one arm and one wing. He is stuck like that, then it's the end of the story.

14 November 1897

Today, I showed Margie my wing. She knocked on the door. Instead of covering up, I had her come in while I was bare-chested. She stared.

"You're staring," I told her.

She immediately looked down at her hands, nervous about it. I didn't like how I had made her feel small and shy. Margie was supposed to be forward and she was treating me like a stranger because she didn't want to offend me.

"You can look," I said.

She went right back to staring. Then, she asked me, "Can I touch your wing?"

I was nervous, but I told her she could.

It was frightening at first, but I realized that she wasn't touching it any differently than the way she would use her hands to inspect the conformation of a horse. Her fingers were light as she felt my muscles and my back. She explored the way my skin gradually changed from man to bird from my neck to my shoulder to that wing. And she looked at the dust that was on her hands after her examination. She told me I was made wrong.

I knew that.

She pointed out every place where my body was shaped wrongly. Apparently, my entire shoulder is not correct. Bones are malformed, and also I'm missing one entirely that birds are supposed to have. She told me I must be stiff at the end of the day. Right here, she said. And she rubbed on the places that were aching, knowing where they were and how to touch them to alleviate the pain.

Her eyes looked so sad. "There's no way for you to rest. Except." And she flopped over on her side on the bed. I laid on my side too. We were face to face.

It was true. This was the only way I could be where nothing pulled on my shoulder and my wing didn't need to be open or lifted up, and it could stay folded on my side.

"Why aren't you afraid of me?" I asked.

She told me the fact that I was so strong I could injure a horse on accident and that I killed three men easily was a lot scarier. Compared to those two things, a bird wing was a silly thing to be afraid of.

When she put it that way, I realized she was right.

25 November 1897

Usually, Margie eats in the dining room, and I sit next to her on a stool at the table. She is on my right side because I'm not fearful of her there and she creates a buffer between me and the other people. But the Thanksgiving Feast in Bitty Bixler's dining hall is too crowded. She was greatly overwhelmed and so was I.

She became quiet. I didn't like her to be quiet because normally she is very talkative. We collected our food and went into my room together. It was nice because I could take off my long coat and sit in front of her with my wing out. She was a lot more comfortable there. I finished my food first. Margie was always slower to eat because she was so particular when eating.

I tried to start a conversation. "It's busy out there in the dining hall," I said.

She didn't respond to me, but when I was the same way sometimes, I liked that she kept talking to me. That's why I kept talking to her. Because I knew a lot about words and where they come from, I told her about the words I knew. How the way the words moved through history was evidence of the way people moved through history. I started with the seasons in my native language. Ver, Aestus, Autumnus, and Hibernus. I told her how, in Nyuskom, the sailors would come in from other lands, 'Sommer' and 'Summer' in their mouths and the ones who dealt with them the most, the commonfolk, started saying 'Sommer' instead of 'Aestus'.

I told her how once I got used to America and the people in it and started being a plain man, I started saying

'Summer', too. When I think of the next season coming up, I no longer think of 'Hibernus', but 'Winter'. But I don't tell her it's because I think about how Cyrus tells me he likes the way I say 'Winter', with the sharp icicle in the middle of the word.

"I didn't know you liked words so much, John," she told me when she finished her food, and she was able to sit still again.

She told me I should talk about words more often because when I do, it's like I'm sparkling. I told her how she was the same when she was talking about horses and men and animals and how they all move. That's why I always let her talk as much as she wanted.

Chapter 19

The Roast

The rich symphony of aromas that filled the dining room was warm, comforting, and made John's mouth water. Though it was Spring, the roast had a wintertime allure to it. It called for grandeur, and the married couple succumbed to its demands.

Abigail spread a tablecloth over the wooden table, which dressed it up for the special meal. Cyrus placed tall, cream-colored candles in the center. The two of them set out brass chargers, then classic porcelain plates on top of those. Abigail put out the cutlery and rolled cloth napkins. Finally, Cyrus set up a decorative trivet next to the serving utensils for when the pot came out.

"I am glad to see you've gotten at least a little more civilized, Cyrus," John remarked. "I've never seen you set the table like this before."

"Oh, this ain't up to me. Abby insisted." Cyrus shook out his hands and eyed the centerpiece candles. "Oh! Do you remember when I taught you how to light a match one-handed?"

"Yes-yes. I thought it was impossible to, but you proved me wrong."

"I had to relearn how to do it after I came home from the war. My hands wouldn't work for a long time." He clenched his hands to demonstrate how they used to be. His fists trembled for a moment before he spread open his fingers. "Ah, why don't you try it?"

"I don't have any matches on me, at-now."

Abigail produced a book of matches from one of the deep pockets of her skirt. "Since there's times when Rus can only tolerate candlelight, I always have some on me."

John took the small paperboard package of red-headed matchsticks. He flipped up the folder and singled a match out. He bent it against the phosphorus strip and quickly rubbed its head with his thumb to produce a miniature flame. John touched the small fire against the blackened wicks of the candles at the center of the table. Before the fire climbed up the wooden stalk to the rest of the matches, John extinguished it with a puff of air.

"I'd say the table is set perfect now," Cyrus remarked.

"Goodness. Isn't it lovely?" Abigail added, "It's rare for us to have something like this."

"We are having a sirre," John said. "It means 'a wonderful evening with friends.'"

"That's a perfect word for this, then," she said.

"You'll be sitting there, ya silly goose." Cyrus pointed to the end of the table.

It was where John sat when he lived in this house over a decade ago. He scooted his chair off-center, towards the right, like he always did. His right leg was turned out so that he could rest the bend of his wing upon his thigh. His feathers fanned out to the side and behind him, but it got him as close to the table as he could be.

Abigail sat closer to her husband's seat than to John's. She kept glancing at how John's wing was configured, almost twisted. "Is that comfortable for you?" she asked.

"It'll suffice. This is how I sat at the table when I was a farm-hand here."

Cyrus came out with the pot in his hands. He made a noise with his mouth that mimicked a trumpet. Abigail started a drum roll on the table. Their enthusiasm was infectious, and John thumped the table with his hand, joining her drumming.

"I present," Cyrus said, making his voice as grand as possible, "the most beautiful roast ever made in the entire history of the whole world!"

The trivet was a throne for the roast. Cyrus hooked two fingers, palm-side up, around the knob of the lid and lifted it in that way. The mouthwatering smell of the meal intensified as the steam floated out of the pot.

Abigail applauded and cheered, pretending to be a crowd. John merely sat back and marveled at the ridiculous show the pair of them were putting on. Cyrus picked up the wide serving fork. The meat pulled apart with hardly any pressure; he could have cut it with a spoon if he wanted.

John unrolled his napkin and set it on his lap. Cyrus took his plate and served the food. John's posture remained politely straight-backed as he waited for his friend to dish out his portion into the deep plate and place it back on the charger.

Now, John could appreciate how well Abigail had cooked the roast he brought in. The soft, luscious meat appeared tender in the glistening sauce, dark and thick, full of root vegetables and enhanced with herbs.

Once Cyrus had finished serving everyone's plate, he sat at the head of the table across from John. He shook out his hands before picking up his cutlery. "I can't remember the last time me and Abby had a roast like this. Because of the way I ended up after—" Cyrus had put the first bite in his mouth and immediately was stunned into silence. He smacked his lips, then took another bite.

John picked up his fork and did the same. The meat melted on his tongue; its flavor coated his mouth. The meal filled his senses: Rich, deep, complex, and hearty. At that moment, he felt like he was John, just John, enjoying the roast. He wasn't some strange mixed up creature that was part man, part magic. He didn't have the drums of wanderlust beating in his head, and its silence didn't mean he had to pursue some purpose he didn't fully understand. He could feel, for once, that he was allowed to be himself in a way that was rare otherwise.

No one at the table had words. The sound of silverware clinking against the plates was the only noise in that room. John ate politely, making sure his bites were neither too big nor too small.

Cyrus got up to serve seconds. "Abby, you've outdone yourself!" he crowed.

She smiled. "I'm just happy with how it turned out!"

"Yes-yes, it's excellent. Truly a meal fit for a king."

Abigail took her plate from her husband and set it on the charger in front of her. "Oh, John, I couldn't help but notice your table manners."

"It's nothing of merit."

"Yeah, you've always been a polite feller." Cyrus placed John's plate in front of him. "I'm betting that's why you insisted on sweeping up after yourself."

John nodded. He liked the idea that sweeping up was motivated by good manners rather than shame.

Once Cyrus sat at his place with his second plate, everyone continued eating.

"Oh! John, did I surprise you? I can play piano now," Cyrus said after his food was done.

"Yes-yes, that was surprising." John looked at Abigail. "I assume you taught him?"

"Yes, I did!"

"Abby started teaching me a few months after I'd come back from the war. I couldn't walk very well yet, and I didn't have a lot of time each day I could see. But if I could sit up and move my fingers, I would let her teach me." Cyrus mimed playing the keys.

"I would like to point out that Rus had absolutely no talent for it, whatsoever; he learned through sheer force of will."

"Sometimes, I can be very stubborn," he boasted.

"*Sometimes?*" Abigail exclaimed. "What do you mean sometimes? You're always stubborn!"

"I mean, it's my best trait. It's just when they tell stories about me being a hero, they call it perseverance. What did you think about my playing, John?"

John shrugged. "You have a lot of room for improvement."

"It's not like you can do better," Cyrus teased with a laugh.

Abigail and John exchanged a glance. Her expression was bright, pleading to share; his violet eyes were nervous, begging her not to.

Regardless, Cyrus was perceptive enough to ask, "Say, John, can you play piano?"

John remembered Abigail's offer earlier to fill in the high notes while he played the lower ones with his left hand. Maybe he wasn't good enough to play with her anyway. He had been out of practice for sixteen years except for rare moments like playing in Ms. Bitty Bixler's dining hall for Margie in the night. Or when he'd find himself alone with a piano on a job, and he'd play in private just to make sure it wasn't a dream—that person he used to be before he turned into this.

The hush that fell over the room was different from the luxurious one when the roast first touched their tongues. This one begged John to talk about his past; it was tugging him along, the same force that drummed in his head during his travels and compelled him to shop for the roast yesterday: America's wild magic.

For its sake, John shared, "Before I lost my arm, I used to play. It was as if I were born to play. My father got me a tutor to sharpen my skills as soon as the nursemaid informed him of my talents. So, I grew up with it, and it suited me. I filled the great hall with beautiful music, entertained our guests."

Cyrus smacked the table excitedly. "Holy smokes, John! You never told me any of this before!"

"I always thought it was one of the things I had to leave behind because I had transformed into what you see before you. It seemed easier to forget. But listening to Abigail play and then you play made me to realize . . ." John smiled. "That I can play better than you with only one hand."

"Well, now we've got to see it!" Cyrus got up and started stacking the dirty dishes, but he stopped mid-chore. "Oh, never mind this!" He hurried to the archway towards the parlor. "We can wash those silly dishes after! Come, come now!"

22 December 1897

I like winters because it makes my friends sit just a little closer to me. Margie is always delighted when she tucks under my wing, and I fluff it up so that the warmth stays in between the feathers. I can feel her delight glowing from out of her and it makes me to feel less alone.

I told her the other day I was a virgin. I was surprised when she said that she wasn't. She said that she feels safe around me because I'm not really man. It was very hard to talk, but she was very good at listening.

I told her I was a lonely thing.

She said she was, too. She wasn't made right. Something was wrong with her mind, she knew that. The way she was didn't match up properly with the way people wanted her to be. She said it was like how my wing was made wrong for my body, but here we were. When you aren't made exactly right, it's a very lonely existence. It's nice to be able to be lonely together.

Usually, she doesn't talk much about herself, but when she does, I always want to keep her tucked under my wing. I told her how my wing was cut off three times. She said she liked my wing because nobody else has one and she knows for sure I'm John, just John.

But mostly she talks about how I have been doing good with the horses. There is a young horse who seemed braver than the others today. Margie said that one is going to be one I could ride one day, but she is not ready yet.

Her name is Lucky, which means it is probably going to be true. Lucky and Malachy. She'll train her so I could ride her one hand, even with my wing and my strength. I have been doing good with leading the horses, staying calm so I can stay gentle, and I haven't injured any of them.

27 December 1897

Margie has given me a nice hat for Christmas. After everyone was done celebrating, I took her to the dining hall where there was a little piano that sometimes one of the lodgers could play while we ate or during festivities. I showed her that I could play a little with my left hand. She asked me when I learned. I told her I learned before my arm became a wing. That I wish she could hear what the music was supposed to sound like. She told me she liked it the way I played even if it doesn't sound the way I wanted it to.

She asked me if I could hear the lamps in the room. I listened, and then I heard them. She asked me if I could stop hearing them. When I stopped trying to listen, I didn't hear them anymore. She told me she could always hear them. That as long as they were on, she always heard it. Like a fizzing sound. I went and turned the alchemic lamps off and the room was too dark because the moon was barely a sliver that night. Our eyes eventually adjusted enough to see the shape of the furniture.

I told her about the drums in my head. She asked if I heard them now. I said I don't hear them next to you. And that's when I realized she needed a miracle from me. I asked her what she would wish for if she could wish for anything.

She just wished that she could see even when it was dark, like a cat. Then she wouldn't have to turn the lanterns and lamps on and hear that fizzy noise.

So, today, I bought a pair of glasses from one of the other lodgers. I used a feather to make it so that she could use it to see in the dark like a cat. I was glad I could find glasses to enchant because I didn't want to enchant Margie herself. I'm afraid of making the horses frightened of her, and the horses are what makes her happy and feel purposeful.

I remember when I had no purpose once and how useless I felt back then. It was very hard to be me back then. It's still hard, but it's easier now.

29 December 1897

Margie loves her glasses. She told me she wore them in the dark of her room last night. That now, the world is quiet at night the way it is supposed to be. She pretended to be a cat. She asked if I ever pretended to be a bird since I have a wing. I didn't want to think about how I was more like an animal than most men. She kept talking about it though. She asked if I turn into a bird a little bit when I preened my wing. She told me how I was more like a pigeon than a swan because I have to break apart the powder down and spread it over my feathers.

She kept talking about it, and I didn't want to talk about it. I told her I was a plain man. She laughed and said I wasn't. If I were a plain man, she wouldn't like me at all. She said that everything about me made me stand out from the everyday people. I brought the feel of a storm coming, I had a wing instead of an arm, I made magic happen like a wizard, I had violet eyes, and I was very strong. I was good at killing people.

When she spoke of my traits, she was sparkling, so I asked her if she loved me.

She got bashful, but then she said she loves anyone who stood out. She said she loved Ms. Bitty Bixler with her case full of glass eyes and how she always picks one that doesn't match so she can stand out from the everyday people.

Now, when she insists I play piano for her, she leads me with her cat-eye glasses and I put my hand on the keys and I just play simple things on my left hand and she acts as if it's the greatest song she has ever heard. She claps along, but she's very much off-beat, like an anti-metronome, and I have to ignore her clapping.

When it's too dark that I can't see the keys, I can feel them and hear them. I had practiced so much as a child that I always know exactly where my hand is.

I don't know if I love her the way a man ought to love a woman but I also don't know if I loved Cyrus in that way either. I don't know if I can love anyone the way I am.

I just know that I don't get to decide anymore where I'm to stay, so maybe it's a moot point. I can't be a good husband to Margie if I can't hold still. I shed a new feather, and the drumbeat is already so loud.

Chapter 20

One More Waltz, Please

I t had been such a long time since John sat at a piano with the intent to play in front of an audience more real than the one in his memories and more discerning than Margie, who would love anything he played. He placed his fingers delicately upon the ivory keys. His instructor had always said he had the hands of a man destined to be a pianist—long and flexible. It was still true about his left hand, but his right arm was now a bird-wing. The wrist joint rested on his thigh the way he had it when he sat at the dining table.

Cyrus and Abigail stood nearby, entangled naturally in the way lovers often were. All three of them were full from the splendid meal they had enjoyed together. The magnificence had followed them from the dining room into the parlor.

John's fingers started slowly, working on arpeggios until he felt fluent with them.

Cyrus started dancing, as usual, despite the fact that John was only playing with warm-up exercises. Abigail wrapped her arms around her husband and leaned into him as they swayed together.

John wanted to play something more substantial than the drills his instructor had made him repeat so often that his hand remembered them. He stopped playing. "I'm out of practice."

"Still better than me," Cyrus admitted.

"In that case, I want to try to play some songs. Do you have sheet music?"

"In the bench," Abigail said.

John got up, and she flipped open the top of the bench. It was full of sheet music. She selected a spiral-bound book. The most well-loved pages were slipping out of it, torn from being turned too many times over the years. After she closed the bench, John sat upon it again.

"I want you to try this one, it's a Romantic piece. You should know it if you were classically trained. You seem to be." She set the book in front of him. "I'll turn the pages for you."

John nodded. The Italian words over the musical notes told him how it was meant to be played: *Affettuoso*. The music was rich, resonant, and dreamy, but he yearned to add some accompaniment to the movement his left hand was creating. Every time he would have used his right thumb in the song, the vestigial thumb on the bend of his wing—called the alula—moved. His wing-tip wanted to be a hand again, if only to help make the piece truly what it was meant to be.

"That was real pretty," Cyrus said.

John was heartbroken because he knew how beautiful it was supposed to sound. "I couldn't play it correctly."

"I want to try to play with you, John," Abigail said.

He looked at his wing. "But there's no room for you."

"Sure there is! You can put your wing around me like when we were dancing. We'd fit then."

"Do it, ya silly goose! I wanna hear you play piano with my wife!"

"Fine." John lifted his wing, succumbing to peer pressure. It trembled as he held it up to make room for Abigail. He looked away so he wouldn't have to see her interacting with it. She slid onto the bench and gently put her body in front of his open wing. She scooted close until she was almost against his ribs. Carefully, he placed the large gray-brown wing so it barely touched her.

"Goodness John, are you really comfortable like that? Please, just put it where it's comfortable."

"It's too tired at-now." This was awkward, and he wanted to give up.

"Can I help you?" she asked.

He averted his eyes. "I suppose."

She guided the tense wing so that it wrapped around her, and he didn't need to hold it up by himself any longer. "Is that good for you?"

He nodded.

A dust imprint of his feathers was stamped on her dark skirt. "Sorry, it's messy."

"It's just how you are. I don't mind it." She turned back to the first page of the song. Her right hand was light on the piano keys. John remained stiff. "Your wing is just touching me; that's all."

He relaxed as soon as she said it.

"I'm ready when you are," she said pleasantly.

He nodded.

John started playing the song again. Abigail filled in all of the pieces that were missing before. The music sounded as if his left hand played the setting of a clear, dark sky, and Abigail's right hand filled it in with twinkling stars. He kept glancing over to her, waiting for her to flinch at how his wing twitched against her during the parts of the song that had the more complicated phrases for the right hand, but she never did.

As they played together, Cyrus was spinning around in the open space of the room, on his tip-toes, moving his arms fluidly, vaguely following the flow of the music.

After a few more slow songs, both John and Abigail were eager for something with a faster tempo. She turned to a Classical piece that ran around and made her flip the pages at a fun pace. She nodded as she peppered her keys with her right hand. John focused on playing the bouncing chords with his only hand, and Cyrus stood nearby, clapping and bobbing his head.

"John," Abigail said. "If you don't mind, can you play something so Cyrus and I can dance together at least one more time this evening?"

"I can."

She flipped the book to a waltz. "Just play this part, over and over. Then, you won't need anyone to turn the pages for you."

John played the piano dutifully as husband and wife began to dance. The waltz had a steady and simple pattern.

Cyrus held onto Abigail. "You always know. What clued you in this time?"

"You should've been dancing to that last song John and I were playing. That one begged for your particular brand of ridiculous."

"*Ridiculous!* I thought you loved my dancing!"

"Oh Rus, I love your dancing the most when it's ridiculous."

John got to the end of the second page. The music paused

briefly as he restarted again. This time, he memorized the song well enough to watch the husband and wife waltzing together.

Cyrus was much tamer now in his movements. He was intentional with how he stepped, which neatened up his dancing and made it look proper for once. It meant he was always capable of dancing with restraint; he simply chose not to.

When John reached the end of the page, he improvised to provide a seamless transition between the last note and the beginning of the song again. Abigail's steps had started to slow down as she took the lead from her husband.

John played the waltz over and over again for them.

They were done when Cyrus kissed his wife. "I reckon that's enough dancing," he said. "We have to wash the dishes yet."

* * *

JOHN INSISTED he helped scrub the stovetop while the couple washed the dishes together. Cyrus tossed some suds at Abigail. She laughed as the bubbles clung to her for a moment before disappearing. She made a ring out of her index finger and thumb and blew a big bubble that hung in the air. John admired their relentless effervescence whenever they were together.

Abigail wiped down the counters while Cyrus put away dishes. At the cupboards, he paused and looked quizzically down at his legs. Experimentally, he lifted one foot and then the other.

"Is something wrong, Cyrus?" John asked as he finished cleaning the stove.

"No, nothing's wrong," he replied. "It's just time for us to fix up the parlor again for sitting down. And then open up another bottle of wine if we can. Then, keep each other company until bedtime."

"That sounds lovely." John almost forgot that he had come here on business, but enjoying wine at eventide with friends was important—perhaps the most important. Like Cyrus said, it was time.

3 March 1898

Ms. Bitty Bixler talks about how there is a war coming because some people in the government want to perhaps outlaw magic. I guess it makes sense. Not everyone has access to enchanted objects. Those who do tend to hold a lot of power because of it. According to her, the consensus in the government is that enchanted objects make it harder to steer the future of the country because of how easily magic can sway things one way or another. Still, I wonder what would happen to me because I am something in between being a man and magic.

It's strange that most of the lodgers only know of a general unease happening. It's rare that any of them can read, so they don't know what to think about things other than what someone charismatic has told them.

I'm just worried that Cyrus will be caught up in it. He is very strong and able-bodied. He works hard, and he is very stubborn and puts so much effort into everything he does. I know he would make a good soldier, and that is what worries me. I want to make sure he is safe. I have a magic feather on me that can make miracles happen. Maybe that's enough, and I can guarantee he survives the coming war.

The good news is that I don't look like a man who could help win a war, so I don't think I have to worry about it. I have one arm, and I've lived like this for a long time. It's almost the anniversary of when my right arm was transformed into a wing. I remember when it first happened, I thought I was a man, but looking back, I was just a boy.

Those days, I thought Father could fix it. I remember how badly I wrote and how bad my English was when I wrote anything. My English is very good now, but I still make some mistakes in my speech. Like I still say 'at now' instead of 'now' because when I write, I can remember that Americans don't say 'at' for explaining when things happen. If I focus, I can remember not to do that when I speak.

Sometimes, I can even hide my accent well enough that nobody comments too much about it. I just keep my answers short. If I talk too much, it's easier to notice I'm from somewhere else. I don't like when people ask me too many questions. It always starts as one thing, but they eventually feel brave enough to ask me about what I hide underneath my coat. I don't like to share it because I am afraid there will be too much excitement about it the first time people see it.

I still can't ride a horse, so I rely on my boots that will never blister my feet, and I rely on the kindness of strangers to let me ride in their carts if they have one. I try to find men with mules when I ask for a ride because mules tend not to be as frightened about something like me. I feel bad when a man has a horse, and his poor animal is nervous and more jumpy than usual.

Before I left, Margie stuck my feather in my hatband. She kissed me goodbye on the cheek and laughed and said she likes it when I'm clean shaven because then I'm not too prickly for her lips to kiss. She said she doesn't mind kissing me because I'm not really a man. She is too honest sometimes, but I've gotten used to it.

I think I want to see how I feel when Cyrus kisses me but I don't know if he will. He doesn't like me in that way, but maybe if I explain myself, he will try. I just want to know.

Letter to Elysia (Translated)

Elysia,

I want to receive a letter from you. I think I forgot to tell you that I was living in Oaks Bend in the last letter. Now that I think about it, between Oaks Bend and Cyrus's farm, I passed by a few towns called Fairview. I think that's probably why I haven't received your letters. It might be too common a name for a town, unfortunately. The good news is that I think Ms. Bitty Bixler at Oaks Bend with her brave, well trained horses are famous enough for you to send a letter and for me to find it. I will definitely be back there.

Ms. Bitty Bixler is a good landlady, and she makes sure I have a lot of work to do to pay for my lodging. I also like Margie, who is like a daughter to her. Right now me and Margie are close friends because we are both very odd. She has seen what I really look like and she doesn't mind that I have a wing. She has always been very kind and is happy to keep me company when I am a little more like an animal than usual.

Remember how J Bellamy gave us candied oranges, and it always helped me? Remember how you'd be around, chatting with me after my bath, speaking to me when words were hard for me to say?

I think I'm more accustomed to the idea of being like this, and it doesn't feel as bad as it used to. Now, I know to pack peppermints and root beers in my suitcase so I have something to help me come back if I'm traveling. Now, if I'm alone, I'm less nervous about what must be done. I let myself enjoy the feeling of taking care of myself. I have even made friends who are nice to help me if I need it. So far, only Cyrus and Margie know how I really am.

I want you to meet both of them if you ever visit America, and you can see how there are people who don't mind my wing. Maybe you'd get along with them too because, compared to Father and Aurelius, you didn't mind it all that much.

I'm on my way to Cyrus's farm near one of the many Fairviews in America to visit him.

Your brother,
John

23 March 1898

I came to Cyrus's farm yesterday in the afternoon. Cyrus let me in and he was happy to see me. He saw my hat with the feather in the band and complimented it. But he also told me I wore it crooked. He let me in, took my coat, and I got to relax for a bit with him.

I told him that since my first miracle hadn't worked, I wanted to try to give him another one. Especially because I missed his birthday this year. He laughed and said that he was fine even if he hadn't found a wife yet. He said it's okay if he has to find a wife himself.

I noticed his garden was smaller this year. He said that he didn't need a large garden and he only made it so big while I was around because I was such a big help as a farm-hand. I asked if he would hire someone else to be a farm-hand. He said that I enchanted enough tools here that it isn't hard to run the farm by himself.

I told him I missed him.

He asked if I were going to stay this time.

I said no, I still have a drumbeat in my head.

He asked if I heard it right now.

I shook my head. I said I'm supposed to do something here. My feather was barely golden, and I took it out, and I gave him a miracle.

I knew magic was tricky so I told it that I didn't want Cyrus to die in the war and that he was only allowed to die of old age after a life well lived and well loved. The feather disappeared like it did the first time when my heart wished for him to find a perfect wife. Whenever I do magic, it always feels uneventful. I am not sure if I changed him. I followed him while he took care of the animals. I was relieved to see they weren't afraid of him the way they were afraid of me.

Cyrus asked what I wanted to do this evening. I told him I just wanted to help him make supper like I always did. He pulled out the cutting board he made for me, and I got to chop the vegetables. We only had the potatoes and onions to cut. The meal was not extravagant, but I got to help with cooking it, and it felt nice to be able to use a knife again.

I asked him if he could kiss me please. I just wanted to see if I loved men or women. He asked if I ever got a kiss from a pretty woman before. I said I had. He asked if I liked her, I said maybe I did but I knew I liked him, and I wanted to be sure I wasn't lying to myself. I told him just on the cheek for goodbye would be enough to compare. He said he could do that for me.

I got a new feather in my hat today, and the drumbeat has started up again. It's so loud already, like magic is chasing me out of Cyrus's home and wants me to go back on the road. It knows that, if it were up to me, I would want to stay much, much longer.

When he kissed me goodbye on the cheek, it felt nice and I felt loved. But it felt the way Margie's kiss felt. So, maybe I wasn't meant to be Cyrus's wife then.

In that case, I wouldn't want to be in her way. He did say I was too plain, after all.

Chapter 21

Wine at Eventide

Abigail held long-stemmed wine glasses upside down like a chandelier between the fingers of one of her hands. Crystal clinked together as she freed them to set them upon the coffee table once John had finished moving the furniture again.

"Where's Cyrus?" John asked.

"He's coming out soon."

The twinkling of the curtain made John look up to see Cyrus step into the parlor with a bottle of dark wine and a corkscrew. Something was off about how he moved. He was too mindful about his steps as he walked over to the seating area. Cyrus's arm jerked unexpectedly when he tried to place the wine bottle on the coffee table. It toppled and rolled. "Shit." He caught and then righted the bottle before it fell onto the wooden floor.

"You're fading," John observed.

"Ha, I guess you was bound to notice what's happening to me," Cyrus said. "My hands still work at least. I just have to be careful with my arms and legs now is all. They're having a mind of their own if I don't keep them in check." He uncorked the wine and poured it into the first glass. The scent was lush, rich as he poured it. "I've been feeling it for a while. Since we set the table. I reckon this part of our evening'll have to be cut short."

"Abigail told me the nights aren't as bad as the morns." John watched the glasses fill up.

Cyrus put the bottle down. "Yeah, I can feel what's coming so I can put myself away before it gets too bad. It starts by feeling like a Charley-horse. I pretend for a while that there ain't nothing wrong with me. It has been getting harder for some time if I'm honest, but I can hide it well enough. Keep adjusting lil by lil. Then, there's a point where that don't work no more. I just wanna make sure I don't end up being too much of a hassle for Abby. Ah well, I still prefer the night." He passed his wife her drink.

Abigail took it with her left hand. "Oh goodness, Rus. I don't mind it at all! John's here so you shouldn't have to turn in for the night so soon. It's not your fault you got shot in the head last month."

John settled into one of the reading chairs. He propped his wing open on the arm of the chair before he backed into the cushioned seat. He let the couple squabble about how far Cyrus should allow himself to go before he went to bed.

He picked up his wine glass, a burgundy tulip in his only hand. The flavor was smoky, illustrious, but inviting. "Cyrus, did you know? It's not just you who prefers the night. Magic prefers it as well. People have forgotten about things like that. That's why magic feels so rare these days."

"What do you mean by that?"

"It became clear to me when I was taking lessons from Margie. She explained the anatomy of a horse to me when she was teaching me how to ride again. The most important thing she taught to me is that horses aren't meant to be ridden. She always complained about how people kept forgetting that fact, and it ruins a horse when you forget."

Cyrus stayed quiet but set his glass down.

"I said it earlier: Horses are meant to be horses." John peeked out the window, gauging how much longer before the sun fully set and the room filled with clarscuro. Then, magic would feel stronger here.

"Well, with all this talk . . . Are you fixing on doing some kind of magic or something, John?"

"Yes-yes. I'm going to fix you, Cyrus. I *am* a handyman, after all," John said with a gentle smile.

Abigail gasped and covered her mouth with her free hand. Her eyes were shining. Next to her, Cyrus was stunned into silence, but his arms and legs kept fidgeting.

John poured himself another glass of wine "I like this one. It's a nice vintage."

"Vintage? You're about to make me . . . make me . . . Holy smokes! I'm gonna be fixed!" Cyrus tried his best to contain himself. "You devil, you could've told me this before! When I didn't need to—" He lurched forward, then crumpled sideways. He grunted as he got his limbs in order; then he pushed himself upright again. "When I didn't need to keep my wits about me to sit up and be still."

"I'm sorry, Cyrus," John said. "But waiting until eventide was important. I told you I was here on business. And there's a particular way I have to do this work."

"*Particular!* You could've explained some of what you was planning!"

"We couldn't talk about it before. If you were too aware about what I was here for, it wouldn't have worked. Even if you did everything the same, there would have been a part of you that did it because you wanted to be fixed instead of simply for the sake of it. It was important that your motivations stayed true. But we're here, after all of it's done, and it's almost time."

"What do you mean by that?" Abigail asked.

Cyrus used the arm of the loveseat to brace himself through another spasm. When he leaned back, he had his body under control again. Wearily, he said, "Well, let's hear it, John."

"Ten years ago, I should have waited for the evening to fall, for that hush after supper when our bellies are full, and we laze about after a day lived fully well. But instead, ten years ago, I took a golden feather in broad daylight, and I was trying to make magic do something for me when it didn't care about me or you or what we really wanted. So, it decided to fulfill what I demanded of it: To make sure you could only truly die of old age.

"Tonight, it will be different because we had a beautiful day. It was full of everything magic loves—hospitality, good food, the small kindnesses that you don't have to ask for, music, dancing . . . but also baring your heart, talking about the dark things we hate to share, and taking leaps of faith. I know that magic will listen and give us exactly what we want if only we wait. Magic is about doing the right thing at the right time."

24 April 1898

I am riding a little now. I just sit atop one of the brave horses, and Margie tells me whether I sit poorly or well while she leads the animal. It is not easy for I am crookedly made. I have had the wing for such a long time that my shoulders are uneven now. I never noticed it really until Margie pointed it out and made me to look at myself in front of a mirror.

I still don't like how it makes me to look like an animal a little bit. I remember when I had just a stump there instead and pretended I was a plain man with one arm for a year with Cyrus. Sometimes, that sounds easier, especially when summer is coming, and I don't like being so hot when I have to cover up.

Margie lets me into her room sometimes. She's always allowed into mine. She talks to me while I preen my wing. We are almost always together because both of us are strange. Friendship is easy between us.

In the dining hall, when I eat, the other lodgers tease us if we are going to be married. I don't know if I can be, given what I am. A husband can't be on the road as much as I am forced to be. Besides, I don't know if I am husband material anyway.

I'm already feeling the drumbeat in my head, and it's making it hard for me to concentrate. I know I need to figure out what the feather is for this time. I tried using it to make small miracles like I did when I lived with Cyrus, but when I go to try, the feather no longer lets itself be used up for such mundane things. Maybe back then, I was supposed to use it on such things and I'm not supposed to anymore.

Currently, I'm on a job for Ms. Bitty Bixler, and we're moving horses. Margie is to come in order to demonstrate the quality of the animals. She is very good at explaining how well the horses move. They are brave horses. Brave enough to not be unnerved by a thing like me. I know why Ms. Bitty Bixler is making them this way.

Thinking of that makes me think of the war that is coming. I feel better now that I know I made it so that Cyrus cannot die in battle. That means, after the war, I could definitely see him again if the drumbeat lets me. I fear it may not. I think this because of how quickly it sent me away and how much stronger it seemed when I even dared look back and dream of my Halcyon Days with Cyrus.

I have to keep moving to keep the drumbeat out of my head. I still can't ride my own horse, but I can help with Ms. Bitty Bixler's horses. Some of it is their breeding. I think most of it is how Margie works with them. She points out all the small things about how a horse moves that tells you what the horse is thinking and feeling. She knows what aches on them. She is the only one who can tell how, by the end of the day, I'm in so much pain.

In the night, we share a tent when we camp. She says she can tell by the way my wing moves that I am folding it too tightly underneath my coat.

I told her I have to.

She said she doesn't understand why I hide it when I am very good at killing people.

I told her it's wrong to kill people.

She said it's wrong for people to make me feel bad about myself, and that I'm her favorite person in the world because I'm not really a man and there's nobody else in the world like me.

Sometimes, I like when she talks about me like that. Other times, it makes me feel so lonely. Last night, it made me think of how she felt under my wing during the winter. Then, I thought of how Cyrus felt. The biggest difference is that her body is smaller than his, so maybe she fits better.

15 June 1898

In the summer, it's easier to be alone than to worry about how I look to other people. It's too hot to wear the coat, so I keep it in my suitcase most of the time. The drumbeat is quiet as long as I keep moving and keep searching. Sometimes, when I'm lost, I close my eyes, open up my wing so the zephyr blows over the feathers, and it makes me to be a little less human. Then, I can feel the direction magic wants me to go.

I know I'm not to hold still and maybe I'm supposed to be alone. A week ago, I sat in a cart, and I passed Cyrus's farm again. When I looked at his house, the drumbeat was so strong that my head throbbed even though I was moving. But I still watched it go by despite the pain. I watched it until it was a speck on the horizon. When I was too far to see it, the drumbeat was gone again.

I found I prefer sleeping in the wilderness after I bathe in the creek. I let myself stay a little wild, so that I'm more sensitive to the way magic moves in this country. It's strange that I, a foreigner, am more attuned to it than those who grew up here their entire lives.

Magic tells me when someone might approach me. I am able to make my choices then. The more sensitive I am to it, the more gently it can direct me. I feel a little bit like the horses Margie has me work with.

I miss Margie because she would put her cat-eye glasses on, she'd see everything in the dark, and she'd lead me to the horses at night so the clarscuro could hide how I look to people. She put her hand inside of mine so I could feel how she moved the reins as she cued the horses.

As I learned how to cue the horses, I learned how to follow magic's cues.

It asked me to go where there was once a forest, but it had gotten cut down. I used my feather on a hand mirror that I placed where magic told me to place it. Water flowed from the mountain spring, all of it wanting to go inside of a looking glass until the mirror was at the bottom of a pool. There shouldn't be a creek there, but now there is.

I think it's hard on me when I look towards Cyrus's farm because it knows, if it allows me to rest there, I would never want to leave again. It needs me for something. I am still reluctant about the purpose, but when I am half-wild on the road, I empty out my head like I do when I preen my feathers, and I let it lead me. And we are becoming better friends maybe.

Today, it wanted me to use a feather on my revolver. This gun no longer needs bullets. It always has them, and it's always clean and ready to use.

17 July 1898

Today is my birthday. I'm spending it alone. I look at the vastness of America's sky above me. It is very late. I have a little light I have made. I decided, since it was my birthday, I could make a witchglow lamp out of a wood flower I purchased in town earlier this month. It is very pretty, sitting out here, and tonight, my head is quiet because I don't have a gold shine feather wanting to be an important miracle.

It's just me with my enchanted boots and my enchanted suitcase writing in a journal next to an enchanted wood flower that shines like a piece of daylight, but it doesn't hurt my eyes.

Because the sky is dark, I am thinking of my last birthday on Nyuskom, when I turned eighteen. The moon was a crescent that night, but something about that evening felt dark and foreboding. Maybe there were clouds that night. I don't remember. I just remember packing up my things.

Elysia helped me because it was still hard for me back then to do many things. She told me she hated that this happened to me. She hated that I grew a wing, and she hated the amputations. She hated that she was helping to pack up my things to send me away. She hated all of it because she loved me so much, and it wasn't fair. I remember how she embraced me and cried.

Tonight the sky is as clear as my mind is. I know Elysia and Cyrus are looking out their windows and wondering how I am doing because it is my birthday, and I turned twenty four. I believe I'm well into being a man. Except maybe I'm not a man really. I don't know. I still don't have a shirt to wear.

I don't think Margie knows my birthday. She's never even seen me in my season. I hope to change that one day, but she won't leave her little world which consists of Ms. Bitty Bixler's manor or the horses. Maybe she's like me if I were allowed to stay home or stay with Cyrus.

I should send another letter to Elysia, but I don't know if she has been receiving them.

Chapter 22

Waiting for a Miracle

Cyrus was stuck on the loveseat; John stayed nearby in the reading chair. Abigail was up, preparing the room. Brimming with excitement and hope, she could hardly contain herself. She made her rounds, stopping at the half-height candles and striking the matches against the phosphorus paper before touching their burning heads to the wicks. The little flames multiplied through the parlor.

A draft blew across the parlor, bringing a feeling of expectation with it. She closed the windows, but left the curtains open. The moon was already in the lavender sky. Stubbornly, the late spring sun didn't want to give up the day yet.

"How you holding up, Rus?" Abigail asked as she sat next to her husband.

"I'm just peachy," he said. "But if all goes well, this'll be the last time I have to go through this. Still, waiting's hard. My balance is shot. I can tell my eyes are starting to do the thing. It gets blurry, and I get a headache. When it's in-between, you know how that goes."

"You'll get confused as before, speech and mind," John said.

"Bingo." Cyrus grinned.

"What will you be like once the sun fully sets?"

"I told you that story about me being a worm," Cyrus replied wearily. "I'll be writhing soon enough." His hands were getting tighter, and he shut his flickering eyes. "Can't we just start now?"

"Not yet," John said. "We need the clarscuro. And also my hat. We need my feather in it to do the magic."

Abigail nodded and went to fetch the hat.

Cyrus grunted as he rocked. "I'm glad you and my wife finally got to meet."

"Yes-yes. She's good company and talented. She's kind. Even to something like me. She suits you, Cyrus."

"See? I always told you that you was too plain to be my wife, ya silly goose."

"I see that now. I understand myself better."

"Since you can't be my wife, you'll have to settle on being someone's husband. Will you ever get yourself a wife?"

"If I do, she won't be as good as yours."

He laughed. "True. Not many women would stay with someone like me the way she's done. It took one of your miracles, didn't it?"

"Mostly, it was your dancing, ver."

Abigail came back with the hat in her hand. She looked at the feather stuck in the band. "You told me this feather was from a rare bird."

"Well, aren't I?" John lifted his wing and waved the tip of it.

"Oh, you!" She gave him his hat.

John held it up in the last of the daylight shining through the windows. The sun was setting, and it accentuated the effect of the gold sheen which sparkled throughout the feather.

"It looks different from the ones on your wing," Abigail noted.

"It's a special one."

"It's even brighter than it was earlier today."

"That's because of the clarscuro. It's close to the right moment, at-now."

"Can I see it?" Cyrus asked.

"Of course." John donned his hat. It sat askew on his head, as it usually did. Once there, he plucked the feather from the hatband and offered it to his friend.

Cyrus reached forward, deliberately, because his arms were difficult for him to use. He had to match his fingers to where John was patiently holding out the feather for him. Once in hand, he held the feather with his fingertips, one set at the soft tip and the other at the hollow shaft. It was about as long as his face was wide, and he tilted his head down, forcing his eyes to focus because it was easier at the extreme angle. "Ah, I see. It looks like the ones I seen before. It's definitely brighter than the one you had that Spring when you came to visit me ten years ago."

"It is; I didn't understand how it worked, at-then. I kept using the magic poorly."

Cyrus handed the feather back. "How do you mean?"

John tucked it into his hatband. "Magic is not really for us to use. It simply is what it is."

"'Horses are meant to be horses,'" Abigail said quietly.

"Yes-yes. That's right. I used what Margie taught to me about horses. I need to keep my requests soft and pay attention to what magic needs and to what it prefers. Maybe what we have so far is enough. But I'd prefer to wait for the time to be perfect, to make sure we get the best possible outcome. I hope you don't mind to endure it for a little more time. Please."

His friend sighed.

"I can imagine it's hard to sit there, to feel yourself fall apart," John said.

"Well, it ain't easy."

"Time will pass faster, I think, if I tell to you some of my secrets."

"Well, I want to know where you're really from!" Abigail said. "I can't place your accent, but it's nice to listen to."

"I answered that one already. Many times."

She shook her head. "You only said you were from nowhere!"

"That's what you're always saying, anytime anyone asks," Cyrus said.

"Because it is the truth. There's an island which floats freely en Ocean di Atlantyke—the Atlantic Ocean—and it's covered in mist. It is my homeland. Sometimes, it's so close to this country, you can see it from the marsh-islands on the east coast before it drifts away again. It's hard to find, but it settles down some winters west of Hibernia. If you read the old stories, pirates and criminals used to hide there. When people would ask them where they were coming from or where they were going, they would say—"

"Nowhere," Cyrus finished.

"Yes-yes, that's right," John replied. "'Nyuskom' en lingua di —sorry, I meant to say, it's 'Nyuskom' in the local dialect actually, but that just means 'Nowhere.' So, that's what they say."

Both Abigail and Cyrus looked suspicious.

"You aren't just making this up to avoid telling us where you're *really* from?" she asked.

"I told you. Whatever you ask, I'll do my best to answer."

"So, why do you have that wing then?" Cyrus asked.

"That one is trickier to answer . . . I think I'll start by saying that magic is a rare thing at-now, even in Nowhere. People can still find artifacts from the old days. All of those enchanted objects that make magic to come alive and listen and change things. Nowhere dealt with a lot of items like that. Stolen, sold, and sometimes repurposed by the few left who still know magic."

"Like you," Abigail noted.

"Yes-yes, I suppose I am among that crowd," John said, thoughtfully.

"Your wing, John! You was saying how you got it." Cyrus's urgency made sense. He was losing things the later it got. His eyes were shut. His arms tightened up, muscles contracting; they squeezed against his chest.

John continued, "My father and I had a disagreement over my piano-playing. I wanted to make a career of it, and he was against such a notion. I had other responsibilities he wanted me to grow into. I was seventeen when I woke up like this at one morn."

"Oh goodness, that must have been frightening," Abigail commented.

"Yes-yes, it was. My father did everything he could to fix it. He had an expert to examine me. He decided to try a surgery to remove it completely. Amputation." He chopped at his right shoulder with his left hand. "It worked for a short time. It was easier for him to explain me having one arm than having an entire bird-wing. But it is a curse, and naturally, it grew back. Amputation was attempted twice in Nowhere. It came back each time. We tried many things, but nothing worked because it was magic that gave it to me. And because it was to do with magic, he had my fortune told then."

"Tea leaves," Cyrus said.

"Among other things. They had different details, but there was a consensus that I ought to be stripped of my birthright."

"You said that earlier today. Birthright. I can tell you're noble by your manners and your education. You really are a prince, aren't you?" Abigail asked.

John smiled. "Well, you're not wrong. But I am no longer anything like that, not anymore. The majority of the fortunes we received said it was bad luck to have someone like me for a son. So, he had me sent away. It was hard because I always had servants to take care of me before, and I also had to hide this ridiculous wing in a new country."

"You know, I always wondered why you was bad at doing so many things first time I met you," Cyrus said. By now, he was twisting where he sat, obviously uncomfortable.

Abigail put her hand on his thigh.

John shrugged. "I suppose I wasn't a very good farmhand. I did my best with one arm when we first met. Then a year passed, it grew back, and I had one arm et one wing. My American amputation lasted longer than the ones in Nowhere."

"I'm glad that wing of yours"—Cyrus's body jolted, and he huffed—"I'm glad that wing came back. I don't mean because your feathers deal magic, and you're aiming to fix me. I mean I'm real pleased you let my wife take a look at you. Even let her keep you company when you"—he grunted—"fussed your feathers."

"Rus, aren't you getting too excited?" Abigail asked worriedly.

"Oh Abby, just let me get excited. John's fixing me up soon.

I'm already all bent and terrible to look at. And I'll be blind in a bit. Still, why the hell it take you so long, John? Six damn years like this."

"I wish magic allowed me to come sooner. But magic likes its plots."

"Six swans," Abigail said, recalling the story. "Six years."

"Yes-yes, that's right. Even though there weren't any nettle shirts to be made or swan princes."

"Well, there's you. Aren't you a swan prince?" she asked.

"No-no, I'm just a handyman from nowhere."

"Oh, not this again . . ." Abigail paused, then admitted, "But I guess it turned out to be exactly what you are, somehow."

"I try not to be dishonest."

Magic sat in the room with them, observing Cyrus slowly losing his ability to move and see. It saw John with his wing out in the open, enjoying sitting with the Coopers despite his chronic pain. They were all good people.

The nice thing about good people was that they set a kind example. Magic was learning how to be good, bit by bit, so maybe this time, it could do something nice for its cursed prince who was also a plain man and a silly goose.

It was the least it could do. John did listen to its cues very well. Perhaps it should listen to his.

4 February 1899

I am making progress with the horse Margie has selected for me. I am very excited to one day be able to ride Lucky on my own without her help.

Margie is teaching me how to cue Lucky in ways where I cannot use my strength on accident to harm her. She has me hold out my hand to cue my horse to stay. Lucky touches my hand with her nose, and she tickles me. When she is still, I tell her she is a good horse. She makes pleasant noises which mean she likes me. It has been so long since I heard a horse make such sounds for me.

I asked Margie if I could teach her words in my native tongue. She said of course, but only if I told her what they were so she could keep training Lucky for me when I wander again. I told her 'mahne' means 'stay'.

When she is ready, I will buy her from Ms. Bitty Bixler. Margie said she will cry and throw a tantrum if Bitty even tries to sell the horse before I am able to purchase her. She said if that doesn't work, she'll bite. I know she's not joking because when she jokes, she has a joyfulness to her. She was very serious about biting. She even snapped her teeth!

Many times, we go into the barn together, and I let Lucky sniff my wing and get accustomed to it. Margie has me walk around for all of the horses so they can learn to be brave even next to something like me.

I am thankful my head isn't pounding, but when I try to take some time for myself, I notice there is a tapping in the back of my skull, threatening to start up again. It feels like I am in two different worlds.

When I am here, with Margie and the horses and employed by Ms. Bitty Bixler, I am more human. When the drumbeat forces me to set out on the road again, I become something else. Something that is not exactly a man.

12 March 1899

So far, the drumbeat leads me to where I am needed and where I will be taken care of. I still don't have a shirt to wear, but I wear my coat, and it's cool enough at this time of year that I am permitted to without raising suspicion. Today, I was helping set up some fences at a farm in exchange for a good meal and to rest inside rather than underneath the stars. When I am on the road, usually I am stuck sleeping outside or in a tent. But now, I am sitting in a bed and my wing is out because I can lock the door of this guest room.

People always ask me to remove my coat, but I do not want to show them what I have underneath. Many times, they are not good at understanding me. Maybe the only reason Cyrus accepted it fully was because he knew me for a whole year before I regrew it. I suppose Margie understood it right away.

The family is always surprised how well I do as a farmhand even though I only have one arm. I just can't handle the animals well. The animals are not brave like the horses at Ms. Bitty Bixler's are. The family is especially pleased with how well I do with the fence line. I make quick work of it.

I love how good food tastes after I have been traveling for a long time. I wish people could see the magic in that by itself. The magic of how a home-cooked meal tastes much better when you've been on the road too long and spent a good day working hard. The magic of how soft and comfortable a bed is when you haven't slept on a mattress for a while.

When I lie on my left side, I always remember Margie's face looking into mine after telling me that this is the only way for me to lie down and not have my muscles working to hold up my folded wing. Every time I get comfortable, I remember her voice because she's the only one who ever noticed how rare being comfortable is for me. When we share a bed in my room, she lies on her right side, and we are face to face and talk. I like that she does that for me because we can almost be the same.

I will have to preen my wing later today. I miss sharing root beers with Cyrus after I do it. The way he spoke to me during and after, I could tell he cared about me very much. I think that's what I miss the most. I wish the drumbeat would let me stay at his house in the summer. Honestly, I wish I had anyway to stay in the summer months.

For now, it is cold enough to wear my coat, so I don't have to be too lonely. I have a room to stay, and the family is very nice to give me privacy.

Also, I gave the family my little wood flower witchglow light. Their daughter loved it more than I did. I thought it was best for her to have it. Besides, I can always make another.

Chapter 23

Finally Nightfall

"It's night now," Abigail said in hushed tones. Outside the panes of glass, the gibbous moon was the color of an old bone in the dark sky.

"So it is." John got up and closed the curtains. Candlelight was perfect for clarscuro because of how playful it made the shadows. "Just a little more preparation. We need for it to be perfect." He eyed the table in the middle of the seating area; it was in the way. "Let's put the wine glasses to the kitchen. I need to move the coffee table. We need to sit ourselves closer together. Yes-yes, I can feel that would be right."

Cyrus leaned into the corner of the loveseat to try to keep himself from jostling around too much. His limbs were tight and bent. "I won't be much help for that right now. Is it almost time?"

"Almost," John answered. "But not quite."

"Damn it. I feel one coming—I's hoping I wouldn't have to go through . . ." His voice faded away. His entire body clenched. Every breath took effort, and his bottom lip was shining with saliva. He pressed the side of his face against the back of the loveseat.

Abigail attended to her husband, rubbing his back. He groaned, frustrated with his body. "I'm right here, Rus. This is just what happens sometimes," she said gently. "We know how it is."

"Did you want me to pause the preparations until you can speak again?" John asked. "I can wait."

Cyrus huffed, unable to answer. He made only small, sputtering breaths as he fought himself to try. His head wobbled.

"Rus, sweetheart, we can't tell if you're nodding or shaking your head right now. Do you want John to wait until you're talking again before he sets things up?"

He grunted twice.

"That means 'no.'"

Cyrus grinned.

Abigail wiped her husband's chin clean. "I can stay with him, John. You get it ready. He said he wants you to keep going. Don't wait for him."

"Very well."

The candles that surrounded them all around the edges of the room scattered John's shadow as he cleared away the low table. He picked up the empty glasses by scooping them from underneath between his fingers; each was burgundy where the stem touched the cup.

He took another look at Cyrus and Abigail on the loveseat before heading out of the room to put the dishes in the sink. The magic wasn't ready to give them a miracle anyway. It wanted to see Cyrus struggling one more time. It took glee in watching men struggle as much as when they celebrated. But it loved it most when it got to see the contrast between the two. That was the reason it loved the clarscuro so much, after all.

When John returned to the parlor, Abigail was wiping a cotton handkerchief across Cyrus's lips again. His friend's breathing had calmed down.

"How are you faring, Cyrus?" John asked.

His friend nodded wearily, still mute.

Abigail shook her head. "Oh, don't you fib at him, Rus. You keep having to start all over because you're rushing yourself."

Cyrus's mouth moved before he said, "Suh, sight. Tin."

"'It's too exciting,'" his wife translated automatically.

"I suppose it would be exciting. There's more than enough clarscuro, at-now. I just have to move things around, and we can sit close together. However you are when you come out of this, we'll make it work. Fret not, my friend. It will be very soon."

Cyrus's body tensed again, and a little whine squeezed out of his tight throat.

"Oh, sweetheart," his wife said. "You'll get through it. You always do. You are The Undying Soldier after all."

John lifted the table one-handed and leaned it against the wall.

"Did you know you were strong right away after your arm changed?" Abigail asked.

"No-no. I had to figure it out," he answered. "I didn't know for a while because everything was done for me."

"Well, it must've been nice to find out not all of it was bad."

"Yes-yes, it made some of the farmwork much easier when I lived here." He picked up the reading chair to move it closer to the loveseat. "I enjoyed the way Cyrus showed me all of the things that happened in and between those chores. It made it bearable for me.

"He took me into town and lived so vibrantly to show me how nice it was to be in America. He played cards with me with his friends and made sure they were kind to me. I liked it when we had root beer after I preened my wing." John sat in the chair. "I'm sorry you had to see me like that. I'm sure it was strange."

"I didn't mind it," she said. "It was interesting."

"I couldn't tell you earlier, but I liked when you said it was like reading a good book. That was kind of you to say. I'm not exactly human anymore; I haven't been for a long time. But when you said that, I realized it *is* like that. And it made me to believe maybe I am still more human than I think."

"Wing and all, you're a plain man, John."

"Grasi."

"That's 'thank you' in your language, isn't it?"

"Yes-yes."

Cyrus made a small noise.

Abigail put her hand on her husband's thigh. "I'm right here, sweetheart. I'm just talking with your friend, John. We've been waiting for you. You should be able to talk soon, but your eyes won't work no more."

"Hmm. Tuh?"

"It's night time, Rus." Like always, she understood exactly what he was saying.

"It's night time? So, that's why my hands won't work. I can tell I ain't in bed. Why'm I still out here? You know I prefer sleeping before I get like this, Abby. It ain't fair living through this twice a day."

She kissed him on his cheek. "Shh, sweetheart, I know. Just be patient with yourself. It'll catch up to you. You're always so good at getting your bearings."

John stayed quiet, watching Cyrus lean back into the corner

of the loveseat. He rubbed the back of his clenched hands against the velvet upholstery. "Well now I figured out that it's you and John here. I'm in the parlor, sitting in my loveseat. I'm all blind now. Which, yeah . . . We're 'bout to do something. Sorry it takes me a while when my—*oh*." He exhaled as the realization hit. His sightless eyes welled up, and his lips trembled; he couldn't bring his hands to cover his tears, so he pressed his wet face against his wife's bosom.

"Is it happening again?" John asked.

Abigail shook her head. Tears filled her eyes, too. She ran her long fingers through her husband's blond hair gently as he sobbed into her. "Oh goodness, Rus. What you've been through. Six years of it! It's fine to cry when you know it's almost over."

* * *

SOMETHING old and sacred occupied the parlor with them as they all sat close together. It was fond of the little fires on the wicks of the candles in that room, and it brushed against the curtains. They could feel it pass through them, tender to them, as it inventoried their desires. John knew it was always there, but now, it manifested as a conspiratorial feeling cast over them, obvious even to Cyrus and Abigail.

"It's so much different from last time you did this to me," Cyrus said. "It feels holy tonight."

"Yes-yes, I know what I'm doing these days." John took the feather from his hat. He held it in the middle of all three of them. "Come closer."

With Abigail's guidance, Cyrus leaned forward so close to John's hand that his nose bumped it.

"How do we know it's working?" he asked.

"You'll know. Put your hands on mine," John said.

Cyrus forced his arms forward, but was having difficulty controlling them and keeping them in contact with John's. They kept withdrawing and clamping themselves across his chest. "I can't. It's too late for me."

"Sweetheart, I'm here." Abigail gently wrapped her brown hands over his lighter-skinned ones, pressing them against John's. The arrangement was uncomfortable for Cyrus, but it would be impossible otherwise. Abigail's hands were a shell that kept his own steady over the kernel of John holding his feather.

That feather glowed gold in the dim room. The candles all went out so that only the feather's incandescent light remained in the parlor. It warmed their hands as it steadily got brighter and hotter, but somehow it never lost its softness, and it never burned them. Magic draped over them like gossamer and whispered in their ears like a secret lover.

John focused on Cyrus's face. His eyes had stopped their constant movement. Steady now, the pupils shrank in response to the growing light. His weariness disappeared as the magic returned the crumbs taken from him in every death he died. Throughout the years, the Undying Soldier had always carried on being himself, but he hadn't realized how difficult the burden had been to bear until it was lifted from his shoulders.

Then, the feather blazed yellow like a sodium flame before it disappeared and left them all in the dark.

"That's it," John said. "It is done." The old ache in the muscles that supported his wing was gone. The arthritis was cured as well. His limb felt strange without its pain.

"Did it work, Rus?" Abigail asked.

"Yes it did!" Cyrus embraced her and kissed her. The married couple laughed and cried, grateful to be able to hold each other in the dark of night just the same as they could in the bright of day. "Still, it'd be nice to have a lil light."

Like most old things, magic had an unhurried pace to everything it did. It made its way around the room, reigniting the candles one-by-one, illuminating the trio again.

"Goodness, does it listen to us all the time?" Abigail wondered.

"It can if it wants," John replied, "but it tends not to waste its time unless we do something to catch its attention. It likes the two of you."

Cyrus looked up at John. He started to thank him, but instead he shook his head and chuckled. "Wait, hold still, ya silly goose." He straightened up John's hat. "I can't believe you can make miracles happen, but you still never figured out how to wear a hat."

12 June 1899

I usually don't come to Oaks Bend when the months get warmer, but I had been heading over in this direction for a while. I had a feeling that this was where I was supposed to go and entered the home of Ms. Bitty Bixler's even though the door was locked. Because I felt it was important, I broke the door even though it is rude to do so. I saw that there was a gang in the building, and they were intent on robbing Ms. Bitty Bixler. Everyone in her home at the time was folded on the ground.

I saw Margie was huddled up and afraid. But it was like she felt me enter the room. She cried out my name as soon as she saw me. Her smile was bright with relief and joy just because it was me.

One of the gang members yelled for everyone to stay down or he will shoot. But he followed Margie's eyes and saw me with my gun drawn. I knew I had one chance, and everything had to be done in a split second.

So it was.

Each man required only one shot to be killed. It is less about aiming and more about knowing where the gun is meant to go. When I am fresh from the road, I'm not entirely human in my mind. It makes it easier to not miss. It is as if I am aligning the tip of my gun with a thread that pierces them through the heart, and my instinct puts it exactly where it is to go. I suppose I am very good at killing people these days.

I did get shot in my wing, and I was very shy to expose how I really looked, but Ms. Bitty Bixler and Margie took me into my usual room together with my things. Bitty undressed me. I saw her good eye sparkling, curious about the shape of me, but she also understood I was injured. So she was very gentle. Every time her gaze passed over me, it would linger on my wing. She said she called a friend who is a remarkable surgeon on her new telephone. He was coming straightaway because this had to do with magic, and magic is rare nowadays.

I am very much in pain, and I still can't fold up my wing very well or move it. Margie has been attending to me. Mostly, she changes the bandages and talks to me, which is nice. She informs me that Lucky is almost ready for me to ride because she is old enough, and we can practice again once I am healed.

I am afraid of another amputation. The healing process is always arduous, and most things are easier with a wing that can sometimes work as an arm rather than having nothing there at all. I told Ms. Bitty Bixler that as well.

She told me the gunshots didn't look too bad, and also it was rare that Dr. Willard Cross would have to cut off a limb. He'd probably just remove the bullets and that would be it. I hope that's the case.

I am still very frightened. I haven't had a doctor look at me since J Bellamy. He always seemed too eager to cut everything off. Because I was so frightened, Ms. Bitty Bixler made sure I was as comfortable as I could be and refrained from asking questions. She said I definitely look strange, and she'd give Dr. Cross a heads up about my appearance.

She also told me that she received a letter that had my

name on it, but it was not written in English. So, I'll read the letter until Dr. Cross comes. I am in pain, but I always compare my pains to the first amputation. Compared to that hell, this is nothing.

Besides, I'm excited to see the letter.

Letter from Elysia (translated)

Dearest brother,

I am starting to send my letters to Ms. Bitty Bixler in Oaks Bend as instructed in your last letter. I did receive a few from you while you were living in the home of Mr. Cyrus Cooper, but based on the last letter I received from you, you have not been able to receive any of the ones I have been sending you.

Reading your letters over the years has made me proud of you. You have always been a tender person, and I was always afraid that having this curse change your body so much would make it hard for you to grow into a man. You were already struggling to define yourself before all of this happened. I was glad to see you admit that the wind and the sunlight feels good on your wing. I remember watching you when you lived here, and I helped with your care. I can imagine you now, a grown man with a bird's wing, taking care of yourself and not resentful of the shape you're in.

I loved hearing how you were chatting with people while living with Mr. Cyrus Cooper. He sounds like a remarkable fellow to befriend you when you had one arm and then to still accept you when you regrew your wing. Then, you told me you moved out, and you kept making new friends.

I remember how you were always very shy when you lived here in Nyuskom. Even though I am only two years older, you always felt so much younger than me because of that shyness. There was an oddness to you, my brother, long before your arm transformed. I am glad that, through the years, you have found out how to accept yourself.

I remember how much you loved animals and how devastated you were when your curse made them wary of you. It pleases me that Margie is helping you get along with horses again. Once you get a horse of your own, you must tell me all about your horse. I remember I tried to get the animals to like you again. I was not successful. It felt like every part of what you loved about your life was taken from you. I tried my best to encourage you.

Your first amputation was the hardest for me. That horrible surgery that stole a quarter of your body from you. And the pain you were in looked more than any person should bear. I tried to show you how nice your wing was when it returned, but I think I also needed more time to understand it and you. I wish I got to spend more time with you, winged, before everyone decided you were best sent away.

I think you would not be surprised to hear that Father decided to allow me to inherit Nyuskom. Father misses you and wishes that he chose you. We all miss your piano playing in the great hall. When I play, it's not as good as your playing used to be. You, dear brother, are a prodigy. I hope one day to play piano with you again. At least see your face. I wonder if you grew a beard. When I saw you last, you only could grow a little bit of hair.

I was considering sending someone out to find you and bring you home, but then I received a letter from you and you stated you were fine. Then, you found Mr. Cyrus Cooper and seemed happy. So I left you because you appeared to be turning into who you were supposed to have become. I didn't want to stand in your way.

Aurelius sometimes goes to America. He still has not seen you, but he heard the story of an angel who helped define a river's path with a looking glass. And it was enough to help irrigate the fields and bring wealth to a town because overnight all the trees grew enough that they could use them as lumber. They say the angel bathed his wings in the new river, and that's why the trees grew back. I feel like that was you, brother, even though you don't have two wings. You only have one arm and one wing, but it's close enough for me to think it might be you.

Would you be able to return home? At least for a visit?

With all the love and pride in the world,
Regina Elysia Pulkara Valerio de Nyuskom

16 June 1899

Dr. Willard Cross came over a few days ago. I asked
that he kept no records of the surgery to remove the bullets
from my wing. He did practice discretion and was kind
about it. I remember the ping of the bullets hitting the
metal tray as he removed them. He said I was a remarkable
young man. I told him I'm rather plain.

He reminded me he was removing bullets from a wing
attached to a young man's shoulder. He said there's
nothing plain about that. He did good work. He asked me
if I had any clothes to wear because I was shirtless. I said
just my trousers and my coat. He told me Ms. Bitty Bixler
was having a shirt made for me.

I told him I missed wearing a shirt.

Somehow the wounds in my wing have almost healed
completely in just these few days. Dr. Cross said it was
faster than it should have healed. It makes me wonder if
J Bellamy amputating my wing that third time in America
was necessary. But I suppose it was because I don't know if
Cyrus would have helped me as well as he did if he met me
when I still had a wing. I think he needed to know me sans
wing in order to become accustomed to me with the wing.
Especially because, back then, I wasn't accustomed to
it yet.

Dr. Willard Cross stayed a few days and kept me
company like Ms. Bitty Bixler did. When I asked why he
was not frightened of my wing, he said that he is old
enough to see I am a young man who is scared and in pain.
I just happened to have a wing. He said that he had seen

magic do things far more heinous and sinister than give a young man a wing.

I told him 'sinister' means 'left' in my language.

He smiled and said he knew a little Latin and that most doctors do. I told him it was not exactly Latin. He asked me where I was from. I gave him the answer I gave everyone in America: Nowhere.

"Nusquam?" he asked.

"Nyuskom," I corrected.

"Not exactly Latin," he said. He asked me how long I was planning to stay.

"I'm not sure, but for now, I'm allowed to stay. There's no drumbeat in my head."

That was when I realized I was supposed to give him a miracle. I asked Dr. Cross if he had a wish because I had a golden feather that grants wishes.

He asked if magic really was that easy to do. I told him that it was. He asked if he had to tell me his wish. I said it could be a secret, I didn't mind. I don't know what he wished for when that feather sparked up and disappeared.

Letter to Elysia (translated)

Elysia,

I finally received a letter from you.

I have a doctor now named Dr. Willard Cross. Ms. Bitty Bixler has become aware of what I really look like underneath my coat. She has a lot of work for me to do, and she hires me to protect Margie when we move the horses. She has explained to Dr. Cross what her ventures are, and he decided to be a business partner for her so they can get rich breeding and selling their horses.

I am surprised they were not as shocked as I thought they would be about the wing, but they are both already well acquainted with magic. I have found that when you spend too long with odd company, you get marked by magic. I think once someone gets marked by magic in that way, they probably will be fine to know what I really am.

Also, you are correct that I must be the angel in that story. Except I am just a plain man other than having one wing. And I didn't change the course of a river, I just encouraged a stream to flow where magic wanted me to put it.

I'm not sure what to call what I am doing other than it is my new job. It is fulfilling when I do it properly. I'm not even sure how it really works. I have to let the instincts guide me, and it takes me where I'm supposed to be. Then, I do a miracle like a wizard might be able to do.

I believe, because of the circumstances of what I am, time doesn't slip through my fingers as badly as it does for the wizards and witches of yesteryear. They always lost their minds a little bit. I do that too when I preen my feathers or bathe my wing, but I come back easily enough. I only need peppermints or root beer or to have a friend talk to me.

You are also right that I am not surprised to hear you received what Father always thought was my birthright. It definitely suits you a lot more, dear sister. You have always been a remarkable woman. I can remember when you used to help me with the cloak pin and how your hands did not shake. I miss you. For now, because of my job, I must stay in America. My work is important.

The job I do also provides well for me. As a reward for the good work I have done, Ms. Bitty Bixler has given me Lucky. She is black and has a white snip on her nose between her nostrils. She allows me to stroke her, and she is fond of me. I am so happy because I used to love spending time with the animals when I lived in Nyuskom. It has been so many years since I had a horse that was all mine. Because she is new to being my horse and new to being on the road, I am going to make sure to take care of her and ease her into her new life with me. I know I am strange now between my appearance and my job. I want her to not mind it too much.

Your brother,

John

Chapter 24

Tranced

John checked on Lucky before he came back into the house with a change of clothes for the morning. Cyrus was waiting for him in the parlor, freshly bathed and wearing a sleep shirt already. He stood at an open window. With hands on the sill, he leaned out to breathe in the night air. The gibbous moon brightened his face. He gathered himself inside, shut the window, and latched it.

"I just can't stop looking at that sky," he said. "It's been a long time since I've been able to see what the night looks like." He turned to face John, whose shoulders were even. Normally, the right one had less mass and was pulled down. "John, you're standing up straight now."

"I am. It doesn't hurt anymore." John opened his wing up. He moved it through its range of motion. Gone was the tremor from exertion. He flapped it, revealing its fresh strength. It felt like the day he first received it. His wing folded loosely at his side. "It looks like magic turned back time on me, too. No more arthritis. You can never be sure what magic gives you, especially if it's something you did not ask for."

"You didn't ask for your wing to be fixed?"

John shook his head. "I didn't ask for anything for myself. If I did, I'd have wished for my arm back. I know magic wants me to keep this ridiculous thing. Maybe it's amused by how I get on with my life, a man lugging around a bird-wing. Somehow, managing some surreal existence where perhaps I'm less a man and more an animal—"

"You ain't an animal."

"You're right," John conceded. "I think this time I'll take better care of it. The anatomy is still wrong, but I won't ruin it with disuse again. I'll try to be kinder to it." He rested his wing on his left hand; he found comfort in the weight of it.

"Magic's strange," Cyrus noted.

"It is," John agreed. "Now that my job is done and I haven't gotten a new feather yet, there is a brief moment of peace for me."

"Peace? So no drumbeat then?"

"Not yet. It's only between feathers that I don't have to worry about the wanderlust. This country took an interest in me: A cursed, exiled prince from an island where people and magic aren't as estranged as they are here."

"As far as I can tell, the only princely thing about you is that ridiculous name you told me a couple times: Muh-Lucky Sekunder Volley-o de . . . Nowhere."

John chuckled. "Close. Malachy Secundus Valerio de Nyuskom. But that isn't me anymore. My name changed about sixteen years ago."

"Still no last name?"

"I like being John, just John."

"If you had a last name, what would it be?"

"I'm too plain to be your wife, so not Cooper."

"John Cooper don't sound near as good as Abigail Cooper anyways," Cyrus teased.

As if mentioning her name had summoned her, Abigail came down the hall. She had her hair wrapped in a green silk scarf and wore a matching nightgown. Her brown skin was dewy, freshly bathed. She waited at the threshold with a bright expression. "Rus? I was thinking we can set up our old bedroom."

"Absolutely, Abby!" Cyrus danced in place to show off his mobility. "Look how limber I am right now. I ain't missing no crumbs no more!" He grinned and then glanced crotchward before winking at his wife. "*Anywhere.*"

"Oh Rus!" She blushed. "We have a guest!"

John tilted his head. "Before I get a bath, I can help to prepare the room. It will be no trouble with my strength."

Cyrus snorted. "You still a virgin, John?"

"No-no, I am not," he said. "What does that have to do with moving furni—" His eyes rounded. "I see. I suppose I ought to take a bath instead, at-then."

Abigail giggled. "John, we're just sweeping up and laying fresh sheets. It's always best to be clean on clean sheets. I can draw your water for your bath if you want. Rus did tell me how much you love baths."

John looked down and away. His ears were burning. "It's not unlike what you saw earlier when I was preening. I get stuck sometimes."

"You do have a whole bird-wing," she said pleasantly. "Don't let yourself get too embarrassed."

"I'll try not to," he muttered.

Her feet were bare, so her soles flashed pale as she headed back down the hallway.

Cyrus turned to John. "I'll knock on the door about a half-hour into your bath. How's that?"

"That would be nice. Grasi."

"Do you need help at all?"

John took a deep breath. "I'll be fine. It's almost bed time, and I won't need to talk for the rest of the night."

"Oh? You don't mind being crittery no more?"

"It's not too bad," he admitted. "Sometimes, I have to be like that for my work."

"Being a handyman," Cyrus said.

"Yes-yes. Exactly."

THE AIR WAS moist and warm from the hot water in the tub. John undid the toggle closure at the front of his shirt. The strip of cloth hung loose as he felt for the snaps under his wing and pulled at them. After removing his shirt, he carefully folded it on the counter, pinning it with the alula on the bend of his wing to make straight creases with his left hand. Next, he undid his belt and the fly of his jeans. Words were already slipping out of his head because of the humid steam.

The bathroom mirror remained clear; he had enchanted it to never fog up many years ago. The part of himself that was in-between a bird and a man—it was still the same, wasn't it? Bones not right; muscles trying their best, but at least the ache was gone. He touched that shoulder gently, a promise to listen to his body better this time.

He went back to undressing his bottom half. He folded everything neatly, finding comfort and peace in the ritual of it. It was grounding because he always felt like he took too much space when he bathed indoors. His clothes, at least, could be neat and small.

Maybe one day, his work would let him take a break. Then, he could have a little house somewhere with a big bathtub. He didn't know if he could be a husband then, but he hoped he could be.

John slipped his naked body into the tub, barely disturbing the surface. He dipped his wing into the warm water, splashing it in and out. It was so pleasant that his feathers fluffed up involuntarily. He turned and twisted the wing to wash every inch of it. The feel of the water coming through his feathers and touching his skin was always strangely euphoric. The delight rang through his head like the ping of the highest notes being struck on a piano.

When he would see songbirds playing in the puddles after it rained and sharing a momentary truce so that all of them could enjoy their bath, he understood why they did that. Once his wing was thoroughly wet, he held it up and out of the water, and then shook it to flick the feathers dry. Before, when his wing was atrophied, he had to prop it along the side of the tub and let it drip onto the floor, but tonight, he could hold it up, spread the feathers, and marvel at how pretty it was when he fanned it open with the alchemic light behind it.

His head started to empty out. His violet eyes scanned the feathers until he noticed a spot that needed a little more attention, and he dipped his wing again, compulsively. Rinse and repeat. Bathing always tranced him.

A knock on the door startled John.

"Just me. It's been a half-hour," Cyrus said through the door. "I know you can't really talk right now, but I know you can still understand me. I'm real happy you figured yourself out,

John. I's worried about you all those years, but I see I don't have to worry no more. I'll leave you alone now to finish your bath."

John stopped bathing to listen to Cyrus's words. He settled back into his routine, but he focused on washing the human parts of his body this time.

John could remember when he wasn't able to bathe on his own. Elysia and the servants used to assist him back home. Cyrus used to help him with the wing until he learned how to do it by himself. Margie would sit outside the bathroom door and remind him what time it was the way Cyrus did tonight.

When he was on his own, he'd occasionally get lost in the process until the bath was so cold and frigid he was shivering before he finished. It was nice to have someone snap him out of bathing his wing while the water was still warm.

He felt tipsy and giddy when he was like this, a mind still half-filled with the magic of instinct. Tonight, it made him feel especially bright and fresh. Like maybe that feeling of an impending storm that had followed him finally brought the rain.

And it wasn't a downpour. It was a soft, steady Spring mist.

Letter to Elysia (translated)

Elysia,

The war Ms. Bitty Bixler has been preparing for started halfway through the first year of the new century. I feel like I got a war for my birthday, which is not a good feeling at all. Like I thought, people aren't interested in me as a soldier. I am a foreigner, and I have only one arm.

Lucky truly is a brave horse. Sometimes, we hear the gunshots, and there's the smell of smoke and blood in the air. I try to help the people I come across, but I have only one gold shimmer feather at a time. Sometimes, the feather doesn't work because it's not supposed to save that life, and my heart breaks then.

I have noticed that the miracles I'm asked to perform seem further reaching than they used to be. I've passed by the creek I made with the enchanted looking-glass, and there is that new town alive next to it. I think the things I'm being asked to do are affecting the war and the outcome of it. There's something a little frightening about being a part of something you don't fully understand.

When I take care of my wing and let my mind grow wide enough to hold all the magic, sometimes I can see the vision. At least the shape of it. Magic is going to win this war because it likes playing with the lives of men. It doesn't want to give that up.

Please do not worry about me. When I see the shape of the future, I see that I am fine in it. I have a brave horse, a bird wing which supplies me with feathers that cause miracles, and a job that is important for me to complete. I will be safe because I also have a gun which never runs out of bullets and I never miss when I aim it. Maybe one day, we will meet again, and you'll get to see all of my new tricks.

Until that day, be well, dear sister.

Your brother,
John

14 November 1900

There is a sickness going around. It is a fever that is easy enough to survive if one is inoculated first. Dr. Willard Cross is attempting to get the vaccines delivered, but he has to pretend he wants to outlaw magic in order to do it. The reasons behind the war have little to do with what people like Margie or Cyrus want.

Margie just wants to watch horses move well. Cyrus just wants to find a good wife and live on the farm with her. Right now, Margie gets to continue to watch the horses move.

I know Cyrus is fighting in the war. Because he lives on a farm in the heartlands, he is fighting on the side to keep magic alive. I know he's safe, at least. Sometimes, I hear the soldiers singing as they march, a song about Cyrus, the Undying Soldier. He is cheerful and stubborn in the song, but he is also loyal to his country. I'm not sure if the last bit is true, but I know how rumors fly. I know that he's just a good man looking for a good time.

So, for now, Margie needs me more because I know Cyrus can't really die. I try to stay at Ms. Bitty Bixler's for as long as I can until the drums are too loud.

I help shovel the snow. I think about how the news of the war is a little quieter now, as if even wars calm down a little for the cold months. Margie actually isn't sure when she was born. But I think she is a Spring child. In Nyuskom, 'Spring' is 'Ver', which also means 'true' or 'truth', and she is the most honest person I know.

I think the war is making it harder for me to get letters from my sister because I haven't gotten another one. I have reread that single letter I have received from her so many times.

For now, I go walking outside when the weather is clear to try to get a break from the drums. The snow crunches underfoot. Margie walks alongside me most days to chat with me. Sometimes, she holds my hand because she needs something to hold. The bad news worries her.

"Are the drums too loud now?" She asks me that every time.

"I'm moving, so I can't hear them. When I hold still, they aren't bad yet" is what I tell her.

Once, she complained that her boots get wet but mine never do. I used a feather, and now she has boots like mine. They will never blister her feet, will always fit, and will never get wet inside. I think my favorite miracles to use my feathers on are the small ones. I think it's because, if it weren't for the wing, I'd have been a plain man who plays piano, travels, and comes home for summer.

But then I wouldn't have made Margie cat-eye glasses or boots that stay dry forever. That would've been a tragedy.

12 March 1901

The war continues, and I often tuck Margie underneath my wing because she has a hard time when the battles come too close to Oaks Bend. Sometimes, Ms. Bitty Bixler comes around to knock on my door. I let her in, but tell her I'm wearing only a shirt so she knows to enter quickly. She has a key that opens every door. She locks it up once she's inside. I don't want strangers to see my wing.

"How's Margie?" is a question Ms. Bitty Bixler asks me often during this time.

Margie has more bad days than good days sometimes. She doesn't talk much. She behaves strangely, but I know I do that as well. I feel the war won't last too long or maybe they will move the battles westward. I can only hope. I miss the way she looks when she talks too much about how horses move. But I find she still likes being with me when I preen my wing. She is always gentle, so I let her play with my feathers even if I have to fix it afterwards. It seems to calm her.

On the good days, she is more herself. I love those days. We ride our horses on the trails north of the manor, and she tells me I sit crooked and that's why every time I come to visit, she has to work with Lucky to get her evened out again. She said I better keep coming back or else Lucky won't last long.

I promised her I would.

She asked if there were drums in my head. She always asks me about the drums.

I told her I hear them, but it's not bad yet.

I find I can withstand the drums a little longer if I let

my head fill with magic and wildness as I preen my wing. I don't mind preening my wing so much when I do it with Margie around. She helps me take off my shirt. Though it fits me well, it is impossible to get on and off by myself easily. She stayed close by while I worked on my wing in the sunshine. Our horses were nearby. I let myself be the least human I ever am because as long as I'm crittery with my head full of magic, it's easier to hold still and be next to Margie.

Margie sits next to me, and she says she doesn't mind it too much that I'm sometimes more like an animal. When I'm like that, I can't really answer her, but she seems to understand me well enough anyways. Because she doesn't mind it all that much, I don't either.

When I'm not worried about how I look, it's nice sometimes to be this strange thing I became.

Chapter 25

Awestruck

John felt like a wild thing coming out of the bathroom, bare-chested and voiceless. The human parts of his mind were quashed by the instinct that filled him with its heady presence. It reminded him of when he drank far too much at the bar in Fairview, and Cyrus said he was 'three sheets to the wind.' Except instead of alcohol, it was the magic lingering in his head which made him half-drunk. He followed the force that had given him this job.

Yesterday, it cued him to buy the ingredients for a roast. Tonight, it led him down the darkened hall, up the stairs, and then, finally, into the room of this house which was once his over a decade ago. And just like the end of the wagon ride, once he was at his destination—the guest bedroom—he was only 'one sheet to the wind.'

The room was the same as he remembered. The comfortable bed was pushed against the wall. A homely rag rug made by Cyrus's late mother laid in the area between the bed and the chest of drawers. The lace curtains were new, and the moonlight shone coolly in, ghost-like through the two windows.

John made his way around the guest bedroom, taking in the familiar space. Finally, he stood in front of the chest of drawers and opened the top-left one, wondering if—yes, it was still there. He took the soft brush and sat at the foot of the bed. His damp wing fluffed and shook over and over until it was dry enough.

Then, he groomed his wing with the brush until the preening instinct invited his fingers into his feathers. This time, no magic one stuck out. It meant that this night wouldn't sound like drums the way most of his nights did.

Clouds shifted across the night sky, concealing and revealing the moon. John sat on the bed with the playful moonlight, letting it run over him. It brightened him, and then covered him in shadows. Magic loved clarscuro. It was strong here, and it was asking him to go underneath the multi-colored quilt. He obediently pulled the blanket over his body as the sky darkened again.

But he didn't feel his feathers brushing against the cotton backing like he had been expecting. It also didn't feel like he was taking up too much space anymore. Underneath the quilt, what should have been the tip of his wing wiggling felt like separate fingers instead. One by one, starting with the pinky, his fingers folded into a fist for the first time in sixteen years before opening up again. His breath locked up as he waited for the moonlight to come back to illuminate what had happened to him. When it did, he saw the shape of his palm-up right hand under the quilt. Hope hammered in his chest and cleared up his mind to leave a little more room so he could be John, just John again.

He jumped out of bed, into the night's dazzling spotlight, excited to see the miracle, but when he looked down at his right side, the wing was still there. Devastated, he retreated back underneath the quilt. The wing became an arm again. It wasn't a transformation as much as it was something that was suddenly true, changing in the blink of an eye.

John stood but kept himself wrapped up in the blanket. Still an arm. He gently pushed his right hand out from where the edges of the quilt met like a makeshift cloak. It remained a hand. He moved his fingers every way he could. Slowly, he peeled the fabric off, bit by bit. Still an arm with his forearm exposed. With his elbow out. But then, sure enough, once his upper arm was uncovered, it became a wing again. He tilted his head, curious, looking at that strange, cursed appendage.

He was thankful he was given some kind of respite from this curse. Perhaps being a guest for Cyrus and Abigail today was enough for magic to decide to be kinder to him. It left him awestruck.

John got back into bed, covered himself in the blanket, and laid on his right side for the first time in almost two decades. But he found it was too odd to lie like that, so he flipped over onto his left side. Despite the night's noiselessness, sleep would not come.

He sighed and took his right arm out from under the quilt. It became a wing again. He opened it over the top of the blanket, letting it drape over his body—the only way it was comfortable.

He was amused he couldn't sleep without his wing.

Letter to Elysia (translated)

Elysia,

I travel a lot now. I try to stay in Oaks Bend and work there as much as I can so your letters can find me if they ever make it over the Atlantic Ocean. I find, even though I have a handful of people who know how I am, it's easier when I don't spend summer around people. The shirts I wear are not easy to put on when I'm by myself, so I tend not to wear a shirt at all when it's too hot. I remember that first summer I was cursed, I was the palest I ever was in my life. Now, I become so brown during my season. I still love summer, but it is very different now. The reason I loved it was because you and I played on the shores, read books in the garden, and celebrated the Aestival Solstice with a feast and music.

I still love the water, books, food, and music. It is just that I am not the same as I was long ago. I wonder what it would be like to splash in the water with you now that I am not so frightened about having this cursed thing. You would help with it because it gets sore and stiff sometimes. Dr. Willard Cross tells me it's just arthritis because I don't move it enough, and I keep it tucked away. It is not too bad, dear sister. You wouldn't even notice I was in pain, but I think you would help me if I asked. Also, when I'm wandering the wilds in the summer, it does hurt less. I just wish I could stop by somewhere instead of wandering.

I have Lucky, so I'm not alone. She is curious about me when my mind is something in-between. She is not afraid, and she has gotten accustomed to me. She knows I won't hurt her no matter what. I am so soft with my cues now. You would be proud.

I still have to visit Margie this summer. She told me that the way I ride makes Lucky a little uneven over time, and I need to come back at least once a season. When I come around, she works with my horse to get her to be balanced and comfortable again. She said I'm doing a good job taking care of her. When I watch her with Lucky, sometimes Ms. Bitty Bixler stands beside me and says, "Is she still telling you that you have to bring that horse back to even her out?" She told me Margie was just saying that because she wanted to make sure I kept coming back.

You would love Ms. Bitty Bixler, Elysia. She is a clever, shrewd woman who can command a room. She's open-minded, which lends itself to kindness.

The war is being fought more in the west now, so it feels peaceful here. Ms. Bitty Bixler said they have stopped buying so many horses from her, which means the war is probably almost over. If that's true, then it felt like a short war. Here and then gone for those of us who stood outside of it and neatly avoided it because we were not able bodied men. We didn't even have to worry about the fever that went around.

I think about the first year I had my curse, Elysia. That felt like the longest year of my life. I imagine that's what war is like to those who are in the middle of it. A nightmare that, when you finally wake from it, you are so transformed you wonder if you ever were something else once. That's the way it felt to me at least when I travel and help some people who are more directly impacted than I am.

For now, I am comfortable this summer. Lucky is nearby. I'm beside the fire. I can light my own matches because Cyrus taught me how to do it one handed.

Your brother,
John

21 October 1901

I am traveling back to Ms. Bitty Bixler's with a man
and his young son. The man's name is Joseph, but he goes
by Joby. His son's name is Lou. He appears to be a nice
boy, and he was very precocious.

After a job moving some horses to Dr. Willard Cross's
at the Holler, I opted to walk back to Oaks Bend on foot. I
knew I had to do it that way. That's when I saw them with
their wheel stuck in a deep ditch. They had a spotted mule.
I had never met an animal so steady around me at first
meeting, but that's how she was and it was really nice. I am
very strong. It was simple enough to lift the cart and set it
right in the tall grass. I used a feather to fix the wheels so
they would never get stuck again.

I was happy that I followed what J Bellamy would call
a thread and chanced upon them. It always feels good to
help people.

Joby said he wished he could pay me. Then, he said he
wasn't a tailor anymore, but he was still very good at tailoring. He wanted to make me some clothes. I was reluctant at
first. He said, "How about a meal instead?"

He spoke a lot about their travels, about how the war
was starting to finish up soon and how lucky that it wasn't
even going to take two whole years. Lou just nodded his
head as Joby spoke.

Next, we started playing poker, using buttons as
betting chips. I noticed that Joby let the boy win sometimes
the way a good father would. He'd throw buttons into the
middle, and I would do the same. Lou smiled as he won his
pile of buttons.

"You're not just letting me win, are you?" Lou asked.

I try not to be dishonest, so I admitted that maybe I was a little.

Joby laughed and said, "You are meant to win all the buttons this time, Lou."

The more they spoke, the more I realized they were odd the way Ms. Bitty Bixler, Margie, Dr. Willard Cross, and I were odd. Thus, I asked about the shirt again because I did not have a good solution that I could put on myself. I really missed being able to dress myself in clothes that fit well because I am poorly made underneath my coat.

I kept getting shy again. Joby told Lou he had to go away and hide his eyes. Lou protested the way any child would, whining and then reluctantly obeying anyways.

He measured me over my duster to humor me, and I saw it wouldn't work.

He said he wouldn't tell anyone how I looked. Magic told me I was supposed to let him make me a shirt. I told him I had a wing.

Joby helped me to remove it, but I turned away because I didn't want to see how he would react to it. I remember his breath changing. I wish I let myself see his reaction because he didn't seem too surprised. He simply told me he likes the kinds of curses that change the composition of a man. They're rare. He definitely did have experience with curses.

He makes clothes very quickly. Every day, he made a new one. He asks me a lot of questions about how my wing works and how it's attached to me so that the next shirt will be better. We're getting closer. Tomorrow, we will arrive at Ms. Bitty Bixler's, and Joby said he'll stay awhile until I have a couple shirts that fit me and that I can put on by myself.

When I wear a shirt, I feel a lot more plain. But when I need someone to help me, it reminds me of how I was in Nyuskom. Everyone did everything for me then. I like how I am in America. I can do many things for myself now. I just want a shirt I can put on by myself, too. This damn wing is in the way, but we'll see if he can make it work. I hope so.

12 July 1902

The war petered out. There wasn't a final battle, just the resignation that America itself doesn't want to let go of magic yet. I feel that some of that is my fault. One side had only guns. The other had guns and magic and brave horses and a man with a bird wing who can deal miracles. I didn't feel instrumental when I did them, but the small things I've done had left their mark. I thought of the threads that J Bellamy spoke of.

Everything I do leaves a thread, more or less. Or maybe everything I do follows a thread already set down, and they were all going to come together anyways. Maybe it's a little of both. Regardless, I need to be something not-quite-human to even partly understand it.

I'm used to letting my mind do that now. I just try not to do it when there are people around who don't understand what I am. I know it frightens them when I am acting inhuman.

The good news is that I have many shirts now to wear, and they are not difficult to put on by myself. So, in the summer, when I go without my coat and wander America's vastness, I can wear something that reminds me I am mostly a plain man other than this funny bird wing attached to me.

Letter from Elysia (translated)

Dearest brother,

I heard the war is over, and I hope you find peace. I received three letters from you but none mentioned receiving any of mine, so I think you haven't been getting them again. Hopefully this one makes it to you.

That year you changed was special in a way because it felt like it was only you and me trying to understand it and how it worked. You were very shy about it to everyone except for me. I remember that first day, you woke up and you were panicking. Father didn't respond appropriately. He saw you, his son, the heir ruined.

I won't lie; it was alarming at first, but then I saw how you were still my brother. I saw you were very frightened. You were always a sensitive soul. I covered you up in the blanket so you wouldn't have to see it, and I held you close. I remember the strangeness of feeling a wing in my arms as I embraced you, but it was my embrace that calmed you that first day. You were still Malachy then.

I think if you ended up King, I'd have to rule the way I am doing right now anyways because you never had a knack for politics. You always preferred finding wonder in the small things. Like the music and the water and the etymology of words. There was always a little oddness in you, brother, long before you grew a wing. You were always the lonely prince. The strange one. But now, you have a full life in America. John, my American brother who made himself into a myth, a legend, a fairy tale, just like the ones we told each other when we were younger. What a rare thing you've always been. What a wonderful man you became.

Once my children are old enough to watch Nyuskom for me, I'll come to America, and I'll embrace you again. I wonder if you'll feel the same in my arms. I bet you will. You sound the same in your letters. Except now you are content with yourself.

With all the love and pride in the world,
Regina Elysia Pulkara Valerio de Nyuskom

Chapter 26

The Bright Morning

The morning sun shone through the windows. John's wing moved before the rest of him did as he rose up to sit. He gasped, wondering if last night had been just a dream.

He ducked underneath the blanket, and his wing became an arm again. His head tented the quilt as he let a little light in to admire his right arm. He hugged himself and swayed underneath the blanket, rubbing his hands over his matching upper arms. The right scapula was completely human instead of being a bone halfway formed between a bird's and a man's. He experimented with moving each of his new fingers, using his left hand to touch every part of what had been a wing for half of his life.

His smile wouldn't fade. All he wanted to do was cocoon himself in the quilt, go downstairs, and then play the piano with his full ability restored, but he had to tend to his duties. Magic wanted him to keep the wing. He was, after all, one of the last living individuals capable of letting it play with the fates of men.

"Very well. I'll keep being an agent for your brand of chaos, as long as you continue to be fair," he said to the stillness occupying the room with him. Then, he shed the quilt and made the bed the way he learned when he lived with Cyrus so many years ago—one-handed.

After neatening up the bed, John got ready for the rest of the day by grooming his wing. He idly inspected his feathers, looking for another to tuck into his hatband. Typically, a new one molted soon after he used one to make a miracle.

His heart fell when he saw that this morning would be no different. A long feather stuck out at an odd angle from his wing. It shed easily like it always did when he got a new mission. He studied the gray-brown feather, unable to know what the future held for it so early in the process. Already, the wanderlust scratched on the inside of his skull. For now, it wasn't too strong, but he'd need to get moving soon in order to keep its maddening drumbeat at bay.

It would start as a tapping any time he held still, grow into a tattoo the longer he stayed until it was like thunder in his head. It would only quiet when he was moving or if he ended up where he was supposed to be. Not only that, but magic would compel him at times, driving him to do things he couldn't explain in the moment, but felt like the right thing to do—instinct.

Usually, he tried to influence the people around him so they could get a better outcome. But it was tricky. He had to do it without letting them realize they were ultimately being judged by a force so strange and powerful that it was nearly unfathomable. Yesterday went well; he had gotten the best possible result.

If only he could stay a few days longer. He missed when he could truly say he had free will, but this was the nature of his work.

John picked up one of his clean shirts, tailored specially for him by Joby. He put his left hand through the sleeve and took the fabric tab in his teeth to shut the opening underneath his wing so he could push the snaps shut. It was a ritual he did every morning.

He heard a knock on his door.

"Come in," John said. He folded the tab and then fastened it with the wooden toggle on the front. This one was carved with leaves of ivy.

Cyrus entered the room, all smiles. "I'm just letting you know you're staying for breakfast."

"I think you're meaning to ask me if I *plan* on staying for breakfast."

"No sirree! You're staying because I'm cooking breakfast *on my own* for the first time in years!"

John wasn't sure how breakfast was going to taste.

"Also, thank you. Oh Lordy, thank you!" Cyrus was starry-eyed enough for John to know how he must have spent his night and morning. "Abby's made some coffee if you want some. It's good, too. I also wanna say: No better way for an up-and-comer like me to start the day than with a bit of cum-then-upper."

John shook his head. "I wondered how far into the morn we'd get before you were to say something indecent."

Cyrus grinned. "I am who I am."

"That you are."

* * *

JOHN, one-armed and one-winged, descended the steps to finish his morning routine. He could hear Cyrus and Abigail setting the table, distracted by each other; they made the house lively.

Still feeling the pull of a magic thread guiding him, John

moved across the parlor and then to the entryway. He put his duster back on and found that it covered him enough to make his wing into an arm again. He was able to wear that coat with both sleeves filled.

The baby grand piano beckoned him. Magic wanted to hear how John really played. He wanted to hear it, too. He lifted the lid and propped it up to open the instrument so its music could fill the parlor. Next, the fallboard flipped up to reveal the black and white keys. The book from yesterday evening was still on the music rack. He turned to that first piece he played side by side with Abigail. Then, he went to move the bench to set it exactly where he wanted it. It was heavy now.

At first, he played the piano left hand only. His new right hand stayed light upon the keys, not striking them, but practicing movement until it remembered its habits. He waited until he felt comfortable with his sight-reading and moving both hands. Satisfied, he finally allowed his right hand to join. His feet pushed down on the pedals to enhance the emotional depth and dynamics of the music. The tapping in his skull was so consistent that he used it as a metronome.

Not too long after he began playing two-handed did Abigail run out, dragging her husband with her. Both of them were about to say something. But when John played the song, it sounded as complete and satisfied and melancholy as he felt at that moment. They all knew, without a doubt, that after breakfast, it would be goodbye.

When he was done, he shut the spiral-bound songbook.

"Looks like you got your arm back," Cyrus said.

John smiled, stood up, and took his right arm out of the sleeve before peeling the coat off of his shoulder for the arm to become a wing again. He moved the bench back and was relieved to find it weighed nothing again.

"It appears there's a few terms and conditions." John pulled the duster back over his shoulder; his wing became an arm, and he slipped it into the sleeve. He held his right hand straight out in front of him. "But yes-yes, here it is."

Cyrus shook it. "Now you can do handshakes like everyone else can."

"Does it feel funny?" Abigail shook it, too.

"It feels like my left hand, except on the right." John rolled his right shoulder. "And all of the parts are human when I have an arm, so everything is made well together. It's nice to not have to worry about the pain later. I think it could have only been the two of you who would convince magic to give me something that worked better than what I had."

"But why not just make it an arm all the time?" Cyrus asked.

"I need the wing for my job. Being a handyman is important work."

"Well, with your new part-time arm, maybe people can believe you when you say you're just a plain old handyman now," Abigail said.

He smiled. "Yes-yes, that would be nice."

THE COFFEE MADE all of them energetic as they ate the first breakfast Cyrus had cooked in years. The eggs were hard and burnt on the edges. The potatoes were bland and wanted salt. The toast was too dry, but edible with butter. Abigail's coffee was great, which made the food even more underwhelming.

Cyrus laughed. "I'm out of practice. The food's terrible!"

"I don't think one of my feathers could have saved your cooking," John remarked.

"Why do you even call yourself a handyman when you're dealing in miracles?" Abigail asked.

"I've just been saying I'm a handyman because people misunderstand how magic works. They change the outcome. I shed a feather, stick it in my hat, and that means that somewhere, a miracle in America needs to happen. I didn't know how the job worked before. But I have a better sense of it now," John explained.

"When you came yesterday morning, you asked if something might be wrong with Rus. Is magic how you knew?"

"I only knew this was his house and that I didn't buy turnips the day before."

Cyrus sipped his coffee. "When do you know the rest of it?"

John buttered his toast. It was so much easier with two hands. "See, it's not like that. I only knew I was to be here and do something, but I never know what it is I'm to do straight away. I have to pay attention to the little things the magic in America tells to me. It's never the same story other than I show up and wait until it's the right time."

"That's all there is to it?" Abigail asked.

"Yes-yes. I used to think I had to force the magic, but it wasn't until Margie that I realized magic is magic, and it's rude to force it. It was like horses. I didn't understand what I was doing before she taught me how to ride my horse."

"Well, even back then you were better at dealing miracles than being a farmhand sometimes," Cyrus teased. "Never did figure out knots."

John clapped his hands together. "I can try knots!" He was excited to try everything that would be easy now.

Abigail laughed at his enthusiasm. "We can get some rope after breakfast."

John sighed because the drumbeat was already getting louder. "I wish I could stay, but I already have a new feather in my hat. So I already have my next job waiting for me somewhere, and I'll go after this meal. But if I pass this way again, you can rest assured, I'll always stop by for a visit."

THE END

Afterword

When I was a girl, I read a lot. I remember my little self, hunkered down like a beetle in front of the bookcase with a book, as if I couldn't even be bothered to find a proper place to sit; I was too excited to get into the stories.

"The Six Swans" or "The Wild Swans" (depends on which collection you're reading from) always captivated me from my childhood: Six (or eleven) princes, all turned into swans; a determined princess focused on completing the torturous and isolating task to free them; and in the end, the youngest brother was stuck with one wing and one arm.

I always thought of that youngest prince and wondered what life would be like for him with his one swan wing. Because I had trouble making friends, I had decided I would definitely be friends with him.

When I sat down to write *Down and Dust*, I knew it would be an authentically-written and candid exploration of disability and finding one's place in the world. I wanted readers to get to know John before I introduced them to his wing—he would've wanted it that way

John's wing provided some distance to discuss the experiences openly and allow readers to process their own emotions through it. Though challenging at times with what it presents, *Down and Dust* is a tender, kind-hearted story.

I wrote this book to tell all of my friends, *"I see you, and I love you."* Every single one of my friends is an odd one: queer, neurodivergent, disabled, or all of the above.

I wanted to say: I saw you were hurting more than usual that day. I noticed how hard you had to push yourself to do that favor for me. Or how sometimes the world moves faster than the pace we need to go. And how lonely it feels to be set apart like that.

I made it a point to write several characters who are othered throughout the novel because:

"Odd characters tend to attract other odd ones."

Down and Dust is the first novel I've ever written. I had to learn a lot about novel-writing in the process, but I couldn't have been happier with this book being my debut. It is a literary fantasy, and it was difficult to find a writing community to help it develop into the novel you read.

The main issue was that other writers found John hard to relate to: He's queer, neurodivergent, and disabled. He's also a foreigner. People focused too much on the differences to the point that they didn't give a chance to this character or his story.

All of those writers were focused on writing to market, and their feedback reflected that. A lot of them made me feel like maybe I was too odd and my story was too odd and my characters were too odd. But I kept going with this book; there was something about it.

Maybe I was like my John with his one wing, wandering around with the drumbeat in his head that kept his feet moving. Then maybe all those people I found who supported this novel helped me collect up the gold-shine feathers. Since publishing *Down and Dust* in September 2025, several people have told me this story and my characters moved them, made them feel seen, caused them to believe in themselves, and more. Every time a reader reaches out, it feels like they've found a miracle gold-shine feather that was made just for them in *Down and Dust*.

It makes me see this story is alive, and it started decades ago with me curled up with a book on the floor in front of a bookcase. I wanted to know more about the youngest prince, stuck with a wing at the end of a fairy tale.

And you got to the end of my story, and that means you're one of the ones who enjoyed that beautiful day John, Cyrus, and Abigail shared. And you watched the magic unfold.

Thank you so much for reading *Down and Dust*.

Acknowledgments

I wouldn't have been able to write this story without my dear husband. Even if I am a little odd, I will always have a place in the world because of my Joshy Washy. You are the reason my life is as full and beautiful as it is.

My writing buddies were near me every time I wrote: Piper the American Pit Bull mix, Koroviev the Basenji, and Kiddo the Japanese Akita Inu. The three of you have always been such good and loyal pups.

I want to thank the friends I made in the writing community, especially T.N.T.'s Writer Rebellion. Everyone there encouraged me to finish this novel. You built such a supportive and wonderful community—a safe place for the odd ones.

My critique partner, Morgan, noticed all the little allusions, nods to the classics, and attention to detail in this novel. You made me realize I have something special here. Thanks to you, the world got to know John, Cyrus, and Abigail.

Also by A. M. McCray

ANOTHER ODD THREAD IN THE TAPESTRY
OF AMERICA'S WILD MAGIC

Never Steal from the Reaper